# SHAI TOOK IN RAMZY'S INJURED CHEEK

"What happened to you?"

"Nothing. How's my brother?"

"Fine. He's staying in my apartment in Haifa. He's a little disoriented and uncertain about what he's agreed to, but he's going along with it."

Ramzy nodded.

Shai leaned forward on his elbows. He spoke in a gentle tone. "Ramzy, did Abu Nidal's men torture you?"

"No. Actually, I received the wounds in Shatilla. You've heard of the Sabra and Shatilla refugee camps, haven't you? Oh, sure you have. Your troops moved into West Beirut to prevent anarchy and bloodshed. Isn't that what your prime minister announced?"

Shai went pale. Ramzy must have witnessed the Phalangist rampage and somehow survived it. "My people are outraged at what happened."

"My people are dead," Ramzy said softly.

# Howard Kaplan

# BULLETS OF PALESTINE

A GOLD EAGLE BOOK FROM
**WORLDWIDE**

TORONTO · NEW YORK · LONDON · PARIS
AMSTERDAM · STOCKHOLM · HAMBURG
ATHENS · MILAN · TOKYO · SYDNEY

**BULLETS OF PALESTINE**

A Gold Eagle Book/August 1987

Copyright © 1987 by Howard Kaplan

ISBN 0-373-62107-8

Printed in Canada

*For Steven Schiffer,*
*who, while we were exchange*
*students at the Hebrew University*
*in Jerusalem, in 1971, wisely*
*convinced me to accompany him to*
*Lebanon, Syria and Egypt.*

# BOOK I: RAMZY

## 1 June 3 • London, England

THE TERRORIST'S BULLETS had killed Yakov Barsimantov six weeks ago. The vice-consul at the Israeli embassy in Paris had just stepped from the front door of his apartment building when the assassin fired the WZ-63 machine pistol. Three slugs had slammed into Barsimantov's chest; two penetrated his skull. The autopsy had determined that the bullet severing the diplomat's aorta had killed him.

As Shlomo Argov, dressed in formal evening attire, left the bedroom in the Israeli ambassador's residence in St. John's Wood, he had no thoughts of Yakov Barsimantov or of any danger. Argov approached the possibility of death with each step and chose to stride without hesitation. The residence was constantly guarded by Israeli security, and an armed British Special Branch officer accompanied him daily whenever he left the house or embassy. Even without the security, he would not have altered his schedule or his attitude.

Argov walked into the salon where his wife, Hava, sat in her housecoat, hooking a throw rug. She gazed up and smiled.

"Thank God for the British institution of male-only dinners."

"I wish I didn't have to go myself. I'll try to be early."

The doorbell rang.

"There's a late-night film on ITV," Hava said. "I may still be up when you get in."

Argov bent and kissed her, then headed for the door. At the front entrance he looked at the television monitor on the table and saw Colin, his Special Branch bodyguard, standing outside dressed in a tuxedo. Argov opened the door.

"All ready, sir?" Colin asked.

Argov saw the bulletproof embassy Volvo idling in the street and nodded to Colin. They headed to the car.

RAMZY YUSUF AWWAD placed his pen between his Walther PPK/S and the tight handwritten Arabic sheets of the short story he was writing. The perpetual lack of time and the need to move constantly for fear the Israelis would locate him had forced Ramzy to learn to develop his entire story first in his mind and then set it down once, in final form, with few corrections. His novellas and stories had swept the Palestinian world. Read by students in the refugee camp schools, where he had once taught, to those deep in the Gulf oil fields, his gun and pen promised that the struggle continued.

The phone purred. Ramzy glanced at the receiver. The sounds echoed through the small room, naked except for the desk directly under the hanging light and a narrow bed in the corner. Ramzy waited until the fifth ring, the signal that he was not under duress, then lifted the receiver.

"Hello," Ramzy said.

"We have him under surveillance."

"He's someplace where we can get to him?"

"Yes."

"Where shall I meet you?"

"Stratford Station."

Ramzy quickly calculated to himself. This was the sixth month of 1982. Count six letters back from *S*. He looked at the circled underground stations on the subway map in front of him. *M* was Marble Arch. It must be one of the luxury hotels overlooking Hyde Park.

"Then I'll meet you at six in the morning," Ramzy said.

"I'll be waiting."

Ramzy hung up. Six in the morning meant he was on his way. He placed his manuscript inside his small traveling bag, tucked the Walther PPK/S in his belt, drew on his overcoat and buttoned it to hide the weapon. As the Hampstead clock tower across the street chimed ten, he checked carefully to confirm that he had left no signs of his stay. Then he lifted his bag in one hand, extinguished the light and headed down the narrow stairs.

INSIDE THE MARBLE-WALLED, chandeliered ballroom of the Dorchester Hotel, Shlomo Argov glanced at his watch, which read 10:40. Around him some four hundred men, in formal dinner dress, chatted as the waiters cleared the dessert plates. Once a year the De La

Rue Company, which printed banknotes for more than a hundred countries, hosted this formal evening.

Argov turned to Colin seated on his left and spoke quietly. "Well, what do you think?"

"About going, sir?"

Argov nodded.

"If the missus didn't fall asleep and can tell you how the film started, you'll catch most of it."

"Not too many people are leaving yet. Maybe I ought to stay a few more minutes."

"I don't think that's necessary, sir, if you're asking my opinion."

Argov smiled. "All right."

Colin pushed his chair back. "Let me have a look-see, first."

"Fine."

As Colin headed toward the ballroom exit that led directly onto Park Lane, Argov listened to the buzz of talk and clinking of china. The Diplomatic Protection Group officer outside had reserved a spot on the curb for their arrival near the entrance so that the Israeli would not have to walk too far in the open. For the first time in days, Argov thought about Yakov Barsimantov, then motioned to the waiter who was carrying fresh decaffeinated coffee and had the man refill his cup.

Minutes later Colin approached and bent toward his ear. "There's a bit of a crowd out there. It's all the fancy cars. We'd better go."

Argov nodded, placed his napkin on his plate, said goodbye to the men with whom he had shared the table, then rose.

They started to walk toward the Park Lane exit, then Argov spotted George Howard, chairman of the BBC, standing alone. He turned to Colin. "I want to speak to him. This may take a little while."

"All right, sir," Colin said, trying to hide his displeasure. His mind was on the crowd outside and the inability of the lone DPG officer there to keep the onlookers back from the door.

WORRIED ABOUT HIS AGENT, Ramzy continued to wait in front of the Marble Arch Station at the intersection of Oxford Street and Park Lane. The man would not have left of his own volition. Ramzy forced himself to admit that his agent had either been apprehended or killed. A small fear tightened in his stomach, and he moved cautiously toward the cover of the station. Looking out at the street, he saw nothing suspicious, but that meant little.

Ramzy weighed fleeing into the underground, but he wanted him now, tonight. He had been standing in the open for a quarter of an hour, and no one had made a move toward him. He gazed down Park Lane, trained his eyes on the long row of luxury stores and hotels that lined the Mayfair side of the street opposite Hyde Park and suddenly the separate pieces locked together. The Dorchester Hotel. That's why Marble Arch. The hotel was only a few minutes from here.

Ramzy moved quickly out of the station, and crossed the street. Outside the Grosvenor House Hotel, he took the gun from his belt, slipped it into his pocket and broke into a run. He must not be too late.

Ramzy raced past the windows of the expensive car dealerships, banks and jewelry stores, clutching the light bag. Sweat coated his face; his heart pounded. Argov could not have left already, he repeated to himself as he ran.

Ramzy neared the Dorchester. Hundreds of cars were queued alongside the hotel, double- and triple-parked near the ballroom entrance, blocking most of the four lanes on this side of the carriageway. Ramzy saw a blue Volvo near the curb, flying two small Israeli flags. Shlomo Argov was still inside. There was time. Breathing hard, Ramzy approached the shielding crowd, and felt for the PPK/S in his pocket.

SHLOMO ARGOV shook George Howard's hand. "Good night, and thank you," Argov said.

"I dare say I don't believe there's any bias from that reporter, but I will look into it personally."

"That's more than I could ask for. Thank you again." Argov waited until the BBC chairman turned, then he approached Colin who was standing a discreet distance away. "I'm ready now," he said, then smiled. "You'll tell Hava that I tried to leave early, won't you?"

"I think she's used to being a diplomat's wife by now, sir."

They moved through the heavy glass doors and stepped outside. The crowd had completely blocked the sidewalk to their right. "Look at this," Argov said, "they probably think there are film stars inside."

"Probably. We'd better hurry, sir."

"You British have your inimitable way of handling things. The French or American police would never allow people this close."

Colin took him by the arm. "It's not secure here. Come on."

Argov quickened his pace toward the car, where his driver was already behind the wheel, the motor running.

Ramzy saw Argov and dropped his bag, pushing fiercely through the people and knocking some over. There were angry shouts. Ramzy saw the Special Branch officer reach down and open the door of the Volvo. It had to be now. Ramzy pulled the PPK/S from his pocket.

Argov approached the car.

Ramzy held the gun low.

The Special Branch officer stepped aside so Argov could step in. Ramzy pushed toward the front. He needed a clean shot. He would only have one chance. Suddenly Ramzy saw a young dark-skinned man near the front of the crowd, holding a pack in his arms. There would be a gun inside the pack. Fear raced through him. There were too many people in the way. He couldn't sight on the man.

Argov bent to enter the car.

Ramzy saw the young Palestinian pull the WZ-63 machine pistol from the pack, and aim. Ramzy tried to fire at him. A tall couple blocked the shot. Ramzy pushed to the side, desperately seeking an opening. He heard a single pop like a firecracker.

Argov slumped to the sidewalk. People screamed, scattered. Blood leaked from above the Israeli ambassador's ear and through his white hair. Ramzy thrust his gun back in his belt. He did not want to be shot by the DPG or Special Branch officers.

Ramzy watched the assassin freeze in front of the glass windows of a BMW dealership, gripping the small machine pistol. He did not matter now. Ramzy shoved his way through the panicked crowd as he rushed to get to the street so he could search there.

The assassin turned, bolted to the corner and fled to the right into South Street. The Special Branch officer drew his gun as he gave chase.

Ramzy dodged the cars and ran into the middle of Park Lane. Scanning, he saw what he was looking for on the Hyde Park side of the carriageway—a sleek white Porsche at the curb, smoke rising from its tail pipe. He ran toward the grass divider. Before he got halfway across it, the sports car screeched away and sped in the direction of Cumberland Gate. Ramzy felt the strength escape him. There was no way to catch the Porsche.

Ramzy turned and saw the Special Branch officer run into South Street, chasing the assassin, followed by the chauffeur. The getaway car Ramzy had expected to see there was nowhere in sight. With a final, deathly inevitability, the assassin stopped running, turned and squeezed a burst at his pursuers.

Only there was no sound. Miraculously the gun had jammed. The Special Branch officer fired and caught the assassin in the neck; he spun to the ground.

Ramzy moved quickly back to the hotel. The singsong wail of sirens broke the night. He picked up the bag with his clothes and the manuscript, which lay where he had dropped it, and continued walking toward Hyde Park corner.

Abu Nidal would be out of the country before nightfall, and Ramzy had no clues to his destination. He wondered with despair how many Palestinians the Israelis would murder with their bombs because of his failure to stop the assassination.

## 2 June 4 • West Berlin, Germany

RAMZY SAT IN THE BACK of the cab as the driver crawled
through the Kreuzberg Quarter of West Berlin. Gazing
absently out of the window, he still found it too painful
to read the *International Herald Tribune* at his side that the
stewardess had handed him on the Heathrow to Tegel
flight. As the taxi picked up speed, he glanced at the
photograph on the front page showing bombs exploding
in the heavily Palestinian Fakhani district of south Beirut. After Yakov Barsimantov was gunned down in Paris,
Prime Minister Begin had warned publicly that any further shootings of Israelis anywhere in the world would
collapse the cease-fire on Israel's northern border.

Ramzy looked out the window again. As they neared
the Wall, apartment blocks rose beside shattered structures, colorful art works splashed on their facades. He
would have to cross over and somehow persuade Renate
Pohle of the East German HVA intelligence agency, who
provided safe houses, documents and succor to the ren-
egade Abu Nidal, to help him. Abu Nidal had to be
stopped.

Eight years ago, Abu Nidal, head of the seven hundred PLO personnel in Baghdad and the Ramadi training camp outside the city, broke with Arafat and expropriated the entire PLO facilities in Iraq. Arafat's flirtation with negotiations and his new dual-track policy of the olive branch alongside the gun, expounded before the UN, set Abu Nidal and his Palestine National Liberation Movement on a rampage. First they attacked the Saudi embassy in Paris, killing six, as a warning to the moderates. Then they executed a dozen PLO officers in Baghdad suspected of loyalty to Arafat. A revolutionary communiqué declared that the legitimate representatives of the Palestinian people would carry out the death sentence on anyone who advocated abandoning armed struggle.

Ramzy's childhood friend, Said Hammami, the PLO representative in Britain, had been the first to seek avenues to peace. In 1973, Hammami published two articles in the *London Times* stating that it was time to admit that the goal they had set out for themselves, the elimination of the State of Israel, was unobtainable. Israel was too strong. The Palestinians, he argued, had no choice but to compromise with this Israeli entity, which was established on their land, against natural justice, and find a way to co-exist in peace with it. In 1974, Hammami established a breakthrough and was the first Palestinian leader to open face-to-face talks with Israeli doves. Then in January, 1978, while Hammami was working in his basement office, one of Abu Nidal's followers shot him three times with a handgun, once in the head and twice in the body. In the years since, they had killed another half-dozen top PLO members in Europe.

Abu Nidal's aim was to trample what he considered a too-moderate PLO and ultimately take it over. If he could push the Israelis into invading Lebanon and crushing the existing PLO for him, so much the better.

It was not, however, the death of Said Hammami that propelled the schoolteacher, Ramzy Awwad, along the path of the gun but events that culminated eleven years earlier at the end of 1967. As a teenager in Lebanon, his one fierce wish had been to obtain an education, become a teacher and return to the camps. His older brother, Fawaz, insisted that Ramzy take the money he sent from the Kuwaiti oil fields and study in England. He had refused until Fawaz persuaded him, as he had wanted to be persuaded, that he could do endlessly more for their people by becoming a teacher than by joining him in the sweltering desert. He ended his passionate letter with the insistence that one of them here in Kuwait was enough.

After earning that teaching degree at Manchester University in 1961, full of pride and confidence, Ramzy made the emotional hajj to Mecca, traveled to see his family in Lebanon and then rode the bus to his post in Syria. In Damascus he found himself and one other teacher responsible for a staggering twelve hundred Palestinian children. Undaunted, they split the horde into units of a hundred, and each of them took a group for two hours and taught from seven a.m. until seven p.m., six days a week. Ramzy felt certain that eventually his Arab brothers, the world, would come to his people's rescue.

Years fell away. Often Ramzy lay awake at night despite his exhaustion, asking himself how long this situation could continue. Gradually they received five additional Palestinian teachers. When they made little difference, he trudged through the desert alone at the end of each day.

Then late in 1967, after the Israelis' humiliating rout of the Arab armies in six days, PLO officers arrived at the school. Ramzy stood with his wife, Dalal, one of the new teachers, and watched the children. For the first time he saw hope and self-esteem in their eyes as the jeeps careened into the courtyard and the men jumped out with their Kalashnikovs. He agreed to the establishment of the base and was soon training with his students.

Early in December, in the midst of a particularly severe winter without enough blankets in the cold concrete huts, he sat up late with Dalal, and she agreed with the most difficult decision of his life—to leave her for unknown lengths of time. Two weeks later, after spending every minute together they could, he traveled to the Karameh Camp in Jordan, where the fedayeen had their main base, and joined them.

As THE TAXI IDLED at the signal, Ramzy thought about what would happen to his people's chances for a future if Abu Nidal took over the PLO. He picked the newspaper off the seat. The headline, ISRAELI JETS BOMB GUERRILLA TARGETS IN REPRISAL STRIKE, knifed into him. He read:

BEIRUT, LEBANON, June 4—Waves of Israeli jets struck at Palestinian guerrilla camps here and in southern Lebanon today in what the Israeli command described as a retaliation for the shooting of the Israeli ambassador to Britain.

For two hours, Israeli planes bombed crowded Palestinian guerrilla camps in Beirut's southern suburbs. Then Israeli jets attacked southern guerrilla strongholds in the terraced hillsides around Nabatiye, Arab Selim and Wadi al-Akhadar, about 10 miles north of the Israeli border.

Lebanese Government security sources said at least 45 people were killed and more than 150 wounded in the Israeli strikes.

Ramzy slammed the paper down and leaned back against the seat. Soon the taxi pulled to the curb on Friedrichstrasse in front of the series of one-story military huts at Checkpoint Charlie.

FORTY-FIVE MINUTES LATER, Ramzy window-shopped in the Alexanderplatz and waited for Renate Pohle, the Palestinian's link to the KGB. With that closed-in feeling he always experienced behind the Iron Curtain, Ramzy peered through the glass into a market. Tall circular stacks of canned grapefruit juice and pineapple slices from Cuba rose from the floor. Behind the counter dozens of varieties of Pickwick tea bags and freeze-dried coffees lined the shelves adjacent to an entire Oriental foods wing. On the rear wall a section of Hungarian wines rested at an angle in wood racks.

"If you go more than three kilometers from here, you won't find any of this," a woman's voice said behind him. "It's rather unkind of us to fool foreigners this way, but then all visitors to democratic Berlin do come to the Alexanderplatz."

He turned and realized that Renate's green eyes were more heavily eye-shadowed and that there was even redder rouge on her forty-plus-year-old cheeks than when he had seen her six months ago. "Shall we walk along the river?" he suggested.

She nodded and took his arm. They had first worked together in mid-1970, when Renate had arranged for members of the Baader-Meinhof Gang to take refuge in a PLO training camp in Jordan. Once there, the prissy Baader had refused to undergo the commando training, claiming that climbing through mud and under barbed wire were unnecessary for the urban guerrilla. As a favor to Renate, Ramzy had rushed to the camp and prevented the fedayeen from throwing the Germans out.

As they walked, Ramzy reached into his inside coat pocket and handed her a small package. She unwrapped the plain paper, and a smile etched her lips as she saw the Lancôme duet eye shadow compacts.

"My, my," she said. "You are good." She did not ask how he knew her favorite brand.

"You told me the West Germans won't allow you into their sector anymore, so I assumed these would be more difficult for you to obtain."

"Intimate presents, yet always the gentleman. You disappoint, Ramzy, my dear." She gazed up at him. "You look tired." The smile continued to play on her lips. "Been traveling a lot lately? Your call came from where—England, I'd guess?"

"Yes."

She took another look at the makeup. "Oh, charming men." She shook her head. "You want to know why charm works, my handsome Arab. It works because even though we know what charming men say and do is probably not true, we convince ourselves that it might be. Women have to delude themselves. It's the only way they can fall in love with most men." She fell silent, then she flung her hair back on her shoulders, and the smile returned. "Come," she said, holding on to the compacts and taking his arm again. "You wanted to walk along the water."

At the geometric-shaped, gold-windowed Palast Hotel, they turned right and saw the river. Benches and flowers lined its concrete banks.

"Abu Nidal's making everything very difficult," Ramzy said.

"Yes, I suppose from your point of view he is. He's killed a number of your friends, hasn't he?" She drew his arm tighter. "But you needn't worry. As far as we know, he has no intention of pointing a gun at you. I understand he respects your writing."

"The Israelis may use the Argov shooting as an excuse to invade Lebanon."

"Oh, that. Yes, I suppose they will." She stopped to pick a flower from the grass alongside the river. "Now, come, I suddenly want something sweet. Buy me some ice cream. It's a pity we don't have those Italian brands. The capitalists make some things so much better than we do."

Renate ducked into the ice cream shop in the line of stores in the walkway alongside the hotel. She made him buy her a liter each of coffee-flavored, chocolate and something new—an imitation of an American flavor called peanut butter crunch.

They descended the stairs to the river. "So, my dark, gorgeous Arab. You have performed all the proper deeds. You have brought me presents, you have bought me ice cream. You have charmed me. Now, what is it you want?"

"Abu Nidal," he said evenly.

"Somehow I thought so." She pulled a liter of ice cream from the bag he carried, lifted the lid and scooped some of the imitation peanut butter crunch out with her finger. "It's not as sweet and creamy as in the West, but still good. Try some?"

"What'll it cost for him, Renate?"

"You talk payment among friends?" She lifted more of the ice cream with her finger. "Besides, it's very un-Arab of you, not wanting to bargain. We have not yet even eaten our ice cream. Come to my apartment. We shall have it there. I know some places to put it that will substantially enhance the taste."

"What do you want for him?" Ramzy repeated.

She licked the ice cream seductively off her finger. "Come back with me. We'll discuss it later."

He remained silent.

"There are so few men I trust, my Ramzy. It's never quite the same when I have to worry about whether the man's arranged the coincidental meeting. Come make love to me."

"I cannot," he said.

"Cannot. Physical disability? Maybe you lost it to a Zionist bomb? Actually, that's a symbol you can use in your writing. The emasculated Palestinian. You've lost your land and with it your..." She looked straight at him. "Is it because of your wife?"

A dirty red-and-yellow S-bahn rumbled over the river. "Yes," he said.

She laughed. "You're hardly together. How long's it been since you last saw her?"

Dalal still taught in Damascus. "Almost a year."

"Then you need it too, my dark Arab."

He looked at her. If it was the only way to obtain the information, maybe he should. It was, after all, the information that mattered. Always, the information.

"We shall talk about Abu Nidal afterward." Renate scooped up some ice cream with her fingernail. "Actually, I do know where he is."

"He cannot be trusted," Ramzy said. "Abu Nidal will turn on you whenever it suits him."

She smiled. "Of course he will. We all turn on each other when it suits us."

"Where is he?" Ramzy asked quietly.

She looked down at the softening ice cream. "It's melting. I'm sorry, my dear, but I'm going to have to go." She began to walk away, then turned. "Coming?"

He made no move toward her. "Would you want me, even if you knew I was detesting it?"

She looked at him for a long moment, silent.

"Would you want me to do it if I detested it," he repeated, "just to get the information? Please tell me."

Her lower lip quivered. Another S-bahn rocked over the river. She followed it with her eyes, then bent her head.

He came close, gently touched her hair. "I know what living this way has done to me. The never being able to trust. It takes its toll."

Her head moved in a small nod, then came up. "I'm sorry, Ramzy. Abu Nidal planned it all in advance. He's after Khalil Wazir in Sidon. But you don't have much time."

Ramzy's mouth went dry. The threat of an Israeli invasion, and Abu Nidal after the commander of the PLO's armed forces in southern Lebanon. With the charismatic strategic mastermind Khalil Wazir murdered, the PLO's troops would crumble in disarray before the advancing Israelis.

"I must go," he said.

"Of course."

"Thank you." He kissed her head, turned and headed quickly back in the direction of the underground station in the Alexanderplatz.

Renate brushed the tears from her eyes and watched him until he disappeared around the corner. She clutched the bag of ice cream with both arms, then walked quickly down the paved path between the grass, her high heels clicking on the cement. Ramzy had arrived as expected. She had to make that call now.

IN KIBBUTZ SDOT YAM, on the Mediterranean coast south of Haifa, a young blond Swedish volunteer left the dirt road that led to the banana groves and strode toward the huge greenhouse. She entered and breathed in the warm humidity and the heavy scent of the roses. At the far end, other Swedish volunteers similarly dressed in blue kibbutz shorts and work shirts moved along the last row, cutting the long-stemmed ruby roses.

The young woman usually worked here with her friends, but today, with a number of young men abruptly mobilized and the entire work assignments roster altered, she had been asked to fill a space in the nearby kitchen. She had been slicing carrots when the overseas call was diverted to the dining room, and she had been asked to carry the message since there was no phone in the greenhouse.

As she approached the rear of the high, enclosed structure, she saw him on his knees, working the silver systemic granules into the earth from a bucket by his side. ''There you go,'' he was saying quietly to the bush as she approached, ''a little food and a little protection against those beastly aphids all at once.''

''Colonel,'' the young woman said.

The old man looked up, his round wire-rimmed spectacles fogged, his bald pate, surrounded by a hedge of white hair, beaded with sweat. He stood with effort, removed his glasses, rubbed them on his shirt and fitted them back around his ears. Though it was common knowledge around the kibbutz that until a few years ago he had been head of Israeli Intelligence, the young woman volunteer found it hard to fathom.

"There's a call for you from overseas," she said. "They're putting it through to your cottage."

"Good, good. Thank you . . ." He hesitated, suddenly having forgotten her name. "Yes, thank you."

She smiled and bounded toward her friends.

The Colonel moved slowly down the main corridor of the greenhouse and gazed at the young workers. He liked these Swedish volunteers, the way they enjoyed life.

Outside, the bright light struck the Colonel's eyes, and he ambled to the small white cottage, built especially for him near the greenhouse. He climbed the wooden steps, passing the glass jars of tea he brewed in the sun. The doctor had insisted that he give up coffee and smoking; basically he had, though occasionally he still indulged in a Dunhill Montecruz cigar.

In his small living room cluttered with books, magazines and newspapers in a variety of languages, he picked up the phone. Immediately the kibbutz receptionist said, "Hold on, I'll connect you."

He heard the static of the international line, and then a woman's voice said, *"Guten Tag."*

*"Guten Abend,"* he responded. "Or with the time difference should I say *Guten Morgen?*"

"Our friend arrived as you predicted," Renate Pohle said. "I sent him on."

"Yes, good. Then everything is as we discussed."

"I'll be expecting to hear from you."

"Yes, by all means."

She laughed into the phone. "I suppose I should thank you."

"No, no, not at all. It is I who am grateful."

"Feel free to contact me again," she said. "If there's anything . . . similar."

"Of course."

She would have the information at the Café Praha in East Berlin in five days. It had come from the old pre-1967 network he had set up in the Soviet Union when Israel still had an embassy there. He had traded the information about the icon smuggling of a KGB major who was pushing for Renate's ouster, in exchange for her sending Ramzy Awwad to Sidon, and equally important, her silence.

Before Renate hung up, her curiosity pushed her into saying, "I don't understand. With my help, it would be much easier to do it here in Europe, at a specific time and place."

"Of course, that did occur to me," the Colonel said, "and thank you again."

## 3 June 6 • Sidon, Lebanon

DRESSED IN PLO FATIGUES, the Israeli agent, Shai Shaham, sat in the jeep in front of the al-Hilal Hospital in Sidon, where Ramzy's sister Nadjla worked as a nurse. Two heavy mortars, dug into the now-broken stone under the arched entrance to the hospital, pointed south toward the coast road.

At midmorning the invasion to propel the PLO artillery out of firing range of the northern settlements had struck. Shai supported the assault only in limited fashion. With air and sea fire cover, three columns of tanks were pushing toward PLO strongholds in Tyre, Beaufort Castle and Kawkaba. The division crawling up the narrow coastal road toward Tyre would probably reach Sidon sometime tomorrow. Shai hoped for a rapid strike and then a modus vivendi with the southern Shiites who would be thrilled to have the PLO, who had persecuted them for years, broken. If Israel withdrew quickly they would win the Amal Shiites' friendship, which could further help to secure the border.

Shai picked up the two-way radio and spoke in Arabic to the team at the rear of the hospital. He had used two resident agents, living in the city as Palestinian refugees, and several Christian informants. Ramzy Awwad had not turned up at any of the usual PLO haunts. Shai had not expected that he would.

The one fact that had stuck Shai repeatedly as he read Awwad's file was his close relationship to his family, particularly to his older brother, Fawaz, now a newspaper editor in East Jerusalem, and to Nadjla here in Sidon. Shai hoped that the sentimental Awwad would arrange to have his sister taken someplace safe to meet him. With three vehicles, Shai counted on being able to follow her unseen.

RAMZY STOOD on Sidon's seaside boardwalk as the Israeli F-15s and F-16s streaked high in the cloudless sky, heading inland. Abruptly they dived at the Ein Hilweh refugee camp in the hills, engines whining. Missiles burst from their wings, trailing white paths. The planes arced heavenward. Ramzy watched the missiles slam into the camp. Horrendous explosions shook the whole city. Black smoke billowed. Flames leaped into the air—the weapons caches.

The planes escaped over the ocean, veered south and shrank until they looked like small birds. Suddenly Sidon was eerily quiet. The smoke rising from the camp began to blot the eastern sky.

Ramzy looked toward Ein Hilweh, tiredness turning his despair into physical pain. The fires were spreading. In the past two days he had been unable to unearth any trace of Abu Nidal; but that seemed to matter little now, confronted with the size of this invasion. He had warned

Khalil Wazir, and the commander had surrounded himself with a phalanx of bodyguards. Ramzy listened to the
sounds of the shelling far to the south. It occurred to him
that the PLO might well be driven out of southern Lebanon and that there would be a need to escalate the vio-
lence again to give the Palestinian masses hope, show
them that the battle was still going on.

He should drive to Damascus immediately. After this,
his organization in Europe would become even more important. Still, he had a little time. The Israelis could not
possibly encircle Sidon today. He turned and looked at
his second boyhood home, at the sea-fronted hills filled
with low stone Arab buildings, and he remembered that
day they had arrived here and become refugees.

He could still see himself, a boy of twelve, pulled from
his sleep in Jaffa by his father's shaking hand. He had
stumbled outside in his pajamas, rubbing his eyes. A
huge truck was idling in front of the house; his father,
sweating in the cold, was feverishly throwing bedding
into the open back. He leaned against the cool stone of
the house, wishing that his brother, Fawaz, who had
made him proud by joining the Arab legion in Transjor-
dan at seventeen, was here to explain this to him as he had
always explained everything. It was horrible now to live
alone with the silence of his father, who spoke only to give
him instructions. Yet he had grown accustomed to the
lack of talk and listened now to the nearby waves chop-
ping at the shore.

His mother, his uncle and aunt climbed into the rattling truck, an intruder in the quiet street. His father
lifted his three younger sisters up, then grabbed him from

his corner against the house. He shrugged free. He would climb in himself.

As the truck labored noisily up the street, he stared at their house. He could have run inside, taken his collection of sea anemones or the brass narghile he had bargained for in the souk reducing the price from three pounds to only one pound when he was eight, or the other personal treasures his father had left when he'd roughly pulled only Awwad's clothes from the drawers, pushed them into two boxes and, without saying anything, taken the boxes to the truck. But if they were leaving, he wanted none of that with him. Palestine was his home. His life here would remain here.

As the heavy truck crawled up the coast, he watched the succession of orange groves, groves his father and his father's father had planted, watered and loved, under whose shade they had stretched their prayer rugs and bowed to Allah in prayer and thanks. They were all gone now, taken, or abandoned in fear.

His uncle leaned against the side of the truck, dazed, tossing his worry beads over and over in his hand. His mother and aunt were holding his younger sisters, rocking them to soften their crying. With Nadjla beside him, he sat at the rear of the truck on his knees, not moving or speaking, looking out, the skin beneath his pajamas wearing away at each bounce. Shots rang in the distance as they neared Haifa.

The engine rumbled and strained. As they continued north, the sun beat on the metal roof from high in the sky. Sweat trickled down his back, his belly. His knees were bleeding, but still he would not move. As they approached Ras Naquora, their truck stopped behind a long line of similar trucks and cars backed up at the border. The women, carrying baskets of food, moved over the suitcases, while he lowered his sisters to the dusty ground. His father climbed down from the driver's seat, gazed in silence in the direction from which they had come, then turned from them, refusing food.

Ramzy grabbed an orange from Nadjla's basket. Carrying it with him, he followed his father from a distance and watched him wait in line and then, when it was his turn, hand the Lebanese policeman his rifle. The policeman added it to the pile of machine guns and weapons on the table and beneath it in the dirt. As his father turned, head down, Ramzy ran back to the truck with his orange and climbed in before his father saw him.

As their truck followed the line of vehicles entering Lebanon, the women suddenly began clicking their tongues in high-pitched ululation. Huddled against the driver's compartment, his uncle was crying. Ramzy grasped the orange in both hands, brought the rippled skin to his nose and inhaled the fragrance, then he placed the orange on the floor beneath his bleeding knees. He kept it with him in Sidon until, while roaming the Ein Hilweh refugee camp, Nadjla sneaked into the space on the floor where he slept and threw the soft, rotted fruit away.

Now, walking toward the silent amusement park at the sea's edge, depression seemed to overwhelm Ramzy. To his enormous pride Nadjla had stayed in Sidon and become a nurse at the al-Hilal Hospital. Torn, Ramzy quickened his step. He had not seen his sister in a year and a half.

As a boy, when he had saved extra money from selling khaki rolls on the bridge leading to the water-surrounded Castle-of-the-Sea, he had braved the taunts of the well-dressed Lebanese children and taken his younger sister Nadjla on the Ferris wheel. He remembered how she would sit on a rug next to his stand, console him and hold his hand when the Lebanese walked by and called him a useless Palestinian son of a whore, sometimes kicking the stand and toppling it. She would help him pick up and clean the hollowed-out pieces of rye bread filled with eggs and spices, then when he had sold most of them, she would run to the bakery so he would not lose any business. He felt enormous pride that she had become a nurse and stayed in Sidon. Despite the danger, some of the tiredness lifted from him as he decided to visit Nadjla. Another hour here would not matter.

He strode back to the main square, turned south through the dark, enclosed souk, empty, with iron gates pulled in front of its stalls. A single sheep stood with its front legs lifted onto the grates of a butcher shop, licking the window. Coming out of the alleylike souk, he continued into the fragrant lemon and orange tree garden of the great Djami el Kebir mosque. Just up ahead stood the al-Hilal Hospital.

As he approached the large hospital with its arched stone entranceways, he hesitated. He should arrange for a car to pick up Nadjla and take her to a safe rendezvous point. But there was no time now, not to arrange the meeting and not to take her away from the hospital where they would be preparing for the casualties that would soon be carried in.

He took a final look to see if anything seemed out of order. The narrow tree-lined street was silent, save for the PLO guards sitting in two jeeps. Ramzy approached the hospital and hurried up the outside stairs, his steps light; he would only stay a few minutes.

SHAI COULD NOT BELIEVE what he was watching. It had not occurred to any of them that Awwad would actually walk right in to see her. Shai used his two-way radio and quickly alerted the team in the rear of the building, then he pushed his bulky frame out of the jeep and, clutching his Kalashnikov, moved toward the hospital.

Shai had never expected to have to take Awwad in a public building in the center of the city. It would be difficult from here, with the certainty of armed gunmen inside, to bring him out alive and transfer him to the Maronite safe house in the hills. It was also too dangerous to wait. Awwad might come out accompanied by half a dozen fedayeen. In the street too, he would be sensitive to danger, but hopefully not while engrossed with his sister.

Shai's fingers curled around the trigger and stock were damp as he bounded up the steps. Inside, nurses pushed empty gurneys down the hall. Keffiyehed fedayeen with rifles slung over their shoulders carried boxes of gauze, surgical instruments and other medical supplies, stamped with the symbol of the Red Cross, toward the operating theaters. He should not be challenged. Armed PLO officers were a routine sight in the hospital.

Shai headed to the stairwell and the basement blood bank where Nadjla worked and descended without hurrying. At the bottom, the corridor was empty. He moved down the hallway and wiped his hands quickly on his pants. A door opened behind him. Shai spun around. A slight dark-skinned doctor entered the hallway, glanced at him without reaction and crossed to another room. Then an armed PLO officer emerged from the room the doctor had left. He looked at Shai for a long moment, puzzled, then moved toward him, lowering the Kalashnikov from his shoulder.

Fear caught in Shai's throat.

The officer approached. "Who . . . ?"

Shai searched for a way to overpower this man, but saw none that would not draw the other fedayeen likely to be near. "Where is Nadjla Awwad?" he demanded. "We need a trained Palestinian nurse in the main square. Now."

The officer approached. "I don't know you."

"You will as soon as Khalil Wazir finds your commander. What's your name and unit?"

The soldier stared at him, finger tight on the trigger.

"Your name and unit," Shai ordered. "Answer me. There's no time for this. The Israelis may hit the city again any minute."

The soldier lowered his rifle. "She's in there," he said, pointing to a door halfway down the hall.

"Good. Tell whoever's in charge here that I've taken her."

"It will be a great victory tomorrow," the PLO officer said.

"Yes." Shai turned, moved down the hall and listened to the sounds of the armed officer climbing the stairs.

Shai's shirt was soaked. He positioned his left hand just above the doorknob and listened.

There were no sounds inside. He had hoped Awwad would be talking to his sister and off guard. Suddenly explosions rocked the city. The building shook.

Shai burst in, crouched, Kalashnikov extended, heart racing. He saw Awwad standing over a bed, acted reflexively, began to squeeze . . . then stopped.

Kalashnikov on the floor, Awwad was pulling a tube from a patient's arm. Emaciated men were shackled to beds at their hands and feet, glassy-eyed, too weak to moan. Thin plastic tubes leading from each man's arms dripped blood into huge bottles on tables.

Awwad turned, pain pressing his face. Shai leveled his rifle at him. He saw the Arab's eyes harden, then glance at the floor.

"Move away from the rifle," Shai commanded in Arabic.

Ramzy judged quickly if he could dive behind the bed and reach the weapon on the floor.

"Now!"

Ramzy stepped toward the center of the room.

"You were trying to help them?" Shai gestured toward the enfeebled men on the beds. "They're taking blood from Maronite Christians for PLO wounded, aren't they?"

Ramzy said nothing.

"Hurry, finish," Shai said, motioning his head.

Ramzy stood there for a long moment, then quickly moved to the last two beds and withdrew the tubes.

"We're going out the main entrance," Shai said. "If there's any trouble, I'll kill you and anybody else in the way."

"Israeli?" Ramzy asked.

Shai motioned him to the door, not knowing why he answered. "Yes."

Ramzy showed no reaction. He walked toward the door. Shai picked up his rifle and yanked out the bullet clip. "Take this," he said, and tossed the AK-47 to him. Ramzy caught it in both hands. Shai moved around him to the door, opened it slightly and looked outside. The corridor was clear. He waved his rifle at Awwad. "All right, outside."

Ramzy headed into the corridor, in front of him, alert, watching for a means of escape. There were armed fedayeen everywhere. He would never have tried to take the Israeli out in a similar situation.

Halfway up the stairs, Ramzy's heart jumped. He heard Nadjla's voice from the corridor above them arguing with someone.

"You'll kill those people if you take any more blood," she was saying.

"Return to your post," a male voice ordered. "Now."

Ramzy heard her footsteps coming down the stairs. He had not seen her until now.

Suddenly, recognizing him with the other armed *fida'i*, Nadjla screamed with excitement, repeating, "Ramzy, Ramzy, Ramzy," as she rushed down the steps and grabbed him around the neck with both arms.

Ramzy felt the warmth of her body against his and had to fight back the emotion.

"I'm Halim, a friend of your brother's," Shai said quickly. "We have some medical supplies to bring in from the car. Help us, then I'll leave you and your brother alone."

"No," Ramzy said sharply. "We'll only be a minute. Wait here, Nadjla."

"Wait for you here," she said incredulously, snaking an arm around his waist. "I'm not letting you go anywhere without me." She rested her head on his shoulder. "Oh, Ramzy, Ramzy. I have so much to tell you. It's been so difficult here."

"I would not let him out of my sight either, if I were you," Shai said jokingly. "He has a tendency to disappear, this brother of yours."

"Come, let's hurry," Nadjla said.

Shai watched Awwad look at him with a coldness that penetrated.

They began walking, Nadjla talking nonstop about the bombings of Ein Hilweh, the terror in the camp, the problems in the hospital. She clung to his arm. Several doctors and nurses moved through the main floor, but no fedayeen. Shai felt his palms dampen. They were almost out. Then, as they approached the main doors, five armed fighters entered from outside.

Shai saw Ramzy about to call out; he took a quick step forward and held his rifle casually cradled in his arm, the barrel pointing at Nadjla's head. He looked back and saw the fear in Ramzy's face.

"To a great victory," Ramzy abruptly said to the fighters.

The fedayeen leader held his rifle up. "We will show the Arab nations how to fight the Israelis." As the fedayeen passed them, they were momentarily surrounded. Then the fedayeen moved on.

When Shai and the two Palestinians finally stepped outside and moved down the stone steps, a white Mercedes pulled close from around the corner and stopped in front of the hospital. The driver remained behind the wheel, the motor idling. Two men in fatigues climbed out, one from the front and the other from the rear. Both left their doors open.

"Ramzy," the one who had stepped from the front seat called and waved.

The three of them reached the car.

Ramzy eased away from Nadjla. The two men approached on either side of him and took him by the upper arms. "I have to go with these men," Ramzy said to his sister. "It's all right."

She looked at him, and slowly a look of horror twisted her lips. "No," she screamed.

The two men quickly pushed Ramzy onto the back seat and jumped in beside him. As they pulled the doors shut, Shai forced his heavy body around the car, stepped in and, with Nadjla's shrieking in his ears, closed his own door. The car sped away.

THE FOLLOWING DAY, Ramzy sat in the front of the Mercedes between the fat Israeli and the driver. Heading south on the citrus-lined coastal road, they ap-

proached the border. He did not understand why he was
not shackled and sprawled in the back seat. They passed
the mammoth, fenced United Nations installation along
the beach, and Ramzy looked at the facility with dis-
dain. Israeli military vehicles continued north in the opposite lane.

As the Mercedes pulled to a halt at the barrier and the
driver handed the helmeted soldiers some papers, Ramzy
was torn by a simultaneous depression and elation so
powerful, all he could do was sink back in the seat and
stare beyond the checkpoint. This was his Palestine.
From Syria, from Lebanon, from Jordan, he had gazed
the few kilometers across the border into the land where
he had been born. Since he had been a teenager he had
longed to be there again.

The Mercedes accelerated past the barrier. Ramzy
leaned forward. He was home, finally. Yet the highway
across the border was suddenly so wide. A billboard advertised a cable car ride down to the grottoes of Rosh
Hanikra—in Hebrew. A green highway sign with white
letters pointed to a turnoff for Shelomi, Adamit, Elon,
Shomera—Hebrew names. They continued down the
coast. He watched, stunned at all the settlements, the
greenery, the size of the cities. In his dreams he had always seen the land as it had been when he had gazed at it
from the back of the truck heading toward Lebanon.

The fat Israeli suddenly broke the long silence and,
without looking at him, asked, "What are you writing
now?"

Ramzy stared at him, trying to fathom his motivation
for the question, but said nothing.

"I read your *Men in the Darkness*," the Israeli went on. "Not many Arabs would dare write about Arabs using their own people."

"I am writing about how my father's exile from his home destroyed him," Ramzy said harshly.

The Israeli nodded. "Good. I hope to read it when it's published."

Surprised, he supposed this was some trick to soften him for the coming interrogation, and he fell silent again. Shorty afterward, south of the now painfully large city of Haifa, the Mercedes turned onto a peninsula jutting into the ocean. The car stopped at a military-guarded gate. Once through it, they approached the high-walled prison.

As Shai led Ramzy inside, he wondered why the head of Operational Planning, Yehuda Shamir, had sent him on this mission, ordering him to do everything possible to take Ramzy Awwad alive.

LATE THAT NIGHT, after a two-hour drive beginning in the crisp air of the Jerusalem mountains, Yehuda Shamir walked through the warm darkness toward the amphitheater in the Roman ruins of Caesaria. The star-studded sky lit his way, and he could hear the waves striking the sand near the ancient aqueduct. If he knew the Colonel, the old warrior would already be waiting.

The small Iraqi Jew made his way through the dark tunnel in the renovated amphitheater and came out into the heart of the silent rows. He saw the Colonel below near the stage, a single body in the vastness of the empty stone seats.

It took a lot to want to live with the Arabs, Yehuda thought as he descended the steep steps. In his mind's eye he traveled back to the 1950 airlift, saw his wife and the other women stripped naked on the Baghdad runway, being searched for jewelry. Machine guns pointed at his son, his daughter and the other children had ensured that none of the men interfered with the slow frisking and fondling. Still, his tiny Israel lost every war, in numbers dead, despite the battlefield outcome. Some bold initiatives to bridge the gap between the two peoples had to be attempted. That was why, above the secret of his failing health, he had agreed to help the Colonel from the inside.

"Good to see you," the Colonel said, touching Yehuda gently as he sat.

"Sorry I'm late. I didn't mean to keep you waiting."

"No, no, you didn't. I was early. Not much else to do really. I meant to bring some of my tea, but it seems I forgot."

"It doesn't matter."

"I suppose not." He stared at the sea for a long moment and listened.

Yehuda waited, then said, "Shai brought Ramzy Awwad into Israel this afternoon."

The Colonel continued to gaze out at the ocean. "Yes, good."

"I went to Carmon's office to tell him about the capture. It was the first he'd heard that we were onto Awwad. He was quite excited at the success. As far as I can tell, he doesn't suspect anything."

"Good. Unlike him, though. He seems to know everything, doesn't he, my successor?" The Colonel turned back. "This could cost you your career, Yehuda."

Yehuda was silent. Even the Colonel did not know about the extensive and inoperable blockage of his coronary arteries. Yehuda hoped that he would have done this even if he had been healthy. "Something you must have believed in forced you to resign," he said.

"I'm glad you believe that. I had rather hoped you would. How did you tell Carmon you found out about Awwad?"

Yehuda wondered again what had made the Colonel suddenly and inexplicably resign. "An Arab informant in Beirut," he answered. "I told Carmon he spotted him arriving at the airport and tailed him."

"Good. And our Shai, he suspects nothing more than that he was supposed to capture Awwad?"

"No, nothing. But you'll have to be patient for a while. Carmon will want Awwad painstakingly interrogated."

"Of course, of course. I'd do the same in his place. But you'll be able to convince Carmon to release Awwad when it's time?"

"I think so."

"You will. You'll manage it."

"I'd better. We can't very well send Shai and Awwad off together after Abu Nidal if Carmon won't release him."

The Colonel smiled. "No, we can't."

"Then we face the difficulty of persuading Awwad to go along with it."

"Yes, he may simply disappear once he's free. There's always that risk."

A sense of optimism Yehuda had not felt for years buoyed him. He stood. "I've hardly seen my wife lately, with this war. It's a long drive back. I better get started."

The Colonel rose. "Yes, by all means."

"Are you walking up?"

"No. I think I'll sit for a while longer, if you don't mind. Not ready for bed yet, and it's pleasant here by the ocean."

Yehuda nodded, touched the Colonel's shoulder, then turned and climbed the steps.

The Colonel sat and listened to the waves hit and roll up the shore. The breeze bore the salty scent. He wished he had brought some of his tea. He closed his eyes. Yehuda's reference to his resignation again drew out the memory of that afternoon five years ago when Meir Carmon had appeared in his office. He had expected anything, except to capitulate.

Carmon had sat in the chair opposite his desk, slowly lit a cigarette and said, "I want you to resign."

"Yes, I'm not surprised that you do."

"The country's not safe with you here."

The Colonel lifted the cigar from the ashtray and struck a match. "Not safe? Yes, well you're going to have to do better than that."

"You've gone soft."

The Colonel touched his pudgy cheeks. "Yes, I suppose I have."

"You know what I'm talking about."

The Colonel drew on his cigar until it lit. "Are you by chance referring to my position on the West Bank?"

"I remind you the area's called Judea and Samaria now, officially."

"Ah, yes, you people have suddenly discovered the Bible, haven't you?"

"There's really no point in discussing this," Carmon said. He reached into his inside pocket, pulled out an envelope and placed it beside the full ashtray on the Colonel's cluttered desk. "I think you should take a look at this."

The Colonel put his cigar down. It felt as if Carmon was trying to blackmail him, which was ludicrous. He picked up the envelope, opened the flap and removed the yellowed black-and-white photographs.

Surprise drained the color from his face. His hands shook.

"One of our agents came across these during a routine check in Paris a little while ago," Carmon said. "It's not important how they came into my possession. The woman, I understand, is Josra Kuhr. She has some contacts with the PLO, which was why we were checking her apartment."

"She's a professor of Arabic literature at the Sorbonne," the Colonel said, anger edging his voice. "Nothing more."

"How do you know? Have you talked to her lately?"

The Colonel looked at the pictures he had not seen in almost thirty years. The two of them, he with the full head of chestnut hair and she, the dark-skinned Arab woman. They were arm in arm in the Jardin du Lux-

embourg, standing on the Pont Neuf, eating at the Café
Deux Magots. He had been sent to Europe in 1947 to
procure arms for the coming battle when he had met her
in the Deux Magots on the Left Bank. She had been a
student at the Sorbonne herself then, and at first he had
suspected a trap. It had proved not to be the case.

It had lasted a mere six months, and at that he had only
seen her irregularly, as Prague had proved to be the more
fertile ground for postwar arms dealing. Still, though he
had married and divorced later, Josra had been the one
great passion for a woman of his life. Aware their love was
impossible from the start, they had broken off when he
had returned to Palestine. On their last afternoon together, they had ridden bareback in the country outside
Paris, picnicked, and drinking too much wine, fallen
asleep in the tall grass, entwined in each other's arms.
Later, they had ridden back to the stables in the darkness.

They had met on several occasions when he had passed
through Paris in the fifties. Each time they had gone to a
restaurant and, without discussing it, left separately at
the door. The pain he had seen in her eyes at the partings
he had felt himself, like a blow to the stomach, when he
had watched her walk away.

"I never would have suspected you were such a handsome young man," Carmon said, "and she was quite
lovely. Still is, I'm told, but then you must know that.
You are in contact?"

"You have nothing here," the Colonel said, controlling his voice. "I haven't seen her in twenty-five years."

"We'll have to investigate that. We did photograph some old letters, enough to make it a full-scale commission of inquiry. Internal, of course. We'll try to keep it from the press, but then there are bound to be leaks. Possibly even foreign ones."

The Colonel felt the rage hot on his face. He saw now what Carmon was doing. Carmon knew he had nothing that would damage him, but if word spread that Josra had been involved with the head of the Israeli Secret Service, she would become a target for radicals like Abu Nidal.

The late night sea breeze blowing over Caesaria suddenly carried a chill, breaking the Colonel's reverie. Tired, he got to his feet and stood in the wind. Then he climbed toward the amphitheater tunnel.

## 4 August 16 • Jerusalem, Israel

As THE HALL DOOR to Meir Carmon's outer office opened and Shai entered, the director's young dark-skinned secretary, Tami, looked up. She smiled at the tall man of fifty with the increasing waistline, graying side-burns, yet still handsome, muscular face, with those blue eyes and quiet mouth.

"Hello, Shai."

"Hello," he said.

"It's nice to see you."

He stood there awkwardly. "He's waiting for me, I think."

Her clipped ponytail bobbed as she nodded. "Yehuda Shamir's with him. He said to send you right in." She pressed the intercom on her desk and said, "Shai Sha-ham's here."

Shai crossed in front of her desk. More than a year ago they had coincidentally left the office together and, as neither of them had had any place special to go, they had stopped for some coffee and sticky baklava at a café on Ben Yehuda Street. Then he had walked her back to her apartment in nearby Nachlaot, and at her easy suggestion he had come in and ultimately spent the night. Though he knew she was fond of him and had encouraged the casual coupling without obligation—maybe because she was Israeli and dark—he had found himself thinking painfully about Sarit during their intimacy, though it had been three years since his wife had been killed. Neither he nor Tami had mentioned that night since.

As Shai entered, Yehuda Shamir rose and shook his hand. "Good to see you."

"Sit down, Shai," Carmon said from behind his large desk.

Shai turned toward the tall thin man with receding gray hair, immaculately groomed, who had remained seated. He wore his usual Savile Row suit, tieless, with a starched white shirt. An American cigarette burned between his fingers. Shai dropped into the chair next to Yehuda Shamir.

"I have something substantial for you," Carmon said, "back in Europe."

Shai had spent the past month in southern Lebanon, ferreting out PLO documents. He would be glad to get away from that war. "What is it?"

Carmon stubbed his cigarette into his West African ebony ashtray. "I want you to get Abu Nidal."

"Don't we have people after him?"

"Schulmann's had a team attempting to stop him since the Barsimantov shooting. Should I say politely, without success. Yehuda thinks he's getting nowhere. He's championed you."

Shai nodded. "Where was our last trace of him?"

"Amsterdam. Schulmann got word of him there. It's about the only thing he's accomplished since April. The trail died as soon as he stumbled across it."

As long as Schulmann had been far from Abu Nidal and the terrorist had not struck again, Yehuda had had the necessary time to work on a reluctant Carmon. He had been fortunate with Schulmann's running into a dead end in Amsterdam; otherwise removing him from the case would have been far more difficult.

Carmon brought a fresh cigarette to his mouth and snapped his lighter. "Tell me, what's this I hear about the way you brought Ramzy Awwad down from Sidon?"

"I let him ride in the front without his hands bound, if that's what you mean."

"What the hell for?"

"I thought he deserved as much."

"Even if it meant it might be easier for him to escape?"

"It seems he didn't."

"Awwad was after Abu Nidal himself," Yehuda broke in.

Shai turned to the small Iraqi Jew. "What did he tell you?"

"Nothing," Carmon answered.

"It seems he almost got him in London." Yehuda's voice rose with excitement. "He didn't tell us and wouldn't confirm it when we asked him, but we think from eyewitness reports that he was at the Dorchester trying to stop Abu Nidal's men from shooting Shlomo Argov."

Carmon leaned back in his chair. "Not that he was trying to do us any favors."

"We haven't been able to break Awwad," Yehuda went on. "We could drug him and eventually he would say something, but with his training we couldn't be sure if he was telling us the truth or not. Or we could hold him in prison indefinitely to remove his services from—"

"But Yehuda's come up with another idea," Carmon interrupted.

Yehuda nodded. "Awwad's Arab and terrorist connections are obviously far superior to ours, so I've suggested to Meir that if we can get Awwad to agree to it, we release him and send you after Abu Nidal together."

Shai turned to Carmon in surprise. He could see Yehuda creating such an operation, but it was not like Carmon to release a coup like Awwad. Shai watched Carmon bring the cigarette to his mouth and pull on it in one fluid motion. "Why did you go along with it?" Shai asked.

A small smile played on Carmon's mouth. "Are you suggesting that it might not be for humanitarian reasons, to save lives?"

"I'm suggesting there's something else you want."

"You hear this, Yehuda?" Carmon said. "That's our Shai, isn't it?" He came forward and placed his cigarette on the edge of the ebony ashtray. "Well, actually, there is one small thing. We want you to see what you can learn about PLO operations in Europe from him."

Shai understood now. "You mean you want me to get what he wouldn't give you under interrogation?"

"In a word, yes."

"What if Awwad won't agree to work with us?"

"That's your job," Carmon said, "to convince him."

"Does he know anything about this?"

"No," Yehuda said. "We thought it best that you put it to him, since you already have some rapport."

Shai remembered the cold fury he had seen in Awwad's eyes when he had used the Palestinian's sister as a shield.

"Where is he?" Shai asked.

"That's another problem." Yehuda laced his fingers together. "He's . . ."

"He told his interrogators he liked being back in 'his Palestine,'" Carmon said. "When he wouldn't cooperate, I had him dumped in Ansar."

Shai's face sagged. The newly erected prison camp in southern Lebanon was a hot, crowded outdoor hell.

"I know," Yehuda said. "On top of everything else, you'll have to find a way to overcome whatever his being there has done to him."

"We're taking a substantial risk letting him go." Carmon picked up his cigarette again. "It's up to you to prevent him from disappearing, and there's one more thing—something to minimize the long-term danger. As soon as you've learned all you can and you get Abu Nidal, I want you to kill Awwad. I don't want any more of this coddling a terrorist."

Shai looked at the spiky, expressionist Marcel Janco vision of the heroes of '48 next to the shimmering Agam on the wall behind Carmon. "He's a moderate."

"He's a murderer," Carmon said sharply. "He fired the shots when those two terrorists burst into our embassy in Paraguay in '70. He killed the first secretary's wife and wounded another employee. Go tell Yosef Ben

Nir that the man who gunned down his wife in cold blood is a moderate.''

"Still, that was twelve years ago. Positions change. Indications are that he's changed. If Awwad helps us now...?''

"When you get the order, you kill him," Carmon said. "I want no argument about this. I don't want to wait to see who he murders next. I trust I'm making myself clear."

RAMZY SAT IN THE HEAT and dust of one of the inner areas of the Ansar Prison Camp, staring through the glistening bales of silver wire. Eight of these areas comprised Camp B, each with a patrol road encircling it. A high fence covered with more bales of barbed wire surrounded the entire camp. Beyond it rose a bulldozed wall of dirt, where the Israeli soldiers sat with their weapons. Watchtowers loomed behind these hills.

Long tents crowded each area. Boys as young as fifteen, men as old as sixty, sat everywhere, stood idly, some splashing themselves with water. Five thousand of them in Ansar. The stench from the outhouses, the densely packed men sweating in the heat, the unwashed clothes, the cooking, the garbage, permeated everything. The Israelis had stormed the refugee camps and Palestinian neighborhoods and had swept up thousands, not even knowing who they had captured.

The Israelis did not seem to know what they wanted to do now. They let the captives run their own lives inside the camp. Each area had a mukhtar, a chosen leader; they cooked their own food, and the Israeli military police seemed unable to control them. They splashed water all over the place so that the Israelis would have to bring them more, and the Israelis did. The mukhtars found they could bargain for advantages. The Israelis wanted to count them each morning, so they demanded pitas instead of army bread in exchange, and received them.

They held training and indoctrination classes. Artisans fashioned wooden Kalashnikovs with kitchen knives that were almost indistinguishable from the fireable weapons. In the tent classes untold numbers who had not been involved before were taught the ideology, and beginning at dawn they trained outside in what physical space there was.

Suddenly Ramzy saw a group of men in their brown prison shirts and pants hurrying excitedly around the corner of a nearby tent, carrying some white clothes. He knew what they were preparing. Often in the evening there would be a homosexual wedding ceremony, the "bride" dressed in white, the dominant partner singing love songs as the guests gathered around. Afterward, the "bride" was no longer available to other men. Ramzy thought with discomfort about how much his time in the West had separated him from the masses of his people.

Reflecting off the bales of barbed wire, the sun caused sweat to drip freely under Ramzy's clothes. Behind him in the dirt rose the sounds of a quiet soccer game. With nothing to do but sit here, the rage reached every part of him. The massive Israeli bombings of Palestinian suburbs, the arrogant attempt to bulldoze Lebanon into the country they wanted it to be, with no regard for who fell under the rubble had done something he had not believed possible—it had made him hate the Israelis even more.

IN AMSTERDAM, Abu Nidal held the article with the information on his target's movements that he had torn from the London *Jewish Chronicle*. He looked down from the second-story window above the Oude Zijds Achterburgwal Canal. For blocks in either direction red lights reflected in the dark water. On both sides of the canal, men prowled the narrow brick sidewalks and studied the semidressed women in the picture windows before they made their choice and were buzzed through the doors.

Abu Nidal heard water from the sink running in the bathroom. He had met Leila Fahdi the night before when he had attended a reading of her revolutionary poetry at the Amsterdam Free University. It had infuriated him that only a handful of Arab students had turned up.

In a well-lit window directly across from him, he looked at a small blond Dutch girl. Wearing a bra, panties and high boots, she was lounging on fringed pillows and imitation French antique furniture, flipping through a magazine. Impatient with Fahdi, he had the urge to have the blonde again, the way he had when he had first arrived in Amsterdam. But once the drapes had been drawn across the window, he had not liked the tiny velvet wallpapered bedroom in the back that she had taken him to. It had stunk of sweat. He had not so much minded her washing him, but had hated her putting that thing on him, and when everything was over, opening the plastic-lined wastebasket, taking it off him wet and full and dropping it on the smelly pile.

The bathroom door opened, and he quickly folded the newspaper article, pushed it into his pocket and turned. She was wearing one of his shirts, unbuttoned to reveal the tops of her breasts, and her legs and feet were bare. He approached and kissed her hard, sensed the shirt lift as her arms reached around his back, felt her nakedness beneath it.

Abruptly she pulled away and, wondering what he had put in his pocket so hurriedly, stared at him. What frightened her were his eyes: black, piercing and always watching every move when she was in the room with him.

She spoke softly. "I wrote a new poem inspired by the Zionist invasion of Lebanon. Let me recite it for you."

He said nothing.

Nervous, she began:

"The hatred pulls open my jaws,
Gnaws me ravenous.
Only their hearts will satisfy
The vast hunger inside me.
I was once a lamb roaming my own fields
But they killed the peace inside me.
Turned me into a wolf who stalks a
Never-ending night."

He remained where he was. "Your words are not enough."

She looked down. Her voice came out at half its strength. "You didn't like my poem?"

"I came to hear your reading. I am moved by your words."

Her head came up. She felt the power in his face, the wide nose, the large forehead, and was frightened again. "Thank you," she said.

"I ask you to come with me."

Beneath her fear a small excitement rose. "Where?"

"It doesn't matter. Anywhere. Wherever I say."

"What are you planning?"

"Something enormous, the greatest thing a Palestinian has yet done for his people."

That boyfriend of hers, Khalid Monsour, suddenly seemed so silly the way he spouted revolutionary ideology from his houseboat, with his engineering books and drinking. "What is it?" she pressed. "Tell me."

"In time. The clock has begun counting down. There is a timetable. It must happen in Europe, before the world's eyes. But for now there are other targets that must be silenced while we wait for the main one to arrive at the time and place."

Leila would not push and risk angering him, but she would find out. Still, there was something she wanted to know that had been rumored in the coffeehouses.

"Is it true that your brothers are in business with the Zionists, selling vegetables and fruit from the West Bank, inside Israel?"

He came near, grabbed both her shoulders and pulled her to his face. He held her there for a long moment, then pushed her to the wooden floor. "Kneel," he said.

She saw his eyes, and scared, quickly got on her knees.

He unbuttoned his pants and stepped out of them. "Lean forward on your hands."

Humiliated, she bent and extended her arms perpendicular to the floor. How could he do this to her? As he neared standing from behind, she was afraid he would force his way hurtfully into that other place. His hands held her thighs. She wanted to run to the bathroom for her clothes but was terrified of what he would do to her.

Her body stiffened, then she felt him probe, find her, and she relaxed a little as he pushed. She closed her eyes and bit her lower lip. His fingers grabbed her stomach and pulled her against him again and again, farther, easier. She opened her eyes and watched the floor move. This was not at all how she had imagined it in her excitement to be with this man who struck at the Zionists. The degradation mixed with the blood flowing to her face.

He jerked her against him, against him harder now. The power increased with the thrusts. He showed no signs of finishing quickly. She thought about the other Palestinian men she had been with. She felt him even deeper, and then suddenly she realized why he did it this way. He was not like all those castrated poets and students who spoke defiant words, then cowered from the Zionist bombers. He was powerful and reveled in his machismo. He was showing her his potency, symbolically showing all Palestinian women the potency of the Palestinian male who had burst his bonds. She was finally with a Palestinian turned on by his strength.

She moved on her palms and, using her inner muscles, felt him wonderfully. She rocked back and forth. His fingers reached around and touched her. Sounds, unrestrained, escaped her throat. She moved faster. Her entire body tingled, and nothing existed, only the moving and touching. He took his hand away for a while, re-placed it, removed it, then brought it back again.

"Keep it there," she whispered.

She continued, not even hearing the sounds coming from her mouth until they turned into a hoarse rasp; and she felt him inside her and touching her, just above it, without stopping, faster and faster, on and on, till finally she tightened, let out a voiceless scream and shuddered in soft spasms.

She closed her eyes, and limp, let him pull her against him again and again and again, amazed at how long he could do this. His legs moved even nearer as he gripped her thighs. Her whole body was loose as he pushed somehow still deeper. She gasped. There was nothing else, only the power and the incredible sensation and his pulling her, pulling her. Then, a lifetime away, his hands let go, and she felt the flow.

His exit tingled pleasurably, and as he sat back on the bed, she stretched out on the floor, the cold wood feeling good against her nakedness. Without a word he headed into the bathroom, closing the door, and she heard the water in the shower. She lay there against the wood, to-tally content, and started to doze. Then it struck her. He had folded some paper and put it in his pocket.

She sat up, reached over and pulled his pants toward her. From inside his front pocket she removed a news-paper article in English. She knew enough English from her travels and study of the English poets to read it. She hurriedly opened the article and looked at the headline before he could return. Her heart pounded as she saw the words: SHIMON PERES TO ATTEND SOCIALIST

INTERNATIONAL. Underlined were the words Al-bufeira, Portugal, and the date September 24. She read the first few lines, then nervously placed the article back in his pants and pushed them to where they had fallen. She lay back on the floor, hardly able to contain her excitement.

The Israeli opposition Labor Party leader, the one who talked of making peace with the Arab nations, would be attending the Socialist International on the Algarve coast in a little over a month. That was what Abu Nidal had meant by a timetable. He would kill him, not in some back street in Tel Aviv, but in front of Europe's leaders.

SHAI ENTERED Ramzy's brother's *al-Shaab* newspaper office in East Jerusalem. The several men working at old manual typewriters in the copy-strewn room fell silent and looked at him.

"I would like to see Fawaz Awwad, please," Shai said in Arabic.

No one spoke or made any move to help him. Then a man in his late fifties, with a receding hairline and a pencil-thin graying mustache, limped into the doorway of an office at the back of the room. Shai recognized him from his photograph and approached.

"I do not see people from the censor's office without an appointment," Fawaz said sternly.

"I'm not from the censor." Shai stopped. "I've come to talk to you about your brother."

"I have nothing to say. I have no contact with him. Good day." Fawaz turned and limped back into his small office.

Shai followed and shut the door behind him.

Fawaz turned. "You have questioned me before. It has yielded you nothing. Go and check your files."

"We have your brother," Shai said.

Fawaz showed no reaction. He moved around his desk, but Shai noticed his hands trembled slightly as he lowered himself into the chair. "Why should I believe you?"

"I don't need you to believe me. I want to take you to see him."

Fawaz looked out the window at the hills that led to Ramallah. "Why?"

"Call it a gesture of goodwill."

Fawaz's head came back. His voice was icy. "What do you want?"

"I'm offering you a chance to see the brother we believe you have not seen since East Jerusalem fell to us. We already have him, so this isn't a ruse to place him in danger. At the moment that's all I want."

"I don't believe you."

"Whether you believe me or not doesn't matter. We both know I could deport you to Jordan at any time for your writings, or take you to interrogation. So there's no need to trick you with a story about your brother."

Fawaz twisted the ring on his small finger and was silent for a long moment. "Where is he?"

"At a prison camp in southern Lebanon."

"Ansar?"

"Yes."

"And you would take me there?"

"There's a helicopter waiting to fly us now."

Fawaz stared at the Israeli trying to determine his motive, then placed both hands on his wobbly desk and pushed his way to his feet. "All right, I will go. But whatever you ask me to do once we're there, I'll refuse.

Even if it means being in the next room and not seeing him, I will not help you.''

"Bring a jacket," Shai said. "It'll be cool by the time we bring you back."

SHAI STOOD at the open second-floor window in the small stone building used by the Ansar camp commander and watched the jeep bearing Ramzy approach. Across the road, cacophony rose from the teeming Camps A and B. Even from this distance the stench was terrible. Everywhere bales of barbed wire wound over the height of the numerous fences. On this side of the road, to his right, stood the small Camp C that housed the more violent prisoners. To his left clustered the tents where the Israeli soldiers and medical pesonnel lived and beyond them the tents of the Israeli prison camp, without fences, that held those guilty of insubordination, threatening an officer, going AWOL, looting, and the like.

Shai turned to Fawaz who was sitting against the far wall. "Your brother's coming."

Fawaz showed no emotion. "Whatever trick you're trying will not work."

"I said I would take you to see your brother. He'll be here in a moment."

Fawaz looked at him but said nothing further.

Minutes later there was a knock on the door. Shai crossed the room and opened it. Flanked by two armed soldiers, Awwad looked tired; but still the deep lines below his eyes held defiance.

"You can go now," Shai said to the guards. As they left, Ramzy showed no reaction, though it was clear that he recognized him. "Please, come in," Shai said.

Ramzy entered, puzzled, wondering why this man who had captured him was here. Then he saw Fawaz. At first he thought it was a mirage from the bright sun. His brother rose and limped forward, favoring the right leg that had been crushed in an oil rig accident. Stunned, Ramzy felt the emotion catch in his throat, and then he forced it back. They would not break him this way.

"I'll return in a few minutes." Shai walked out the door and eased it closed behind him.

Ramzy neared, touched his brother's face with one hand, then the two men abruptly hugged and held each other for a long time.

Ramzy pulled back gently from the embrace. "What do they want?"

"I don't know. That man came to my office this morning and said he would take me here to see you. He said nothing else."

"What they want will be clear soon enough."

"You must not let my coming here or concern for my safety affect you in any way."

A hard smile outlined Ramzy's lips. "They will get nothing from me."

Fawaz limped to a chair. "My leg hurts less if I sit." Fawaz lowered himself onto the hard wood and saw his brother's concern. "It's all right. I live with it. And you, my brother, how are you?"

"They are probably listening to what we say," Ramzy said.

"It makes no difference."

Ramzy pulled the chair from around the desk, brought it near his brother and sat. "I was in the land," he said softly. "The first time since I was twelve. I could think of only two things. I was actually there, and I knew I was near you. I ached to come to Jerusalem, to see you."

Fawaz reached out and touched his younger brother's hand. "And now you have. We are together, and the important thing is you're not hurt. It does not matter that we are here or for how long, or what they want from you. They cannot take this moment from either of us, no matter what they do."

"You must tell Nadjla," Ramzy said suddenly. "I saw her for a moment before they took me. She doesn't know if I'm alive."

Just then the door opened, and Shai entered, alone.

"I'll get word to her," Fawaz said to his brother.

"Please say goodbye now," Shai said.

Fawaz forced his way to his feet.

Ramzy hugged him to his body. "I love you," Ramzy whispered into his brother's ear, then pulled away.

"I expect to see a new novella soon," Fawaz said.

"Ramzy Awwad, come with me." Shai turned to Fawaz. "You will be taken back to Jerusalem in a few minutes."

Ramzy looked at his brother for a last moment, then brought his eyes to the Israeli. "More interrogation?" He spat the words.

Shai shook his head. "Please, come." He walked out the door.

Ramzy squeezed his brother's shoulder, then moved into the corridor where the Israeli was waiting. They continued down the stairs and outside where two armed soldiers stood leisurely, Uzis cradled in their arms. There was an empty jeep parked off the main road.

Shai headed to it and motioned for Ramzy to climb in beside him. As the Palestinian pulled the door closed, one of the soldiers handcuffed him. Shai drove along the dirt wall toward the main barbed-wire fence. The guards pulled the heavy gates open and let them pass.

The Israeli sped across the flat, rocky plateau, east, in the direction of the Israeli-held village of Nabatiye. Just south of Nabatiye, with a commanding view of the border, rose the mountaintop Beaufort Castle, where the Palestinian spotters had directed shells at the northern Israeli settlements.

Silent, Ramzy felt the coolness of the early-evening air blowing on his face and through his hair. This was an old interrogator's trick. Give the prisoner the sense of how close freedom was, if only he cooperated. Ramzy glanced at the gun on the Israeli's left hip, gauging the odds of smashing him over the head with the handcuffs and trying for it.

Suddenly the Israeli pulled to the side of the road.

''What is this?'' Ramzy demanded.

Shai knew Carmon would have his head if he reported having taken this chance. ''In a few minutes I'm going to let you go. I won't try to stop you. But I want you to listen to what I have to say first.''

Shai watched Awwad's dark eyes settle on the pistol in the holster at his waist. He removed the gun, pulled the

clip from the butt and tossed it to the Arab, who, handcuffed, made no move to catch it, and the bullets smacked
against his thigh.

Ramzy listened to the terrain for sounds of Israeli vehicles, the trap. He heard only the small rustling of the
wind through the olive trees. He reached for the hard
metal clip and held it in his fingers.

"I want Abu Nidal," Shai said.

Ramzy felt the cool breeze against the anger inside him.
The Israeli would slit his throat if he did not get what he
was after, or do it later on. Ramzy looked at the rolling
pine-filled hills ahead of them. It was beginning to grow
dark; if he could get away, escape would be possible.

"Ramzy, it's the future that counts now. You can hate
us, you can hate me." Despite the coolness of the evening, Shai felt the sweat prickling his skin like tiny
needles. "If I were in your position in Lebanon, in Ansar, I would probably detest every Israeli ever born. But
somehow it has to stop. We're losing too many sons,
you're losing too many sons."

"You started this war, not us." Fury squeezed Ramzy's
voice. "You *knew* it was Abu Nidal who shot your ambassador."

"Yes, we knew. But the war has nothing to do with the
shooting in London. It's about the amount of artillery
sitting on our border and what it was doing to the people
living under those guns. You left us no choice, only how
far to go in. Ramzy, the question now is where do we both
go from here? Lebanon's over. I want Abu Nidal. I want
you to help me get him. We believe you were after him
yourself in London."

"You're the greater threat."

"I think not. Abu Nidal has killed your friends. He'll continue to kill them. He'll get you eventually. The greatest threat to those on both sides who believe, even after this, in the possibility of a just settlement are the Palestinian extremists. We must have someone left alive we can talk to."

"You don't care what Abu Nidal's doing to the PLO. You want him because he's killing Jews."

"You're right. That's my primary concern, but I also believe what I said about Palestinian moderates. It really doesn't matter if you accept that or not. If we eliminate him, your friends in Europe, those who can affect Western opinion for your cause will be safe. Abu Nidal will not stop. We both know his success in igniting this war will only embolden him."

Ramzy stared at the Israeli. "And if I say no, you kill me or lock me back in that pigpen?"

Shai removed a key from his pocket, reached over and unlocked the handcuffs. "You can leave anytime you want. I won't try to stop you."

Ramzy held the metal clip in his fingers. If this was some trick, he could still use it. If it was not, all he had to do was agree, disappear and return to his operations in Europe.

"I understand you were very close to Said Hammami," Shai said. "It was courageous, being the first to meet openly with us. Abu Nidal cut him down and gloated over it, didn't he? Work with me, Ramzy, and we can help each other stop him."

Ramzy remained silent.

"Our last trace of Abu Nidal was in Holland. I'm leaving tomorrow. I'll be in the bar at the Victoria Hotel in Amsterdam between seven and nine in the evening, starting a week from tonight. I'll wait ten days."

Ramzy looked back toward Ansar. His voice shook. "With all those in there, with what you've done to us in Lebanon, you think because you bring my brother then let me go that I'll help you?"

"There are workmen's clothes in the back of the jeep, identity papers in the name of a Christian mechanic from Jezzin. There are also *hummous*, olives and goat's milk."

Ramzy pocketed the metal clip, then, watching the Israeli the whole time, he climbed out of the jeep. He went to the rear and pulled out the small bag.

Shai looked at his brown prison shirt and slacks. "You better change here before you run into one of our patrols in those clothes."

Ramzy said nothing.

Shai turned the ignition. "My name's Shai Shaham," he said over the rumble of the motor. Then he turned the wheel, pulled the jeep around and headed back to Ansar.

# BOOK II: ABU NIDAL

**7**  September 4 • Vienna, Austria

LEILA FAHDI FELT excited and nervous as she walked through old Vienna beside Abu Nidal. The time for her to play her part in the strike had finally arrived. Ahead of them, the Gothic St. Stephen's Cathedral towered in the pedestrian square. Leila was still afraid to ask what had forced him to suddenly fly to Baghdad and then to Damascus, leaving her here. He had told her that much about his absence. She also knew, from looking at his passport while he was in the shower, that he had been to Portugal just before they had met.

At the edge of the Kartnerstrasse pedestrian street that led from the square, he stopped and surveyed her. The navy skirt he had bought her fell below the knee, but was tight enough to reveal her fine figure. Her wavy black hair touched the white blouse that was parted to reveal her breasts. He reached over and fastened the second button.

"He will find you attractive, because you are."

Her smile flashed. She wanted him to hold her before she went, but dared not ask, afraid he would interpret it as weakness.

"He's conservative, a banker," Abu Nidal said. "You know how to act, now go."

She looked at him, nodded quickly, then strode through the fashionable pedestrian street lined with stores, hotels and restaurants. Everywhere people sat in outdoor cafés surrounded by flowers in narrow sills.

Leila was amazed at how wonderful she felt, with all the talk and reciting in the coffeehouses behind her. Being with Abu Nidal had suddenly lifted her with a fresh sense of pride. For the first time in her life she did not feel like that small, poorly clothed Palestinian girl who had stolen wallets and purses from swimmers on Beirut's beaches. She increased her gait. She knew she would do anything to hold on to the way she felt now.

At the National Opera House, Leila turned onto the Ring. She walked up the lovely broad tree-lined avenue, with red trams running along its edges, that encircled the inner city. Almost there, she headed down the stairs to the underpass.

Her heart beat quickly as she came up the escalator and saw the Arab Commercial Bank. Its director, Taha Hamshari, was the PLO's banker in Europe—the man who invested, then dispersed the vast contributions of the oil states and the twenty percent European allotment of the Liberation Tax levied on Palestinian wages in Arab countries. As she strode along the sidewalk, she examined her blouse to make certain the button above her breasts had not come undone.

Inside, she asked a middle-aged, balding mustachioed man behind a desk for a loan application. From his accent, he was either Tunisian or Algerian; she was not sure. He hurried to find one for her from another department, and when he returned, she smiled warmly, then sat at a couch near the door and began to fill it out.

When she finished, she returned to the same mustachioed man and smiled again. "I know this is not normally done," she said in soft Arabic. "But I have heard the bank president is interested in helping young Palestinians start businesses. If I could just see him for a few minutes . . . ?" She looked down demurely.

He studied the form, his expression businesslike.

"I'm tired of waiting in the camps for someone to sweep me back home on a magic carpet. I want to start something on my own." She said the words exactly as Abu Nidal had rehearsed them with her.

He looked at the sheet for a long moment, then nodded, picked up the phone and dialed an internal connection. "It's Azmy, sir. There's someone here I think you should see." He nodded, said thank you and hung up. He smiled at her. "Come with me."

He led her to a heavy oak door at the rear of the bank and knocked. After a moment, a handsome man in his forties, wearing a charcoal business suit and glasses that hung from a gold chain around his neck, answered.

"This is Nima Kanaan. She has an application for a loan that I think you'll have to look at yourself if we are to consider it. Miss Kanaan, our president, Mr. Taha Hamshari." Hamshari was Algerian, as was the bank.

"Thank you for seeing me." Leila extended her hand.

"My pleasure," Hamshari said, taking it. "Come in, Miss Kanaan." As she walked past him, the scent of anemones swept the air. He took the sheet of paper from the balding employee. "Thank you, Azmy, and please ask Nayef to bring us some coffee." As Azmy left, Hamshari closed the door, slipped his glasses on and moved into his office, studying the loan application. "Please, sit down," he said without looking at her.

Leila sat in the chair and crossed her legs, trying to control her nervousness. This was not starting right. He was hardly paying attention to her.

"So you want to start a combination café and bookstore," he said, settling into his chair and turning the sheet over without looking up. "What languages do you intend to stock books in?"

"Arabic and German," she said.

He slowly set the sheet down. "I see you've just come from Amman. Do you speak German?"

"I plan to hire someone to handle those books until I learn the language."

He frowned. "So why did you choose to open your café in Vienna if you know no German?"

She felt a line of sweat forming on her upper lip; he was being totally unreceptive to her femininity.

"I want to make something of myself, be part of life here in the center of Europe's music. Once the café is successful, I will have small concerts in the evenings."

"How is it that you learned of classical music?"

"From a Viennese woman physician. She came to the Jabal Hussein camp to help us. We became friends."

Just then there was a knock on the door, and a young Arab of fifteen or sixteen came in carrying a tray with a brass pitcher and small porcelain cups. He set the tray on the mother-of-pearl inlaid table to the left of Hamshari's desk. As he left, the banker rose, poured the thick Turkish coffee and gave her one of the steaming handleless cups.

Hamshari returned to his desk, sipped the sweet coffee and set it down beside his pens. "Tell me about this house in Amman you list as collateral."

She leaned forward in the chair, holding on to the coffee cup with both hands. "My brother works in the oil fields. He is still very old-fashioned. He got Cabinet permission as a non-Jordanian to buy the house, then he gave it to me as a dowry."

"And you claim it is worth two hundred thousand dinars?"

"That's what he says. He may, of course, have exaggerated. He believes, somewhat simplemindedly, that this would get me a better husband."

Hamshari nodded. "I understand your brother."

She sipped some of the coffee, then set it down on the inlaid table next to her. Abu Nidal's words replayed in her ears. "I'm tired of waiting like a visitor in King Hussein's country," she said, "of waiting for someone else to sweep me back home on a magic carpet or help me produce more refugee children. I want to make something of my life and at the same time offer something to my people."

For the first time, he smiled. "It's admirable what you propose. I fear the political situation consumes the Palestinians, takes them away from learning. They need the book as well as the gun."

"If I thought I could be of more use with a rifle, I would raise one."

"Well, I don't think we need you to do that. I'll have someone cable a cooperating bank in Amman to verify your property holdings. It should take, I'm afraid, at least several weeks, but as soon as we receive the answer, I'll authorize exactly what you need." He lifted his cup. "I think you've underestimated what it will take you to get started, but we'll arrange that, too."

She looked at the carpet. "How can I thank you?"

"By being a success."

Her head came up slowly; she felt in control now. "I will, and if you would honor me, I would like to show you how, with an example of my cooking. May I prepare dinner for you sometime soon?" Abu Nidal had told her that Hamshari's wife had died the year before from a protracted bout with cancer.

He looked at her; she was quite beautiful. "I suppose we could consider it part of my researching your loan application. Yes, I would be delighted."

"How about tomorrow night, at eight?"

He frowned. "Unfortunately, I have an engagement tomorrow evening. A business colleague from Geneva has invited me to dine with him." He flipped the page on his calendar. "But the following evening, the sixth?"

She rose. "I look forward to it. My address is on the loan application."

He came around his desk. "Let me accompany you out."

He opened his office door, then escorted her across the bank floor to the main exit, the scent of her perfume staying with him as she walked.

"Thank you," she said at the heavy glass entrance.

He nodded. "I am happy to help those anxious to help others, as well as themselves. Until the day after tomorrow."

He turned and headed back to his office.

TEN HOURS LATER, the night of September 4, Shai sat at the bar in the Victoria Hotel in Amsterdam, sipping his third glass of oude genever. He looked at his watch— 9:30. He had been waiting here like this for ten days. So, the Arab was not coming, he forced himself to admit.

Shai returned to his lightly scented genever. Carmon would scream bloody murder when he found out he had lost Awwad already, maybe even threaten to throw him out of the service. Shai wondered if he could return to the kibbutz without Sarit being there. He doubted it.

He was surprised that Awwad had disappeared. The Colonel had often said that Shai's major weakness as a spy was that he believed too much in people. It was the Colonel's blend of cynicism with stabs of hope that endeared Shai to the man who had recruited him in the months after the Yom Kippur War disaster.

As a teenager in pre-State Palestine, Shai had trekked with his father in silence through the vast Sinai Peninsula. The blond, bearded Zionist from Hungary had formed an unheard-of bond with the nomadic bedouin, from whom Shai had learned respect for the surrounding culture, as well as his flawless Arabic.

As a result of these years in the desert, during the 1956 Sinai campaign Shai had been drafted into military intelligence as a field intelligence officer. He later continued to serve his reserve duty in military intelligence while living in the Negev desert and developing low plastic tunnels into a science for growing early crops the country could export to Europe at considerable profit. Disguised as a bedouin, he had sneaked behind enemy lines before the Six Day War to report on Egyptian preparations for attack.

When Israel's civilian army had mobilized yet again in 1973, Shai, then a brigade intelligence officer, had traveled during the war in a small reconnaissance plane over the familiar Sinai wadis and mountains.

After that the Colonel had driven down to Shai's kibbutz in the Negev unannounced. Shai had heard him speak several times at intelligence briefings, but they had never actually met. The two men had talked for a long time under the winter desert sun.

The Yom Kippur War had been a national trauma, a shock, but for the intelligence fieldmen, not a surprise. They had known, predicted the attack. Yet the top government and military intelligence echelons had misinterpreted the data. They had spent six years since the lightning Six Day War flexing their invincibility. When the decision makers had received the reports, they had been convinced that the Egyptian and Syrian movements were mere maneuvers, that they would not dare attack such a power. So, reluctant to undergo the huge cost unnecessarily, they did not mobilize, and more than three thousand had died. In the Six Day War they had lost seven hundred.

The morale in all the services had plunged. The Colonel needed strong, seasoned men to revitalize the youthful agents who had seen everything they had risked their lives for ignored and their friends and neighbors killed in battles that could have been prevented. Shai could help them enormously in the external service, the Colonel had told him.

He had sat on the bed next to Sarit that night, and she had placed her cheek on his shoulder and listened. If he could help stop what had just happened to the country from ever occurring again, he needed to go. She had nodded against him. Afterward, as they had made love, tears had dropped down his cheeks.

Shai stared at his oude jenever, rested his head in his hands and let his fingers push through his thinning hair. He would try to keep the news about Awwad from Carmon as long as possible and go after Abu Nidal on his own. Carmon was used to his vague reports anyway.

Saddened that he had been wrong about Awwad, Shai put on his hooded parka and went out into the drizzle. Across the channel, the nineteenth-century central station was silhouetted in the darkness. He had spent over two weeks searching for where Abu Nidal had stayed, whom he had contacted, slept with, anything that would place him at one end of a trail—but had unearthed nothing. He had hoped Awwad would have greater success penetrating the Arab circles here. Shai turned left along the ocean channel. A yellow trolley rumbled by, its windows bright, its patrons dry.

The rain was slanting in the beams of the car lights, pounding cold and hard on the sidewalk. A taxi suddenly slammed to a halt behind him, and Shai whirled. The driver beckoned him through the glass, evidently thinking the lone man might want a ride. Shai shook his head, and as the vehicle splashed through a puddle and sped away, he thrust his hands deeper into his pockets. Maybe he should try a movie, but he was restless and in no mood to sit in a small seat for two hours.

The area he was approaching was poorly lit, the neon streetlamps casting a sickly light that hardly stretched halfway across the sidewalk before it was gathered by the darkness. He looked back in the direction he had come. Nothing moved. A sliver of lightning flashed in the distance, followed by the soft, faraway roll of thunder.

He walked on for over an hour until, following a series of narrow dark streets flanked by huge buildings, he came into Dam Square. He entered the first cab at the stand and told the driver to take him to the Carlton Hotel. After they arrived, Shai retraced his direction by foot back to the neon-lit Muntplein, making certain he had not been followed, and tired, headed for his own Schiller Hotel. He had no idea where to begin in the morning.

IT WAS AFTER 10:00 P.M., the night of the fourth, when Abu Nidal walked through the dark Vienna woods, his flashlight's beam playing on the thin beeches.

"Here," the Iraqi intelligence officer said, flicking his light twice in the darkness.

Abu Nidal switched off his own beam and headed through the clearing. In the moonlight he could make out the small bag at the man's feet.

"I cannot officially help you anymore," the Iraqi said, "but unofficially I'll do what I can. I don't fully understand these new orders."

"Your government collapsed under pressure from the Americans and French," Abu Nidal said sharply. "That's how you understand them."

"Oh, yes, now I see. The Super Entendards and the Exocet missiles. The American State Department and the French have been most insistent that we be removed from the list of countries that support terrorism before we receive such weapons. Are they demanding that you completely close your offices as well as the training camp?"

"Yes."

"What will you do?"

"I've been to Damascus."

"Good. Syrian Intelligence must be impressed with what you've done for us. And, of course, they too are anxious to destroy Arafat and the mainline Fatah." The Iraqi picked up the bag and handed it to him.

Abu Nidal removed the WZ-63. The small Polish machine pistol, designed for use by paratroopers and issued to Iraqi tank personnel, was thirteen inches long and weighed only four pounds. It fired 9 mm bullets one-handed like a pistol, or with its forward grip folded down and wire stock extended, it became a fully automatic submachine gun.

Abu Nidal flicked the safety and squeezed a burst at a nearby tree, shredding the bark. Assured the weapon was in good working order, he replaced it in the bag that held the extra clips. He would kill the banker Hamshari with it in two days.

HIS CLOTHES SOAKED, Shai passed the enclosed terrace café-restaurant, walked into the Schiller Hotel and took the stairs to the third floor. At his door, he removed his key, which he always kept in his pocket rather than at the desk, pushed it into the lock and turned it. He would take a hot shower, then read the newspaper and go to bed. The room was cold as he entered and switched on the light.

Ramzy Awwad was sitting in the chair opposite the bed.

"This is to let you know I could have killed you had I chosen to," Awwad said.

Shai slowly closed the door. "You should have turned on the heat. No reason for you to sit here in the cold."

"You get used to the cold in the camps."

Shai bent and turned the steam radiator up. "You're good. I never saw you." He removed his coat and tossed it on the bed. "When? And while you're at it, why?"

"Last night I followed you here. Tonight, I wanted to see what you'd do when I didn't show up. I wanted to learn something about you. Rather an unpleasant night for a walk, wasn't it?"

"I assume you've been to Amsterdam before? You seem to know your way around the city."

"I like Amsterdam. It's lovely."

"You spend a lot of time here?"

"Looking for evidence of my centers of operation?"

Shai paused, uncomfortable. "Let me change my clothes and we'll go someplace and have some coffee. If you're here, I assume we have something to talk about."

"Go ahead and change."

As the Israeli took some clothes into the bathroom, in his mind's eye Ramzy saw the photographs of his friend, Said Hammami, lying in his London office, blood draining from the three bullets in his body. He would even cooperate with the Israelis to stop Abu Nidal.

As Ramzy waited, his thoughts turned to the week and a half he had spent with Dalal in Damascus after the Israeli had released him. He could still feel her move inside him. He had rushed to the school in the hills, then had waited outside her classroom. When she had finally emerged, and he had held her with the children crowding around, tears had rolled down his cheeks. He still had no idea if he had cried because of the devastation in Lebanon, the relief at being free or the happiness at seeing her.

Shai came out of the bathroom. ''Shall we go?''

Ramzy let the memories dissipate and rose. ''Yes, but not for coffee. There's no time.''

''You have a lead?''

''You think I've been spending all my time watching you?'' Ramzy headed for the door.

They drove in Ramzy's rented car along the nearby tree-lined Amstel Boulevard that fronted the river. Large barges moored at the Amstel's banks had been converted into houseboats.

''A Palestinian poetess, Leila Fahdi, left Amsterdam on August nineteenth,'' Ramzy said. ''Do you know of her?''

''No.''

''She was heard bragging among students at the Free University that she was going to help kill her people's enemies. She made a point of emphasizing not only Zionists. It's unlikely she could have suddenly decided to do this on her own, especially since Abu Nidal was here then.''

''Where did she go?''

Ramzy pulled off the road and squeezed into a spot near the water. ''That's what we're going to try to find out from the man she walked out on. I'm told he likes this bar.''

The rain had softened into a fine mist. They headed toward the Metro Bar across the street. Antinuclear graffiti was scrawled over its walls.

Inside, long-haired Dutch students and a number of Arabs filled the smoky room. Electronic blips and bleeps rose from the video games along the back walls. With Shai following, Ramzy approached a table where a group of young Arabs sat. There were no empty chairs.

''I'm looking for Khalid Monsour,'' Ramzy said. ''Can anybody tell me where I can find him?''

''Sure,'' one of the Arabs said, ''he's usually flat on his face under the table.'' He looked below. ''Hey, Khalid, you down there?''

They all laughed.

''Has he been in tonight?''

''In where? From what I understand, he hasn't been in anywhere lately. That seems to be his problem.'' One of the Arabs slapped the speaker on the back and laughed, spilling some of the beer he held in his other hand.

''I have some money from his father. Maybe if I left part of it here, you could give it to him.'' Ramzy took out two twenty-guilder notes and set them on the table.

The Arab student who had spoken first snatched them up. "He's not even in Amsterdam. He went to London, to heal his ailing heart."

"He'll be back eventually," another said. "Knowing Khalid, it shouldn't take him more than a year or two to get over it."

They all broke into fits of laughter again.

"Do you know where he is in London?"

"Sure. Where are the hookers? Earl's Court?"

An older Arab student who was sitting at the next table with a group of Dutchmen leaned over and touched Ramzy's arm. "Don't listen to them. I saw Khalid earlier. He was home studying."

Ramzy nodded.

"It's the blue houseboat, a half-dozen blocks up. *The Lantaarn*."

"Thank you," Ramzy said.

Outside, as they headed to the car, Shai turned to him. "Our students can be just as impossible."

Ramzy remained silent.

They drove along the river, spotted the houseboat, but there were no parking spaces nearby. Ramzy crossed the boulevard, rode up over the sidewalk onto a narrow pedestrian street and stopped.

"You better wait here. He'll respond better to me alone." Ramzy started to leave.

Shai looked at him. "If you're not back in half an hour, I'll come after you."

Ramzy smiled. "No need. He's Palestinian. You're the enemy."

Shai watched him move through the misty rain, then cross the street. He slipped out of the car and followed. Staying behind at the edge of the pedestrian street, he looked out. Lights shone long paths across the water, and he could clearly see as Awwad moved on the deck, and spoke to someone. Then both of them disappeared down a staircase into the boat.

Inside, Ramzy followed the young Egyptian, a medical student, along the narrow corridor until he stopped and knocked on a door.

"Who is it?" a hostile voice said from inside.

"Someone to see you, Khalid," the medical student said.

The door opened abruptly. The tall thin Khalid Monsour, with a scraggy beard on his chin that apparently would not grow over his cheeks, looked at Ramzy as the medical student left.

"I don't know you, do I? What do you want?"

"First of all, to come in. If you have become so European that you are unable to show hospitality, then I will leave."

"No, no. Please." He backed away from the door.

Ramzy entered the cramped, dimly lit room. There was a cot in one corner and a desk opposite it, filled with books and lit with a Tensor lamp. A bottle of clear arak stood between the books, open.

"I am Ramzy Awwad. Do you know the name?"

Khalid stared at him in disbelief. Here in his houseboat, Ramzy Awwad. He had read his stories in *Falastinuna*, *An Nahar*, even the weekend *Al Ahram*.

"Forgive me, I didn't know." Khalid nervously pulled the chair away from his desk. "Please, sit." He grabbed the bottle of arak. "I'll wash some glasses."

Ramzy sat on the edge of the bed and motioned Khalid toward the chair. "I need your help. It's a matter of importance."

"My help?"

"I must find Leila Fahdi."

Khalid banged the bottle down on his desk. "What do you want with her? She's nothing. Less than nothing."

A motorboat sped past on the river, and small waves rolled against the houseboat.

"Have you seen or spoken to her in the past two weeks?"

"That daughter of a whore." He fell into the chair, his face flushed. "No."

Ramzy waited.

"One day she's telling me how much she loves me," Monsour burst out, "the next day she's disappeared, her clothes gone from the room. Then I hear talk around the university that she's met someone else and left with him. That—"

"Did you try to find her?"

"No, what did I care?"

"Do any of her friends know where she's gone?"

"No. They know nothing."

"And you haven't heard from her since?"

Khalid fidgeted in the chair. "What do I care if I hear from her or not? What do I care what she said?"

"Then you have spoken to her?"

"No."

''Then how do you know what she said?''

Khalid hesitated, then looked down at his hands. ''I don't.''

''How long have you known her?''

''What difference does it make? I don't know. Six months.''

''Six months is a long time. If she left without a word, she is not worthy of you.''

''I told you, she's no more than a whore.''

''But you have spoken to her since she left?''

''No.''

''I think you have.''

''I said I didn't.'' Khalid rose restlessly and went to the small window. He was silent, then squeezed his eyes. ''There was just that damned postcard.''

''Do you still have it?''

''No, I don't know. I threw it out.''

''Will you look, just in case you didn't?''

He stared at the water. ''It's no use. It's not here.''

''When did it come?''

Khalid turned back, angry. ''I don't remember. I have better things to do than pay attention to anything that has to do with her.''

''Will you look for the card?''

''What for? How could anything she said matter?''

''It probably doesn't. Still, on the off chance that it might, I ask as a personal favor. If you still have it . . . ?''

Khalid abruptly went to the shelf above the bed and pulled down a volume of Mahmoud Darwish's poetry. He removed the postcard from the front page and thrust it at Ramzy.

On the back there was only a poem:

These chains of slavery
Now vanish
I lithely curve and turn
In rhythm to his lust.
I am like an ocean
Lapping at the shore of his manhood
And he like a waterfall
Crashing into my water.
There is no day
No night
Only the rush of being unbound.

Then one word, Goodbye, and the signature, Leila.

Awwad read the printed description on the upper left-hand corner of the card: The famous Lippizaner Stud of the Spanish Riding School, Josefsplatz, Vienna. He flipped the card over to the picture of the majestic white horse, its mane and tail interwoven with gold. He turned the card over again and read the postmark: Vienna, August 24.

"Please, do not tell anyone I was here or who I was asking about. If your boat mates or anyone else inquires, tell them I am a friend of your father's and he asked me to bring you news of the family."

Khalid nodded. "If you see her, tell her if she ever wants to come back I'll spit in her face."

Ramzy knew he would take her back in a moment. He rose. "One last thing. I need a picture of her, one that shows her face well."

Khalid went to the desk, yanked open a drawer, rummaged through it and came up with a photograph of her taken in front of the houseboat. That made him even angrier.

"Here," he said.

Ramzy took it. "I'll see that it's returned to you."

"Keep it for all I care."

"Nonetheless, I'll see that it's returned, and thank you." Ramzy let himself out.

Across the wet street, he saw the Israeli standing at the edge of the building. Ramzy approached and smiled. "It's about time an Arab kept a Jew waiting in the rain."

A similar smile touched Shai's lips. "We Jews don't mind. We're resilient. We waited outside for a homeland for two thousand years in all kinds of weather."

Ramzy's face suddenly hardened. "Maybe that's the problem now. Begin thinks he's still standing inside Auschwitz, in the rain." Ramzy walked to the car. As they ducked in, he said, "Eleven days ago, Leila was in Vienna. We better get there as soon as possible."

As the car bounced down the curb and they headed for Shai's hotel, the night turned into September 5. Ramzy hoped Abu Nidal was after some Israeli diplomat or the Soviet Jewry transit operation in Vienna and not who he feared he was.

# 8 September 5 • Vienna, Austria

RAMZY AND SHAI were the only ones in the elevator as they rode to the tenth floor of Vienna's Hilton Hotel. The early flight from Amsterdam had been delayed more than an hour, and after the two-hour flight, airport procedures and the taxi time, it was after three and they were only now arriving at their rooms.

The elevator slowed and Ramzy picked up his bag. ''I'll check with my people, see if they've had any sign of him. If you do the same with yours, we can meet outside in the park in two hours.''

The doors parted. ''If you want me in a hurry,'' Shai said, holding the elevator door open with his foot, ''call the embassy and tell the ambassador's secretary you want to speak to Gabriel.''

Ramzy nodded. ''Can you obtain weapons immediately? I believe you can get them easier than I can.''

''All right,'' Shai said, and walked out of the elevator.

Ramzy moved down the hall and watched the Israeli open the door farther along the corridor. Fear tightened in the depths of Ramzy's stomach when he thought about Abu Nidal. If he was still in Vienna and had sighted on a Palestinian target, it would almost certainly be Hassan Jibril. Head of the large PLO legation here, Jibril was in great part responsible for Austrian Chancellor Kreisky's position as the chief Western advocate of a Palestinian state in the West Bank and Gaza. Due to Jibril, the PLO had made greater inroads in Austria than in any other Western country.

Inside his room, Ramzy dropped his bags on the floor, then went into the bathroom and ran the cold water for a long time while he stared into the mirror. He saw the web of lines at each eye, the less certain mouth. He splashed the cold water on his face. He had been much surer about everything at twenty-six than now at forty-six. After the seizure of so much more of their land in 1967, he had had no doubts. Strike them anywhere on the globe, men, women, children.

He wiped his face, dropped the towel on the bed and headed for the door.

In front of the hotel, he climbed into a cab and gave the driver the address of the PLO office in Vienna. As the small Mercedes pulled from the curb, it struck Ramzy that for the first time in fourteen years he did not have to fear the Israelis locating and killing him. He felt an almost heady sense of freedom, though a voice at the back of his mind nagged that they could turn on him at any time.

The cab halted in front of the PLO office. Ramzy had already phoned Jibril the night before and warned him.

Ramzy emerged an hour later, worried. Jibril had seen nothing suspicious, and Ramzy knew that unless he was extraordinarily lucky they would not. An assassin always held the advantage. He could remain in hiding, then suddenly burst out at his designated place and time and fire. Ramzy wondered if the Israeli was faring any better. He looked at his watch and knew he still had a little time before their scheduled meeting.

Ramzy saw the red number one tram that circled the Ring glide to a halt at the street's edge. He hurried to it and jumped on just before the doors closed. As the tram slid forward, he checked to see if anyone was running toward the stop or if any car had suddenly pulled into traffic, but saw nothing. He made his way to the back of the crowded car and continued to search the road. The PLO office was public. Where he was going now, he did not want to be followed.

Ramzy stepped off on the Burgring. The gardens and huge white-marbled Imperial Palace stretched to his right, with the spire of St. Stephen's rising behind the buildings. He looked around him again, then descended into the underpass. There was the possibility that Jibril was not the intended victim.

Ramzy strode to the Arab Commercial Bank. Inside, he knocked on Taha Hamshari's office door. The banker opened it, and surprise and delight lit his face when he saw Ramzy. The two men hugged. Ramzy's and Hamshari's wives had been childhood friends. Years ago, the women had arranged for the four of them to holiday together on the Beirut beach and the men to meet. Through the social start, Hamshari had been drawn to the cause.

"How unexpected," Hamshari said, playfully slapping Ramzy's cheek. "Come in. How long are you going to be in Vienna?"

Ramzy walked across the office with him and settled into the chair. "I'm not sure."

"Do you have time for dinner? I'm booked tonight and tomorrow, but after that?" Hamshari sat behind his desk.

"We'll see. Taha, my time's a little short at the moment. This isn't a social visit."

Hamshari leaned back in the chair. "Banking?"

"No. Abu Nidal's in Vienna or was here a short while ago. I just want to take every precaution. I have no solid evidence that he's going to strike here, but it's a strong possibility that he will."

Hamshari took a paper clip off his desk and unfolded it. "You think I may be the target?"

"I have no reason to believe so. It's much more likely that he'll be after Hassan Jibril or the Israeli ambassador here."

"But he may be after me?"

"It's a possibility. Have you seen anything unusual? Had a sense of anyone following you?"

"No."

"Has anything out of the ordinary occurred in the past two weeks?"

Hamshari thought for a long moment. "Not that I can think of."

"If you see anything suspicious, I'm at the Hilton Hotel under the name Raju Metha."

"I don't know how I should feel."

"You probably have nothing to worry about. I have to meet somebody in a little while, but there's one more thing." Ramzy removed the small photograph and slid it across Hamshari's desk. "We believe this woman is with Abu Nidal. If, by any chance, you see her . . ."

Ramzy saw Hamshari's face collapse. Hamshari picked up the picture, his hands shaking. He kept staring at it. "She was here yesterday," he whispered.

Ramzy felt his palms dampen. "What happened?"

Hamshari sank back in the chair and told him. As he spoke, he unbent a series of paper clips. Afterward, he asked, "What should I do?"

Ramzy was already working out the details in his mind. "I'd like you to go ahead with the evening as planned. I'll see to it that nothing happens to you. Will you trust me?"

Hamshari was silent for a long time. He wanted to drive to Paris, this minute. "If I go along with this, you have a good chance of getting him?"

"The best I've had so far."

Hamshari brought his lips together and exhaled through them. "Okay." He nodded. "We'll eliminate this menace once and for all."

"This is a very brave act, Taha."

"No, it's not. I'm more afraid if I run he'll come back another time when you're not here."

"It's still a brave act. Let me take care of everything. The less you know, the less you'll give away, if they're watching you. I doubt they are now. Still, I or someone else will be nearby at all times."

"All right."

"It will be hard, but don't look around to see who's guarding you. We don't want to tip Abu Nidal off. We have the element of surprise now. Where are you supposed to meet Fahdi?"

"Her apartment." He turned the page of his calendar. "Twelve Rosastrasse, number three. That's in the Meidling district near the Schönbrunn Palace." Hamshari suddenly looked up. "You can go there tonight. Take people with you."

"Taha, he won't be there. He wouldn't allow her to give you his address. He never pulls the trigger himself. But he'll be in the area tomorrow. He likes to watch."

Hamshari was silent, then nodded.

"As far as everything goes, act normally. Keep your daily routine, and go ahead with whatever plans you've made. What time are you leaving the bank today?"

"Around five."

"Fine. Don't leave any earlier. I'll be in contact with you by phone before then."

Hamshari looked past him. "I'm scared."

"I know."

Ramzy rose, and Hamshari came out from behind his desk. As they hugged, Ramzy felt Hamshari tremble. "A little more than twenty-four hours and it will all be over," Ramzy said.

Hamshari broke the embrace. "All right, whatever you have to do, get started."

Ramzy smiled and nodded.

Outside, Ramzy walked, hardly noticing the people or the city around him. His excitement increased with each step. He had never before known exactly when and where Abu Nidal would strike. Still, he feared that this, too, like so many things in his life, would be taken from him. At the taxi stand at the bend in the Ring, he climbed into a cab and gave the driver the address of the PLO office. He would be late for the meeting in the park outside the Hilton. He had to make arrangements to get half a dozen of his best men from Sofia, Bulgaria. Then he would decide how much of this he would tell the Israeli.

SHAI HEARD THE ARAB approaching from behind him. While Ramzy lowered himself onto the bench, Shai tossed bits of bread into the mossy pond edged with oaks and weeping willows. Two ducks glided near him and snatched the food, the splash creating concentric ripples that widened toward the shore.

"The Austrian police are checking hotel registration cards for all Arabic, African and Asian names," Shai said. "Photographs have been circulated to all street officers. But obviously those are extremely long shots."

"I suspect though that you've had no sign of Abu Nidal," Ramzy said.

"Why?"

"Because one of my people was contacted by the girl. He's to meet her tomorrow night."

"Where?"

"Her apartment."

Shai nodded. It was Awwad's countryman Abu Nidal was after. "How do you want to handle it?"

"I have some people coming in. I'll put sharpshooters in or on top of the buildings across the entrance and two teams on the street in vehicles. Once the door is opened, someone will be right behind him. We'll get Abu Nidal either in the apartment or on the street."

"When was it set up?"

"Yesterday."

They had been lucky. "When's your team arriving?"

"It will take them a little time to get here." They had been attempting to trace a reported large shipment of Abu Nidal's weapons from Iraq to Bulgaria in the hope of following the weapons to him. Travel from Sofia was not like flying from London to Paris. It would take his men too long to drive, and they could not get a connecting flight through Rome until the morning. "They'll be here in the early afternoon," Ramzy said.

"Who's the target?"

"I cannot tell you that."

Shai tossed small pieces of bread into the water. "All right, but you'll have to guard him. Starting now, in the event Abu Nidal changes his plans."

"It's taken care of. I have a man on him."

"A man?" Shai stared at Awwad. "But that's not enough. You have to have a crack team around him. Men that won't be seen."

"I will, as soon as my people arrive."

Shai was silent for a long moment. Two teams alerted late last night had arrived already from Paris and Tel Aviv. "I understand your problem. You don't have the personnel here, but we do. Let us help."

"I am. We need high-powered rifles, telescopic sights and handguns. It would be dangerous and time-consuming for us to smuggle them across several borders. You will help by providing them."

"We're happy to. You can have the guns today. But let me give you a surveillance team. Three top men. They're here now, ready."

"There's no need," Ramzy said quietly. "Abu Nidal cannot be suspicious. Leila Fahdi will lead his prey right to him. It is arranged for tomorrow night. By then I will have the men to handle it."

"Awwad. Ramzy. Don't take the chance. Please, take the men. Better we should know who he is, than he be dead."

Ramzy rose. "I cannot reveal his identity when I don't know what you may do to him later. How may I take charge of the weapons?"

Shai threw the last whole slice of bread into the water and watched the ducks converge and peck at it. "A white Toyota," he said. "Across from the main entrance to the Sudbahnhof. In three hours. The key will be in an envelope under your door."

"Thank you." Ramzy turned to leave.

"Find me if you need help," Shai said.

Ramzy looked at him and nodded. Then he moved off along the sculpted path between the trees.

Shai watched the Palestinian and wondered whether Carmon was right, that after a humiliated PLO was pushed from Lebanon, Awwad would launch his teams on more massacres. Shai thought about the Olympic athletes in Munich, the PLO's incursion into Maalot. They had crossed the Lebanese border and seized a school building in the northern settlement with ninety teenagers inside. When negotiations broke down, the Palestinians had begun to slaughter the children. Israeli security forces had rushed the school. The death toll had been twenty-one children killed and more than fifty injured. That was why Carmon believed they could not take the risk of leaving Awwad alive.

Shai rose and made his way toward the white Toyota parked across from the Strauss statue at the edge of the park. He would see to it that the weapons and car were fitted with directional transmitters so they could follow Awwad.

IT WAS AFTER EIGHT, the night of September 5, when Shai, in the back of the van parked at the edge of the cobbled intersection two blocks from the Sudbahnhof, saw the red light come on that signified the Toyota was moving. The rear of the small van was windowless, with a seat that stretched across the back and a small light in the interior roof that illuminated the computer console fitted into the wall. From the chair in front of the keyboard a boyish Israeli with short-cropped blond hair spoke to the driver via a microphone. This close, Shai did not want Awwad to blow their chance at Abu Nidal. Eventually, and with luck soon, the weapons would be taken to where Leila Fahdi would lure the target.

Shai leaned forward to watch the map of Vienna superimposed on the computer screen and felt the van bouncing lightly over the cobbled pavement. They had hidden a directional transmitter under the body of the car and another smaller beauty inside the slightly hollowed-out stock of one of the M-16s.

They drove for fifteen minutes, curving away from the central city. Shai remained silent, watching the red line move slowly as his van stopped, and he heard a tram wobbling in its tracks in front of them. The young agent continually gave the driver directional changes through the microphone.

Soon, Shai watched the red dot hold in one place, longer than the Toyota would have to, to pause for a traffic signal.

"He's stopped now," the blonde said. "Either he's unloading or switching to another vehicle."

"Have the Delilah team pull by and see," Shai ordered. "In the meantime, get a little closer, then park."

The blonde switched the button on the transmitter-receiver to the right of the computer screen, gave the orders to the fast Audi that had been following them, then instructed their own driver.

When they stopped moving, the young man lit a cigarette in the confined space and smoked it quickly. A voice cackled over the speaker.

"They've loaded them into a truck," the voice said. "They're pulling away now. They've left the Toyota. What do we do?"

"Tell him to drop back behind us," Shai said. "Then—"

"I know," the youth interrupted, already punching the new instructions onto the keyboard. As he gave the Delilah team their orders, a new map of Vienna began to form. The blonde punched in more instructions, and a green light from the transmitter inside the M-16 moved north slowly.

The blonde spoke into the microphone without waiting for orders from Shai, and the van pulled back into traffic. Shai leaned against the vibrating wall of the van, feeling a small spasm in his back, and waited. Between the van and the Audi, they would have no trouble following the lumbering truck.

The blonde periodically gave new instructions to the driver. He finished his cigarette. Lit another.

Shai leaned back in his seat, sitting in the silence and the smoke he hated. Ten minutes passed. Twenty.

"They've stopped again," the blonde said.

Shai bent forward. "Get Delilah in, and tell them to be careful. I don't want them recognized from the last pass."

The blonde was on the transmitter, then ordered the van to park. He lit another cigarette and waited. He knew the routine now.

A nervous voice cackled over the speaker. "There are four cars. They're pulling away."

Damn, Shai swore to himself. He knew Awwad was short of experienced agents, but any Arab could be mobilized to drive a car. He stepped down to the floor and pushed his heavy frame toward the transmitter. "Did you see which car had the primary target?" he asked Delilah.

The voice came back, cackling. "Yes. A brown Opel. License: *W*, seven, six, five, three, nine, three."

"Follow him," Shai ordered.

"The light's still moving," the blonde said. "The transmitter's still in place."

"Tell the driver to follow it." They had one, Shai thought, and Delilah had a good chance of staying with Awwad. That was two out of the four. "Then check Delilah and find out where they are," Shai said. "Let's make sure we're not following the same damn car."

The blonde followed his instructions, and seconds later they jerked away from the curb.

"We've got him heading north on Triesterstrasse," Delilah answered between the static. "No indication that he suspects he's being followed."

The blonde turned to Shai. "That's not ours."

Shai nodded and stayed where he was, his body close to the young man's. He held on to the back of his stationary chair as the van bounced over the pavement. "Good. Now, put out that cigarette," Shai ordered as the smoke curled up from the ashtray near his face.

The blonde reached out slowly, then stubbed the cigarette.

"Tell the driver to stay as close as he can to them, without being seen," Shai said.

The blonde spoke into the microphone, and Shai felt the van picking up speed. The blonde punched a new set of instructions into the computer, and a new map jumped across the screen, line by line. "They're heading back to the center of town."

"How far behind them are we?"

"Seven blocks."

"Bring it to four."

"The car's faster than we are."

"Four," Shai said.

The blonde spoke into the microphone, then looked at the screen and turned abruptly to Shai. "They've stopped."

"Close. Fast."

The van picked up speed. The blonde returned to the computer. The seconds dragged. The green line was suddenly moving again, slower. The green dot stopped, then continued slowly again. The blonde turned to Shai, puzzled. "I think they've boarded a tram. The J-line runs right up Josefstadter to the Ring from here."

Why would they abandon the car and risk carrying the weapons on a public tram? Shai wondered. "How close are we to them?"

"A block."

"Tell the driver to pull over when the tram stops next. I want to get on." Awwad was in the Opel. Whoever had the weapons should not recognize him. "Then follow me."

When the van halted at the curb, Shai ran to the red tram and bounded up the steps as the doors folded behind him. He paid and walked to the back of the car without looking around. He was about to sit and study the people when at the rear of the tram, sitting on the window ledge, he saw the transmitter.

At the next stop, Shai lumbered down the stairs, frustrated, not because Awwad had outsmarted him, but because he feared he was that much farther from stopping Abu Nidal. As he stepped into the van, a voice cackled over the speaker: "Delilah here. Subject has just parked in the Hilton Hotel underground lot." There was a long pause. "And . . . I think he's staring at us. He must have spotted us. He's going into the hotel. What do you want us to do now?"

"Tell them to go home," Shai said to the blonde. He moved to the rear of the van. He should have figured it out. Awwad had put the weapons in the rear of the truck in order to search them. He sank into the seat. "Then tell the driver to take me to the Hilton."

HIS BACK HURTING from leaning forward in the van, Shai moved into the green-carpeted rubber tree and fern-filled lobby of the Hilton and wondered what he would say to Awwad. He would find out soon enough, he breathed to himself. Awwad was seated beneath the winding staircase to the second-floor restaurants, reading a paperback, apparently waiting for him.

As Shai approached, Awwad stood and faced him. "If you attempt to follow me again, it is the last you will see of me."

"Ramzy, if whoever you're protecting is not directly involved in murdering our people, he will be watched, that's all. There are no killers we know of in Vienna. By not letting us help, you are risking your person's life."

"My people will be arriving earlier than expected."

"But not early enough. They're not here now."

Ramzy looked off at a girl and a boy playing cards in front of the empty fireplace.

"Is it someone involved in assassinations or bombings?" Shai asked.

Ramzy continued watching the children. "No."

"Then don't take the risk. Let us help."

Ramzy turned to Shai. "I did before. With the weapons." He headed for the elevators.

ABU NIDAL SAT in the dark bar of the run-down Hotel Neubau with Abu Jihad, the man who would kill the banker Hamshari. Mixed nationalities and students crowded the chipped Formica tables. Rock music blared from a jukebox. The linoleum floor was stained; squares curled at the edges. Abu Nidal had chosen to stay in this hotel because of the cover of the foreigners who walked from the nearby Westbahnhof, where trains screeched in from Western Europe.

"How is the Fahdi woman?" Abu Jihad asked.

"Fine. I like the types who've played at revolution. It makes the conversion easier."

"Will she be all right tomorrow night?"

"She only has to open the door. You'll do the rest, but I think if I asked her to do it personally, she would."

"Then maybe she should?"

Abu Nidal's mouth tightened. He did not like suggestions. He took a piece of paper from his wallet and handed it to Abu Jihad. "This is the banker's address. Go there tonight and watch the house until he goes to sleep. Then return in the morning and stay with him throughout the day."

"But why? If he's agreed to the dinner..."

This Abu Jihad would not remain with him long. "I always watch the target the last twenty-four hours," he said, controlling his anger.

# 9 September 6 • Vienna, Austria

THE PHONE RANG, the sound penetrating Shai's skull. He groped for the receiver and looked at the digital clock on the nightstand whose green numbers read 5:43 a.m.

"Yes," he said, dropping back into the bed.

"It's Joram," the voice said. "We have something. I'll be outside in ten minutes."

"All right."

Shai fumbled the receiver into its cradle, fought the tiredness, shoved the blankets off and sat on the edge of the bed. Then he struggled up and forced his way into some clothes. Joram, who worked out of the embassy, had been doing the legwork in the attempt to locate Abu Nidal.

Shai rode the empty elevator to the lobby and ran his fingers through what was left of his hair to comb it somewhat. The lobby was deserted except for a man reading a newspaper behind the reception desk, and Shai hurried outside into the semidarkness. A blue Opel Ascona was parked across the street at the entrance to the Stadtpark, its motor idling. Shai pushed his large frame to-

ward it at a slow run, and as he got in, Joram pulled away
from the curb.

"I have a friend with the Viennese Polizei—a German,
from Munich. He was on their force back when they
botched the Olympic business. He always felt it was their
fault. He's been going through hotel registration cards
and sending his people out on anything that looked worth
checking. They just came up with a possible. Good-
looking young Arab, Libyan passport, in the Neubau
Hotel. Night clerk's seen a woman visiting him that fits
Leila Fahdi's description."

Shai crossed his arms against his chest in the cold car.
The sun was just brightening the skyline behind them.
Though optimistic, Shai knew better than to celebrate
before the job was finished. Joram glanced at him and
flipped on the heat. He turned west along the broad
boulevard that, at the Opera House, led away from the
Ring.

"The building under surveillance?" Shai asked.

"Four men. It was still quiet when I called you. We
have weapons under the seat."

Several blocks beyond the Westbahnhof, Joram turned
into a suburban shopping street and parked. He picked
up the walkie-talkie and spoke into the device. The street,
with bars, a Korean restaurant and a store that sold old
comic books and fingered German *Penthouse*s and *Play-
boy*s, was still. In the distance, church bells pounded six
deep thuds. A voice cackled over the walkie-talkie, in-
dicating there had been no movement of the subject.

"Where's the hotel?" Shai asked.

"Around the corner, half a block up."

Shai looked out the window. "The desk clerk is certain he hasn't left?"

"Yes, and my police friend managed us a little present." He handed Shai a key. "Third floor. Room three-six-two. How do you want it handled?"

Shai would have preferred to gain access, plant explosives, and when Abu Nidal returned to the room, detonate them from a safe distance.

"We'll wait for him to come out. Once we're sure it's him, tell the people on the roofs to shoot. But be certain first. I don't want any mistakes."

Joram picked up the walkie-talkie and relayed the instructions and the cautionary.

Shai looked at his watch—6:15. He rolled the window down a little to get some air. "We might have a lot of time to kill."

"I'll get some coffee. What do you want in it?"

"Milk . . . and two sugars, and some pastry if you can manage it easily." Shai knew he should cut down, and he would, but not in the middle of an operation. He was vaguely aware that he had started eating like this after his wife's death.

"I'll be back in a moment."

When Joram returned, they drank the coffee, then Shai took a short walk to the corner. From under faded posters of bare-breasted women outside the Roxy Bar, he surveyed the run-down street and hotel. The hours dragged. Periodically the two teams of agents, at the front and rear of the hotel, checked in. There had been no sign of Abu Nidal or the girl.

A little after nine, Shai reached under the seat, took the Hi-Standard .22 caliber and slipped it inside his pocket. "You and I are going in," he said. "Have your men stay where they are and watch for him coming out in a hurry."

"In case we fail?"

"Yes."

Joram reached under his seat for his gun. "You know, I volunteered for this work because of the generous pension."

"You mean it wasn't just to see such exotic locales?"

Joram smiled, pushed the gun under his belt, zipped the jacket over it, then spoke quickly into the walkie-talkie. They walked at a moderate pace, reached the corner and turned. The white HOTEL sign, jutting from the peeling building, was half a block ahead. Shai watched Joram rub his right hand on his jacket.

"How do you want it?" Joram asked.

Shai felt the key in his pants pocket. "The night and morning desk clerks are certain he hasn't come out of there?"

"Yes, and there's no other way out. They can see the back entrance from the desk."

"Okay," Shai said. "I'll open the door and go in first. You follow."

"All right."

Shai wondered if he was making a mistake, if he should wait longer.

The hall leading to the reception desk was dim. It was covered with a dirty, spotted red carpet. The small bar to the left was closed. Beyond it and before the stairs stood a small, broken yellow-tiled kitchen. The man behind the reception desk lowered his eyes behind a pornographic magazine and pretended not to see them.

They climbed the dark stairs. At the third floor landing, used sheets lay piled near the iron banister. Shai removed the Hi-Standard. A toilet flushed somewhere behind thin walls. Shai continued along the corridor, silently, despite his size. He followed the numbers and found the room on the left side at the end of the hall.

Shai crouched at the side of the door, his mouth dry. As soon as Abu Nidal heard a key in the lock, he would go for his gun. Joram, easing his jacket to the floor, was ready. Shai nodded. His breathing tight in his chest, he raised the key to the lock. In a quick motion he inserted it, turned sharply and twisted the knob. He dived in on his stomach, gun extended.

The main room was empty. Joram ran in over him. Men's clothes were scattered around, a lamp knocked over. Shai rose slowly and pointed to a closed closet door. Joram inched to the side of it, pulled the door open. A few pairs of pants and a shirt hung from wire hangers. The door to the black-tiled bathroom was open. Shai moved in cautiously. It was empty. There was a stained tub, no shower. A toothbrush, shaving gear and deodorant had been left on the sink. Shai kicked at a towel on the floor, the anger at Awwad's unwillingness to cooperate more fully running through him.

Shai came back into the dingy room. There was no suitcase anywhere. "Look around and see what you can find," he said. "But it won't be much. He's not coming back here."

Joram rose from bending to look under the bed. "You knew he wasn't here. That's why you took the risk of coming in this way."

"I suspected it."

"How?"

"His file. He hates being enclosed. Rises early. He wouldn't stay in a small room like this so late."

"Where is he?" Joram asked.

"In another room, for the night only. He must have left sometime in the evening, or before, and in quite a hurry. Somehow he's onto us. He'll be moving each night now."

Shai picked up the phone. After a long wait, the receptionist answered, and Shai had him dial the Hilton Hotel. As the phone rang in Ramzy's room, he hoped to God the Arab was there.

"Hello," Ramzy said.

"It's Shai. There's no time to worry about a secure connection or explain. Abu Nidal's onto you."

"How do you know?" Skepticism sounded in Ramzy's voice.

"We found his room. He bolted suddenly last evening. Something alerted him. Somehow he must have found out that you're onto him."

Despite Shai's words in the Hilton lobby, Ramzy knew the Israelis might kill someone as important as Hamshari. "How do I know this is not a clever ruse so I'll take you to guard the target until my people arrive?"

"Damn it," Shai said. "The dinner is undoubtedly off. He may strike now, any minute. Wait for me. I'll be there in a quarter of an hour."

"Thank you for the warning."

The line went dead in Shai's ear. He slammed the phone down.

THE MIDMORNING SUN filled the cloudless sky as Leila stepped off the tram onto the Opernring. She wondered who Abu Jihad had seen standing outside the banker's house, guarding him. She pushed the question from her mind. It did not matter now. Hamshari would be dead within the half hour, and she would play the crucial role in the shooting. As she moved with quick, short steps toward the florist booth on the sidewalk, she surveyed her new gray pleated skirt and peach silk blouse. It made her feel clean, wonderful to wear such clothes. She stepped past the baskets of daisies outside and entered the kiosk.

"A dozen red roses in a box, *bitte*," she said, repeating the German words she had memorized.

The white-haired, spectacled Viennese woman smiled. "I'll find you nice ones."

Leila, who did not understand her, nodded and took out the cash Abu Nidal had given her.

The spectacled woman carefully removed the roses from the small glass refrigerator compartment, one at a time. She sprayed each bud with mist before she placed it in the box lined with wax paper. She worked slowly without talking, and Leila watched the moisture trickle down the glass behind her, like a tear.

She realized how much the past weeks had changed her. A month ago she would have rushed to a café, sat with pen in hand and written a fierce, emotional poem using the image of the tear on the florist's glass. Now that Abu Nidal had taken her a distance from that time, she looked back at herself with embarrassment. It was the image that had been so vital to her—that she was a poetess, an artist, someone important.

She realized she had not written a single poem since that silly postcard to Khalid Monsour in Amsterdam while Abu Nidal was away in Iraq and she, to her great surprise, was feeling so alone. She blushed. All of it seemed foolish now—reciting in those smoke-filled university cafés, pretending that her poetry fought the enemy. She had been just like most of her people, who when the wars they longed for finally came, had no idea what to do. In 1973, like millions of young Arab men and women, she had listened to the news, smoked cigarettes and gotten excited while the civilian population of Israel had mobilized and fought.

"Here you go, my dear," the woman said, placing the box tied with a ribbon on the counter.

Leila awkwardly held out the money to her and again said, *"Bitte."*

The spectacled woman looked at her puzzled, then realized. "Oh, you don't speak German. No matter, dear." She counted through the currency, took the correct amount and patted the rest in her hand. "That's enough. *Danke schön.*"

Holding the box of roses under her arm, Leila walked outside. At the corner, where the black iron-pointed fence separated the old people sitting on benches in the manicured park from the sidewalk, she saw him waiting in the orange convertible. The excitement leaped inside her. She was always afraid he would not be where he said he would, and each time relief spread through her when he was. She jumped into the front seat, and quickly he drove along the huge gardened square and marble-columned buildings of the Hofburg Palace. Across and down the street from the Arab Commercial Bank, he pulled to the curb and opened the box of roses. He touched one of the partially opened buds and rearranged them. He loved their beauty, their softness. He handed the box to her.

"You know what to do?"

She wrapped both arms around his neck and kissed him. "Draw their attention. Make them think the weapon is in the box of roses."

"Then go. Hamshari's on his way to the office."

"I'm very happy." She left the car and headed toward the stairs to the underground passageway, holding the box in both arms.

Leila came up the moving escalator not remembering having crossed the underpass. Her legs propelled themselves. People were drinking coffee at the tables of an outdoor café. Then suddenly, far down the block, she saw two men start to get out of a dark Mercedes in front of the bank. Hamshari. He had arrived too quickly. "No," she shouted, and began running, clutching the box.

On the sidewalk in front of the bank, hand around the gun in his pocket, Ramzy watched the two men leave the Mercedes. There was no need for his agent to remain out of sight now. His team from Bulgaria was not due in Vienna for almost two hours. He hoped it would take Abu Nidal time to formulate a new plan.

Suddenly he saw Leila Fahdi running toward them, holding on to a long box of roses. A WZ-63 would fit easily inside.

Leila neared, then stopped running. The two men were halfway to the bank entrance. There was no time. She had to improvise.

"Taha," she called out. "Taha Hamshari." She hurried toward him.

The two men hesitated.

Ramzy dived at Hamshari, caught him in the shoulder and sent both of them sprawling to the pavement. Leila reached in among the roses. From the ground, Ramzy watched the guard rush at Leila and slam into her chest, knocking her over. The box flew in the air. Taha was safe.

Behind them, a man with a pack on his back suddenly stepped out of a store and pointed a small machine pistol. Abu Jihad stared at the two entangled men on the pavement, not knowing if he should search for the man whose photograph he had studied or simply spray both of them. He squeezed off a single shot.

Ramzy rolled and fired behind him, by instinct rather than aiming, and knew he had hit. People in the outdoor café screamed.

Ramzy scrambled to Hamshari who had been shot, at the same time looking up. An orange convertible, parked across the street, screeched away from the curb and sped away. The bodyguard was holding both Leila's wrists with one hand, dragging her toward the bank. Hamshari lay on the ground, blood soaking his shirt from the wound in his shoulder. Beyond him, the young Arab with a pack on his back was spread on the sidewalk, his face silent in death, blood forming a pool around the metal of his gun.

Ramzy bent to Hamshari. People on the sidewalk, screaming seconds earlier, began to gather a short distance away.

"Taha, I'm sorry." Ramzy's face was ashen.

"Go," Hamshari whispered hoarsely. "The police."

Ramzy took out a handkerchief and tried to bandage his friend's shoulder.

"Get away from here," Hamshari half shouted, then began coughing. "I'll be all right."

Ramzy looked at him and nodded. "Someone call an ambulance," he said to the crowd.

As a woman hurried into the café, Ramzy pushed through the people and ran toward the maze of streets across the Ring, without heart, in his mind's eye seeing Abu Nidal escape again in that car.

# 10 September 7 • Jerusalem, Israel

YEHUDA SHAMIR MOVED into Carmon's outer office and smiled at Tami, who motioned with her head that he should go in. He knocked, then entered.

"What is it, Yehuda?" Carmon said, looking above his small half-moon glasses, then returning to the papers he was reading.

"We've had a report from Shai." Yehuda sat in the chair.

Carmon stopped reading. "Is Abu Nidal dead?"

"Not exactly."

"What is not exactly?"

"You want the long explanation or the heart of it?"

He took his glasses off and set them on the stack of sheets. "I'm listening."

"They had him, but he escaped."

"Then evidently they didn't have him."

"They tracked him to Vienna and got close."

"Close, I understand, is of some value with a hand grenade. They know where he's gone?"

"Not yet. The Austrian police have been questioning an accomplice, without results. We'll try when they release her."

"What about the Arab, Awwad?"

There was no gain in lying. Shai's report would bear the truth. "He's been cooperating, but not fully. Shai believes if he had, they would have killed Abu Nidal."

"I don't like this. I don't know how the hell you talked me into letting him go." Carmon reached for his cigarettes. "Shut it down. Awwad's murdered enough of our people. Have Shai eliminate him and go after Abu Nidal on his own."

"According to Shai, he would not have gotten close without Awwad."

Carmon flicked his lighter and brought the flame to his cigarette. He pulled on the filter, then blew smoke. "Let me understand this. Are you telling me that we *need* this Awwad, that we can't find this terrorist on our own?"

"I'm only suggesting that with Awwad we may finish Abu Nidal sooner, before he has a chance to strike again, and there's something else. We set this up to discover what Shai could learn from Awwad. According to him, the man Abu Nidal was after is someone big, a banker named Taha Hamshari. This could be the key to where their money in Europe is and how it's dispersed. Hamshari was shot, but he'll be all right."

Carmon dropped back in his large leather chair, pleased, then his smile faded. "If he was shot, we would have checked him out anyway."

"You're right. We probably would have come up with the link." The small Iraqi Jew spoke in a soft voice.

"Meir, Barsimantov and Argov. The truth is, there wasn't much we could do to stop it or we would have. Will you be able to live with yourself if Abu Nidal murders someone else and we could have prevented it, if we'd stayed with Awwad?"

Carmon put his cigarette down, swiveled in the heavy chair and looked at the colorful Agam on the wall behind him. The geometric lines seemed to shimmer and change perspective as he watched them. It was only now, with the full realization that keeping Judea and Samaria meant permanently curtailing Arab rights, that the country so united in the purpose of survival during its first twenty years was divided along ideological lines he believed threatened that very existence. Awwad and those like him could not be trusted. To return substantial portions of the land and have the Arab menace at their throats would deliver the same "peace in our time" that Chamberlain had gained from Hitler. Still, Yehuda had a point about Barsimantov and Argov.

"All right," Carmon said, turning back. "They have a little longer together, but that's it."

THE COLONEL SAT in the Arab coffeehouse, hidden in the passageway in the Old City of Jerusalem, and waited for Yehuda Shamir. It had been a long time since he had driven into the familiar Jerusalem mountains. Expecting to be more excited here, back in the game, he realized how he never would have thought, when he had resigned, that he would come to enjoy a quieter life.

A line of ceramic plates surrounded the blue walls. A boy emerged from the kitchen, carrying a tray with glasses of mint-leafed mahogany tea, and hurried into the arch-roofed lane. The Colonel followed him with his eyes.

Yehuda strode through the entrance. The Colonel smiled, happy to see him. Yehuda sat beside him at the small, wobbly table.

"Will you have some coffee? Turkish?" the Colonel asked.

"Fine."

The Colonel turned to the waiter who was sitting on a stool at the entrance to the kitchen, reading a newspaper. "Two Turkish coffees, please," he said in English, though he knew the man spoke Hebrew. He never felt comfortable speaking Hebrew to the Arabs, always felt that was reminding them they were living in Israel, not their own country.

"They almost had Abu Nidal in Vienna. Awwad was after him on his own, got close, but he got away."

His arm shaking, the Colonel removed his round wire-rimmed spectacles. "Good."

"I thought you'd say that." Yehuda felt a stab of pain in his chest, but ignored it. "There's something else. Carmon wants Shai to kill Awwad when it's over."

"I see. Well, we can't have that, now can we?"

"I managed for the moment to persuade him to give them more time."

"Good, good. Now, you'll have to keep me informed if Carmon changes his mind."

"Of course."

"What about Shai? Will he kill Awwad if ordered to?"

"He's independent, does things his way, won't report in if he wants to hide something. But he's never disobeyed a direct order. You know that."

The white-aproned proprietor neared and slipped the small, handleless cups in front of them. The Colonel looked up at the man. *"Sukran,"* he said, using his limited Arabic. The proprietor bowed slightly and walked away. The Colonel sipped through the foam at the top of the coffee. "Now, where were we?"

"Talking about what Shai would do?"

"Ah, yes, well, we'll just have to have faith in him, won't we? I want them to get Abu Nidal, of course, but not so quickly."

"How long do you think it will take for a real relationship between Shai and Ramzy to develop?"

The Colonel surrounded the small cup with both hands, feeling the warmth. "Can't be certain it will, you know. Can only hope. Depends a lot on how it unfolds along the way. The danger, of course, will help."

Yehuda drank his coffee and thought about what the Colonel was attempting in bringing the two men together. Though this was not an operation that rescued Jewish children from Damascus, protected an agent in place or unearthed a traitor in their own house—it held a subtler, long-range importance. Awwad had a massive following among the Palestinians and held an influential position on the Palestine National Council. Few could carry his people to peace as Ramzy might.

"Awwad's going to question a woman accomplice of Abu Nidal's," Yehuda said. "Maybe that will provide a fresh lead."

---

RAMZY SAT ALONE in the living room of the safe house that the Israelis had set up exclusively for the purpose of interrogating Leila Fahdi. Under Austrian Polizei questioning, she had steadfastly claimed that she had been bringing flowers to Hamshari in gratitude for the loan he had promised her. Since no weapon was found among the roses, the Polizei had released her.

The Israelis had swooped her off the street, three blocks from the police building. Ramzy still was not certain whether the Polizei were cooperating with the Israelis or not. In the night she had been here, the Israelis had not spoken in her presence; she still did not know for certain who her captors were.

Shai had not mentioned Abu Nidal's escape. To Ramzy's surprise, the Israeli had expressed pleasure that he had not been hurt, then immediately launched into a discussion of what they should do next. There were no recriminations, though they both knew that had there been enough men on the street Abu Nidal would be dead now. It was not what he had expected.

Leila Fahdi came out of the bedroom wearing the traditional long hand-embroidered dress he had left for her earlier that morning. Her unkempt hair tumbled wildly over her shoulders.

Ramzy rose. "I hope you are reasonably comfortable here."

"You speak Palestinian dialect excellently," she said with contempt in her eyes. "The occupiers have learned well."

"Come have some breakfast with me."

She did not move from the doorway. "I do not eat with the enemy. Your speaking to me will make no difference."

"I hope that I am not the enemy. I am Ramzy Yusuf Awwad. I am not certain, but perhaps you have heard the name?"

She leaned back against the doorjamb. He had looked familiar, but she had thought in her disorientation from lack of nourishment that her eyes had been fooling her. Now she knew why; she had seen his photograph with his stories in the *al-Muharrer* weekly magazine. There was no Palestinian writer more respected by their people.

"I'm sorry," she said, her whole body shaking. "I've just been..."

He moved to her, smiled understandingly, placed an arm around her waist and led her to the kitchen table. She had refused all food since they had brought her here. "Eat something first."

She sat down, managed a smile and sipped from the orange juice. Ramzy waited for her to take a little food.

She swabbed some of the *hummous* up with the edge of the pita. The olive oil ran into the space.

"The man you helped Abu Nidal attempt to kill is very important to our people, Leila."

She continued to eat, but said nothing.

"Now, because of Abu Nidal's action, your action, the Israelis have identified him."

"It doesn't matter. He's a traitor."

"Do you even know who he is? He has dedicated his life to working for our return to our homeland and has financed most of the PLO operations in Europe for years."

"That was before. He's abandoned the struggle."

"Your Abu Nidal has abandoned his people. What he's doing will only push our homeland farther from us."

She held the cloth napkin in her lap. "He's acting, not sitting in Lebanon as the Zionists slaughter us."

"Acting, to gain what? Can your Abu Nidal do them any real damage? Even if he kills all the Zionist ambassadors in Europe, will they not only be replaced by others?"

"We will strike fear in their hearts, make them afraid to leave their homes."

"But they will still leave them. Leila, when those of us who first took up guerrilla activity planned them, we splashed bloody headlines across the international press to shock an indifferent world into recognizing our history, to show our people that the struggle was still going on. Our goals have been achieved. The world is sympathetic to our cause now."

"Abu Nidal is eliminating those who would sell us out."

"He is killing our own brothers," Ramzy said angrily. "Your Abu Nidal will bring us nothing. No, not nothing. Towering Israeli settlements everywhere on the West Bank. The Israeli right-wingers love what he's doing. He's proof that their intransigence is justified." He watched her look down; her hands gripped the twisted napkin. "If we don't act soon, we may be too late to act at all."

Her head did not come up. "It can't be too late."

"I hope it's not. Where is he, Leila?"

"I don't know."

"Where did he talk about going next?"

She was so confused. "He didn't say. He didn't talk much. We..."

"Oh, I see. So that's how you helped the revolution?" She avoided his eyes.

It was unlikely that she knew much. Still, there was a chance. "We found the new clothes, Leila, the shoes, the new coats in your apartment—" he paused "—the lace underwear. I suppose you don't mind that that's how you shall be known in the camps? Do not mind that the young girls will talk about what Leila Fahdi did with the revolutionary funds while they still did not have enough food."

The napkin was damp, twisted in her hands. Silence.

"It couldn't really matter to you, then, if the girls talk about how, while the camps were being bombed, you spent your time shopping in Vienna's most exclusive stores."

Her head came up. "You can't..."

Ramzy saw the fear in her face and edged his chair nearer. Scare her, then win her confidence. "I understand you write poetry."

She was silent, then said, "I did."

"Maybe I can look at it, work on it with you."

She shut her eyes. "My poetry's worthless. I've stopped writing."

"All writers have periods when we think our work is horrible. It's difficult sometimes to believe anyone would be interested or affected by what we have to say."

Her head came up, and she laughed. Too loud. A month ago she would have given anything to have the greatest writer of her people look at her work. "My poetry's terrible." She was laughing, on the verge of tears. "It's rage thrown across a page. No style, nothing."

He touched her arm for a brief moment. "My political writing used to be like that. I took the kernel of talent in that earlier work and faced what I wanted to say, honestly. If we looked at your poetry, possibly you could do the same."

She sat motionless in the chair, hands clenched around the damp cloth. The poetry had been the most important part of her, then she had given it up as worthless compared to the work with Abu Nidal; and now this man, a great writer *and* a guerrilla, was turning it all around again. Tears welled. The police had not let her sleep, and she had refused to take food thinking they were Israelis. The tiredness was tugging at her.

"What's best for our people is what matters. We must stop Abu Nidal, then you must go on with your poetry, have it translated into as many languages as possible, make the world feel what it is like to be Palestinian."

She said nothing and looked down at her hands.

"Where is Abu Nidal?" he asked gently.

The tears rolled down her cheeks in two lines, glistening against her dark skin. "I told you, I don't know."

"Would you tell me if you did?"

No reply. She wiped her face quickly with the cloth.

She did know something, and he was close. He could sense it. A little more pressure, and it would come. "Would you tell me?" he repeated.

Still the silence, the looking down.

In the gentlest of voices. "He used you, Leila."

Her head came up. "No."

"He uses a lot of women like you."

"I don't believe you."

"I can show you the files. When he's done with one, there's always another. He abandoned you. All right, maybe he figured there wouldn't be enough evidence to hold you and you'd be released. If that was the case, if he cared, he'd arrange for you to meet him. I don't think he did that. Did he, Leila? Tell me if I'm wrong."

Her crying was barely audible. "He said that the Israelis could use me to find him, that much later on—"

"Come on, Leila. The Israelis are patient. Why wouldn't he worry they'd follow you then?" Ramzy edged even closer, was almost on top of her. "When your namesake Leila Khaled was arrested in Britain, three days later the PFLP hijacked a British flight from Bahrain and demanded her release. They threatened to blow up the plane and the passengers. The British let her go, Leila.

George Habash arranged it in three days. That's how true revolutionaries act. Khaled's still with him. He's not worried about the Israelis, but then maybe he cares about her. Abu Nidal will just trade you in for someone else. He was getting rid of you. I don't mind if I'm wrong. Tell me if this much later on has a date and place.''

She let the napkin go and watched it fall to the floor. It was true. He had not cared about her; part of her had known it all along.

''Tell me where he went, Leila.''

She squeezed her eyes; her whole body trembled. ''Portugal,'' she said just above a whisper. Her head inched up. ''The Socialist International. He's going to kill Shimon Peres.''

Ramzy drew Leila near. Her arms circled him, her head hid in his chest, the tears warm against his shirt. Now that he had the information, he felt empty. He touched her hair and promised himself that he would make the time to help her with her poetry.


SHAI SAT IN THE STADTPARK and watched the early-evening shadows of the trees on the water. A middle-aged couple strolled along the pond, hand in hand. The man drew an arm around the woman's shoulder, and Shai remembered with pain how he and Sarit would walk that way. It had been twilight like this the last time they were together.

Home on one of his leaves, they had driven down to the Sinai to vacation in the guesthouse at the Moshav at Neviot. He loved the desert peninsula. He and Sarit on that leave had spent two weeks walking through the alternating sandscapes and jagged mountains, lying on the beach at Nuweiba and snorkeling along the coral reef, following the bright orange and purple fish.

Then, on the way back to the guesthouse, after strolling by the sea, she had gone ahead to buy a few things at the kiosk across the main road. The paved highway the Israelis had laid from the military base at Sharm el Sheik to Eilat was unlit and not traveled much in the evening. Shai had liked to watch his wife when she was unaware of his eyes on her, so, instead of heading back to the cottage, he sat on a rock looking at her as she crossed the asphalt. He was thinking about how much he loved her when he saw the car speeding around the bend.

A futile scream of warning erupted from his throat as the brakes screeched much too late and the car struck her with that horrible thud that went through him and sent her flying in the air. The car skidded to a halt. He ran wildly to where she lay crumpled on the asphalt, and with her blood running onto his hands, he caressed her face. Her eyes were open, and she was alert. She reached up and touched his arm. "You're here," she said, sounding surprised. He bent and kissed her twice on the lips.

A helicopter lifted Sarit to the hospital in Eilat. She came out of surgery in a coma. The following morning, without regaining consciousness, she had died.

Shai heard the sounds of Ramzy approaching. He surrendered the memories, stared at the pond and fought his way back to the present. The Arab sat next to him.

Ramzy was silent, worried that the Israeli had identified Hamshari, then said, "Leila talked."

Shai turned to him. "I thought you might be able to persuade her."

"It's the sixteenth Socialist International in Portugal. It's going to meet in Albufeira on the Algarve coast."

"When?"

"September twenty-fourth."

A little more than two weeks away, Shai realized, nervously. "Who's the target?"

"Shimon Peres."

The words struck Shai like a slap across the face. Again he felt anger at Awwad's refusal to work together fully. They might have eliminated Abu Nidal here and averted the danger to the opposition Labor Party leader, a man Shai deeply believed was his country's best hope now. Peres had supported the war only as far as pushing the PLO forty kilometers from the border, and he favored negotiating with King Hussein to return significant sections of the West Bank in exchange for peace.

"Did she know how Abu Nidal would attempt it?" Shai asked.

"It was lucky she knew anything. He wouldn't have left her alive if he thought she knew that much."

Shai turned to the dark Palestinian. He had brought them to Leila Fahdi and thus so close to Abu Nidal. "Will you help me?"

"Save Peres?"

"Ramzy, Abu Nidal wants him because he's eager to talk peace."

"So Peres says. It's what you all say. But will he ever be elected with any kind of mandate to do anything about the West Bank?"

"I don't know, but if he's assassinated, I promise you the Israeli electorate will swing even farther to the right. And what will it do to your relations with Brandt, Palme and the other heads of government who are sympathetic to your cause—if Peres is killed by a Palestinian right in front of them?"

Ramzy remained silent, the lines at his eyes, the edges of his mouth, tight. It was Argov in London all over. Abu Nidal knew, when the world sees a Palestinian with a gun, it thinks PLO. "I'll help you kill Abu Nidal," Ramzy said. "Isn't that why I'm here?"

"I've had some doubts, if you'll excuse my saying so."

At another time Ramzy would have delighted in a duel of words. He looked at the Israeli and chose, however, to swallow his feelings one more time. He was becoming increasingly good at it.

"The PLO has an unofficial delegation at the International headed by Dr. Issam Sartawi. It will give me a public reason for being there."

"You know," Shai said, "it's just possible that if we work together this time, we'll stop him."

"That's true. You Israelis don't seem to be doing very well on your own, do you? If you'll excuse my saying so."

# BOOK III: FAWAZ

## 12 September 13 • Ramallah, the West Bank

ELEVEN DAYS BEFORE the Socialist International convened, Ramzy's brother, Fawaz, drove through the West Bank toward the demonstration that was building in Ramallah. The tire burning had erupted to protest the Israeli government's ejection of the PLO from Beirut.

As one Arab village melded into the next, Fawaz questioned what he was doing racing to the demonstration. Soon he approached a military base surrounded by barbed wire, standing amid the low Arab homes of the area. A sign read Camp of the Meadows of Jacob and an Israeli flag rippled in the wind next to some red and black flags, which he thought meant it was a paratrooper unit. Adjacent to the camp rose the clustered, fortresslike buildings of the Jewish settlement of the Meadows of Jacob. He saw the Hebrew billboards: Build Your Own Home, Build the House of Your Dreams, Top Scandinavian Standards, Construction Completed Within Six Months, Especially Comfortable Payment Terms.

Where at first they had built settlements in isolated strategic areas, now whole towns of apartment houses and villas were springing up, overlooking their villages. At moments like these, helpless to do anything to stop their tanks and bulldozers, he understood why his brother had walked into that embassy in Paraguay and shot an unarmed woman and man.

Tens of thousands of *dunams* had been taken from Arab inhabitants by expropriation and legalistic ruses. Their army had closed off land for military purposes—firing ranges, training grounds, security zones—then leased much of it to the settlements, raising Kiryat Arba on a hill overlooking Hebron that way. When the Israeli Supreme Court had struck down the military expropriation method for creating civilian settlements as illegal, the government had unearthed an old nineteenth-century Ottoman Land Code, which had enabled it to declare practically any unoccupied land for which ownership could not be proved *mawat*, dead, and seize it for Jewish settlements. Title remained in the hands of the Sultan, that is, the Israeli government. Most of the Palestinians' long-held *dunams* had not been entered into the land registry.

Fawaz pushed the accelerator hard. Near the entrance to Ramallah, he followed a large open truck filled with sheep. A young girl wearing a red scarf bounced on a crate in the back among the animals. Under a canvas stretched across poles, a woman waited for customers next to a mountain of watermelons. Up ahead at the intersection, armed Israeli soldiers sat on the low stone fence.

Fawaz descended the small incline into Ramallah, the tension hard in his chest. To his left, dozens of Israeli soldiers in helmets and thick black riot jackets stood in front of the military government police station. He continued toward the center of town; the streets were strangely empty. Usually men sat on low stools on the sidewalk, smoking, some reading newspapers, others wheeling carts laden with bananas or apples, while women in long embroidered dresses and scarves balanced heavy loads on their heads. Every store was shut. Before the roundabout, where six streets converged, Fawaz pulled to the curb and parked.

He walked, limping slightly, into Jerusalem Street. The street paralleled the highway and led back toward the Holy City. First he smelled, then saw the black smoke of the burning tires. When they came, the soldiers would line up everybody, have them remove their shirts and then wipe the street clean with them. Then the soldiers would march them to the military government compound with their shirts tied around their waists.

Fawaz headed down the deserted market street; the iron grates on the shops were all pulled closed. The crowd was marching in his direction. He continued toward them. Rubber balls, plastic pitchers and plastic net shopping bags were still tied to a tree on the sidewalk. In front of a butcher shop, blood covered the flagstones where whole cows' heads had lain.

The demonstration neared, the chanting in English and Arabic: ''PLO! Israel, no!'' and ''No to the occupation!'' Over and over in mesmerizing rhythm. Fists thrust into the air with the beat. Then behind him he heard the soldiers' jeeps skidding to a halt at the roundabout. He wondered again if he should be here.

The protest caught him and swept him into the street with it, and he began to move toward the soldiers, shouting too, "PLO! Israel, no!" The Israeli troops were prying open the gates of the shops with crowbars, trying to force an end to the strike. His limp seemed to ease as he marched. The soldiers came away from the grates of the shops, their rifles extended. One of the Israelis was shouting in Arabic through a bullhorn, telling them to disperse. The acrid odor of the burning rubber hung over the street.

Fawaz glanced at the demonstrators, hundreds of them. The boys held rocks in their dirty fingers. The order came again, over the bullhorn, for them to return to their homes. This time he could not see who was speaking.

The shouting rose in rhythmic frenzy. The orders boomed over the bullhorn, this time threatening that they would shoot. The chanting grew louder. The frustration Fawaz continually reined back burst out, and he roared, "PLO! Israel, no!" Soldiers fired into the air. Women, peering behind curtains in the windows above the closed shops, screamed. The demonstrators kept coming, shouting wildly. They were fifty, then forty meters from the soldiers in their neat lines.

The frontline soldiers aimed at the street, just short of the demonstrators. Bullets exploded in the ground, ricocheting everywhere. A hail of stones flew at the soldiers. They ducked and raised their arms to protect themselves. The boys scattered, found more stones and flung them, shouting. Fawaz looked at the young soldier nearest him, blood dripping from a cut on his nose.

The soldier with the bloodied nose looked directly at him and raised his rifle. An order was shouted in Hebrew. Other soldiers raised their rifles. Stones sailed at the soldiers and banged off their helmets, guns and riot jackets. Fawaz watched as the bloodied Israeli aimed at him. He did not move. There was a shriek as the demonstrators realized what was happening.

Two soldiers fired into the crowd. The first soldier's bullet sailed past a young boy's ear. Fawaz felt the second bullet smash into his chest over his heart, and then the velocity of the close-range shot kicked him backward, and he crumpled to the street. The blood soaking through his shirt stained the asphalt.

The demonstrators ran in all directions. In seconds they were gone. For a long moment there was an eerie silence. Then women ululated from the windows. A doctor with a red Mogen David on his helmet ran to the still body, knelt, opened his bag, gently turned the older man over and felt his neck for a pulse. The company lieutenant, who was not much older than the soldiers, neared. The doctor looked up at him and shook his head.

THAT SAME AFTERNOON, in Paris, Ramzy climbed the steps to Dr. Issam Sartawi's office. The former heart surgeon, now the PLO's roving envoy and highest-ranking member in Europe, was expecting him. He knocked on the door. Sartawi was also the leading advocate on the Palestine National Council for recognition of Israel and peaceful coexistence, but Ramzy remembered when Sartawi believed differently.

Born in the village of Sarta on the West Bank, the American-trained physician had returned to the Middle East after the crushing 1967 defeat. Certain there could be no reconciliation with the enemy, he formed his own guerilla group, still remembered for the sand-colored uniforms they wore during the attacks on Israel from Jordan. In 1970, learning that a Mr. Dayan was on the passenger list of a Munich to London El Al 707, he sent three guerillas to hijack the plane. One person was killed and eleven wounded in the failed attempt that found only Moshe Dayan's actor son, Assaf, on the flight.

Joining the PLO in the need for unification, in Africa Sartawi became the driving force behind the black nations severing ties with Israel after the 1973 war. Then with Arab honor restored in 1973, he began to search for a Middle East solution. It was a long, arduous journey and finally he came to the conclusion that the Palestinians must recognize the cruel necessity of a choice between the vision and the limits of reality. In 1976 he began direct talks with Israeli Zionists.

Sartawi opened the door and saw Ramzy. They hugged and kissed on both cheeks.

"Come sit," Sartawi said, tugging at Ramzy's neck. "We don't see you nearly enough. You better have time to come visit the kids."

Ramzy looked at him for a long moment, then gave a small nod.

"Good. Now, sit, I said."

As Ramzy lowered himself into the chair, Sartawi pulled his out from behind the desk and placed it next to his friend.

"So what brings you to Paris?" Sartawi asked with a smile. "You're not exactly famous for your social calls."

"I know." Ramzy's own smile flashed, then faded. "It's Abu Nidal. We have evidence that he's planning an operation at the Socialist International. He's after Shimon Peres."

Sartawi was silent, then lit one of his ever-present cigarettes. "You're sure it's Peres?"

"He explicitly said he was waiting for the target to arrive in Europe. You, obviously, live here."

Sartawi tugged nervously on the unfiltered Gitanes. "He knows the expulsion from Beirut has weakened Arafat. Killing Peres will make him a world-renowned figure, put him that much closer to taking over the PLO."

"I know. Considerable numbers of our fighters, disillusioned after Lebanon, will rush to join him."

Sartawi pulled on the cigarette again then exhaled heavily. "Have you alerted the Israelis?"

"I've been working with them."

Sartawi's eyes widened. "Really?"

"It's only until Abu Nidal's stopped. I'm leaving for the Algarve coast in the morning."

Just then the phone rang. Sartawi leaned over to the desk, lifted the receiver, said hello and listened. Ramzy gazed up at the photograph on the wall of Sartawi shaking hands with the Israeli Knesset member, Arieh Eliav, and shifted restlessly in his chair. In early 1979 leading members of the Palestine National Council had threatened to expel Issam from the PLO if he accepted Austrian Chancellor Bruno Kreisky's award to he and Eliav as peace campaigners. Immediately after the public ceremony, with Arab newspapers demanding a trial, Issam had been summoned to Beirut. Once there, Arafat defended him passionately and sent him back to Paris with his approval—his dual-track policy.

Ramzy watched with concern as his friend's hand suddenly shook as he brought the cigarette to his mouth.

"Then you're certain?" Issam asked.

There was a pause.

"There's absolutely no doubt?"

Another pause. Sartawi mashed the cigarette into the edge of the ashtray, again and again.

"All right. Thank you."

Sartawi cradled the receiver and turned to Ramzy, his voice wavering. "It was my assistant downstairs. A report just came in over the telex from Amman. He knew you were here. Ramzy, your brother's been shot by the Israelis during a demonstration in Ramallah. I don't know how to tell you this. Fawaz is dead."

Ramzy sank down and stared at him.


IN TEL AVIV, Shimon Peres leaned back in the chair in his office and looked at Shai.

"Are you asking me to cancel my participation in the Socialist International?"

"I'm saying only that I cannot guarantee we can protect you."

"If I cancel, what then? Do I only leave the country secretly? And then how do I know they won't discover my plans anyway? What if I'm elected prime minister? Do I decline state visits overseas? To curtail my movements would be a greater victory to the terrorists than my death."

Shai smiled. "I was hoping you'd say that."

"Was there any doubt?"

"Not really."

"I arrive in Portugal in eleven days." Peres reached for the cup of coffee on the corner of his desk and sipped. It was cold. "I assume that you have our best people working on this."

Shai nodded.

"So, with any luck, you'll have the terrorist eliminated before my arrival."

With he and Ramzy working together, Shai felt they had an excellent chance of doing exactly that. Shai stood. "If you'll excuse me, I have a lot still ahead of me today."

Peres rose, extended his hand across the desk and held on to Shai's as he shook it. "A lot more rests on this than my life. If they succeed, I fear the direction it will push the country."

Shai felt an excitement, standing here with the man he hoped would be the next prime minister. "We'll have to see to it that Abu Nidal is killed, for a lot of reasons."

"Thank you for coming," Peres said, releasing his grip.

Outside the government building, an old man sat on the sidewalk next to a blanket piled with coins and stacked with the afternoon editions of *Yediot Ahronot* and *Maariv* newspapers. Shai had not heard the radio news broadcasts all day. He handed the man the exact change and picked up a red-bannered *Maariv*. He glanced at the headline, then saw the smaller story below it.

He quickly read the first sentence: "The PLO terrorist Ramzy Awwad's brother, Fawaz Awwad, was killed early today by the Israeli Defense Forces during an antigovernment demonstration in Ramallah."

IN MADRID the young female revolutionary drove down the handsome Boulevard de Alcala and approached the sculpted grass-and-flower-surrounded fountain in the center of the roundabout. The two assassins she was supposed to pick up for Abu Nidal were seated on the grass, as instructed, waiting.

She slammed to a halt and motioned them into the car. They clamored into the back seat with their suitcases. Once in, she sped away from the fountain and joined the heavy traffic on the tree-lined boulevard.

"I'm told one of you speaks English," she said without turning back.

The older mustachioed Ismail al-Qasim turned to the younger Marwan Nasir, puzzlement on his face.

"I understand, but not speak so good," Nasir said.

"I'm going to drive you to the Algarve," she said. "Abu Nidal will meet you and give you the weapons there."

"He's in Portugal now, yes?"

She smiled into the rearview mirror. "Yes, he's there, waiting."

# 13 September 14 • Damascus, Syria

RAMZY SAT RIGID at his window seat as the Air France
707B-stretch jet descended outside Damascus. He closed
his eyes. He had not flown to Amman where Fawaz's funeral would be held, but had remained in Paris, walking
the streets alone. Finally he had slept for a few hours.
Then he had taken a taxi to the airport. The family gathered in Amman would understand when they learned that
after what had happened to Fawaz he had traveled to Abu
Nidal's office to join him.

Through the small window, Ramzy looked down at the
approaching city where he had spent so many frustrat-
ing years. All he had wanted was to teach their children
under reasonable conditions. As the plane dropped low
on its final approach over the irrigated orchards surrounding the dusty city, he took in the narrow streets,
minarets, mosques, mausoleums and virtually colorless
skyline. The elongated 707B banged down on the tar-
mac and bounced hard. Then there was a screech of
brakes, and he was thrust forward against the seat belt as
the plane slowed on the desert runway.

He came down the steep steps, holding his small bag by the straps. As the hot wind kicked the sand up from the runway and sent it sailing toward the terminal, fear knotted in his stomach. He reached the ground and walked past the khaki-uniformed soldiers at the base of the ramp, their Russian AK-47s ready.

Ramzy's Tunisian passport was not questioned, and after the customary delays, he made his way through the teeming arrival lounge. Ignoring ragged boys who wanted to carry his one small bag, he stepped outside in the heat, the sweat coating his face. He lingered near some food stalls and watched the rotating skewers of lamb. He loved this world. This, not the cool protocol of London and Paris, was home. Past the rows of sandbags piled against the terminal, the taxi drivers were beckoning customers with their loud singsong *Shaam . . . yallah as-Shaam!*

He approached, and before a half-dozen could converge on him, shouting to each other that he had seen the customer first, Ramzy pointed to an older man wearing a worn keffiyeh who had been straggling a step behind the avid drivers and said, "*Shaam.*" He allowed the old man to take his bag and followed him as he hobbled to a battered Toyota. Ramzy wiped his forehead, then stepped into the rear of the cab. He rested his arm on the ledge of the window, then quickly jerked it up. The metal was too hot.

As they approached the city from the south, Ramzy saw the ring of SS-12 missiles and antiaircraft guns that circled Damascus. Entering the city they passed rows of yellow stone houses. Soon the traffic stalled. Villagers riding mules, boys pulling donkeys and men of all ages on bicycles, some with fruit and vegetables in the baskets, others with narghiles strapped to their backs, wove in between the horn-blowing cars. Drivers leaned out their windows and shouted curses up ahead. A tourist bus full of Iranian pilgrims, the sides of the vehicle plastered with posters of the grim-faced Ayatollah Khomeini, belched black exhaust in front of them.

"Where may I take you?" the driver asked as they crawled forward. "A hotel? I know many fine hotels and some not so fine, if you prefer?"

"Take me to the Souk Midhat Pasha."

"As you wish."

They picked up speed near the Palace of Justice where black-veiled women hurried up the steps and several Druze mothers squatted in the shade of the entrance, breast-feeding their babies. The driver turned right, and they drove along the street that fronted the western side of Old Damascus. Here the bazaars and mosques had long ago spilled out toward the cooling sea breezes and eaten away the Roman and medieval walls.

The driver pulled to the curb and Ramzy climbed out. He would walk a little first along the southern walls, shed his European self, fully enter this world. He felt Dalal's presence so close, at the school in the hills. A half hour later, beyond the as-Saghir Gate, he turned from the broken medieval towers, minarets and the lines of washing flapping in the hot wind. He continued along the Mameluke Cemetery, then turned into the narrow street in the slightly run-down quarter of the city.

He approached the second building from the corner, noticing the small cameras on the outside facade that recorded all arrivals. Armed guards in jeans and T-shirts lurked in the shadows. Above the entrance to the building hung an illuminated crest: crossed rifles held by fists with a hand grenade at its base. Abu Nidal had maintained this small office here, even while being supported by Iraq. His heart beating quickly, Ramzy approached the entrance. No one stopped him.

WITH THE SOCIALIST INTERNATIONAL opening in ten days, Shai pushed his key into the door of his apartment on the slopes of Haifa's Mount Carmel, then bent to pick up two bags of groceries, leaving two in the hall. The Rosh Hashanah holiday arrived this weekend, and shopping in the mobbed supermarket had taken him much longer than he had expected. He moved inside.

Instead of taking the bags into the kitchen, Shai walked into the bare white salon. The man standing at the window, staring out at the ocean, turned.

"I'm leaving for Europe in a few minutes," Shai said. "This food should hold you for a while."

The man limped forward. "All right," Fawaz Awwad said.

"You know, of course, not to leave here under any circumstances, even for a few minutes."

"I know." Fawaz's tone was hard. If word leaked out that he was alive, it would bring Ramzy's immediate death. His brother had needed a reason Abu Nidal would not suspect for Ramzy's abrupt radicalization. His "murder" by the Israelis would provide cover for Ramzy's infiltration.

Shai went to the end table near the vinyl sofa, wrote down a number and held the small sheet toward him. "If the food runs out, or if you need anything else, call this number and ask for Tami. Tell her your name is Ibrahim."

Fawaz took the paper from him, his chest hurting where the bullet had slammed into the steel-mesh vest. As the Israeli carried the bags into the kitchen, Fawaz thought back to the way this man had again appeared at his office. This time he had asked that he come with him to a secure phone where they could make a call to Ramzy in Paris. Not trusting him, believing Ramzy was still in Ansar, despite what the Israeli told him, he had only reluctantly agreed. It had indeed been Ramzy on the phone. There was no mistaking his voice or his mentioning the bag of sea anemones Ramzy had kept under his bed as a boy in Jaffa. Ramzy had asked that he do exactly as the man who had brought him to the phone requested.

The Israeli had originally planned to foment some kind of public killing, but when the spontaneous antigovernment demonstration had erupted, they had rushed him to his car, holding back their troops until his arrival in Ramallah. The artificial blood in the sack over his chest had been convincing. He had told only his wife the truth.

The Israeli returned, carrying a small suitcase, which he set down on the floor. "Thank you," he said.

"I'm doing this for Ramzy, not for you."

"Thank you, anyway. I'm sure this is not easy for you." Shai started to leave, then stopped. "You'll be all right cooped up here? It might be a while."

"I can wait as long as is necessary."

There was a loud honking outside from the *sheirut* that Shai had arranged to take him to the airport. He would change planes in Athens, then continue to Lisbon.

"Use anything you want in the house freely."

Fawaz looked at the picture of Sarit on the coffee table. "It's your apartment?"

"Yes."

The expression on Fawaz's crease-lined face softened, and he nodded. "I shall treat it like my own home."

Shai hurried down the stairs, surprised that the *sheirut* driver was not pounding his horn. Outside, the seven-passenger Mercedes was idling, passenger side facing him, baggage piled and tied on the roof rack. Someone was bent, talking through the window to the driver. Then to his surprise, the heavy shared taxi accelerated down the street.

He saw her standing there in her shorts with those long, bare legs in sandals and an oversized T-shirt, her dark hair clipped in a ponytail. He moved toward her, surprised how pleased he was that she was here.

"I'm driving you to the airport," Tami said as he approached.

Behind her, the ball of the sun hung high above the sea; the hot *hamsin* winds from the desert rippled her T-shirt. "How'd you know what flight I was on?"

"I don't work for Carmon just because I'm pretty."

He laughed. He liked her assurance. "You leave work early to do this?"

"I came down very ill about three hours ago. Don't I look pale?"

He shook his head. "Actually, you look rather attractive."

"Thank you, kind sir."

He held his bag out to her. "You going to carry this, too?"

"No, I think coming here uninvited was quite enough."

He looked at the flat ocean. "I'm glad you did."

"Come on," she said. "My car's just down the block."

When they reached her Subaru, he tossed his bag into the back seat, his spirits considerably lightened, and climbed in. Tami sped down the mountain.

After Carmon had reluctantly agreed to the gambit with Fawaz, Shai had suggested that Tami supply the Arab's needs; they need not tell her for whom she was leaving the parcels. Carmon had called Tami in to discuss it. Later, Shai and Tami had sat at dinner to go over the details. He had been amazed at how easily the conversation had grown personal during the meal and how good it had felt to talk to her. They had not really talked much that other time. He remembered that night with discomfort. After he and Tami had made love, he had lain awake, pictured Sarit bleeding on that road, holding on to his arm, and heard the surprise in her voice as she had said, "You're here." Until that moment in the Sinai, he had never fully realized how painful his being away had been for her. At dinner with Tami he had unburdened himself for the first time about how guilty he had felt afterward.

As the dry heat volleyed through the Subaru's open windows, Tami brushed the strands of hair from her eyes. "How long are you going to be gone?"

"I hope not too long," he said quietly.

"I'm not like your wife. If this gets more serious, I'll complain."

He smiled. "That will help."

In front of Ben Gurion Airport's single passenger terminal, Tami pulled to the curb and turned off the ignition. Silent, her assurance suddenly deserting her, she stared through the windshield. He leaned over and kissed her, feeling her turn, her bare leg touching his. He stroked her face with the back of his fingers. "Be careful," she said. He nodded and kissed her again.

Halfway across the Mediterranean on the plane, thinking about Ramzy, Shai ground the ice that remained from his gin and tonic between his teeth. The doctor, the ambulance driver, the man who had fired the bullet, his officer, Fawaz's wife and, of course, Carmon knew the killing in Ramallah had been faked. Too many people to keep this a secret for very long.

RAMZY WALKED SLOWLY up the stairs in Abu Nidal's information headquarters, sweat at his hairline. The banister creaked as he touched it, and he let it go. The fear that had shadowed him since stepping off the plane, caught and entered him now. It was not so much the fear of torture and certain death, if the ruse was revealed—he had grown almost accustomed to greeting death—but more, he feared having come so far and failing. Though to his people his life was crowned with guerrilla and literary achievement, he felt everything really important he wanted to achieve for himself and his people had failed.

On the second floor, two armed fedayeen stood with rifles raised. A third sat at the security screen. The seated man looked up.

"Search him," he said to the guards.

They did, quickly and thoroughly, then took the bag from his hand. One dumped it on the floor and rummaged through his clothes, notebook and pen, then left everything where it was. Ramzy bent and replaced his belongings.

"You are not expected," the seated guard said.

"Tell Abdul Rahman Rahim that Ramzy Awwad would like to see him."

The seated man evidenced no recognition of the name but rose and entered the office. Moments later he came out and nodded to the guards to return to their positions.

"Go in," he said.

Ramzy picked up his bag and moved into the sparsely furnished office. A large colored map of pre-Mandate Palestine covered one yellow-painted wall. The rest of the walls were bare. A fan suspended from the ceiling circulated the hot air. Abdul Rahman Rahim, whose slick black hair was parted and combed to one side, spilling onto the edge of his dark-framed glasses, rose and moved toward him, but stopped short of the traditional hugged greeting the fighters gave each other.

"It is a surprise to see you here," Abdul said.

"I hope that I am welcome."

Abdul Rahman looked down at him. "Your writing is highly respected here." He shook his head slowly. "It is your continual alignment with the defeatist faction that we do not understand."

"Much has changed now."

Abdul Rahman nodded. "Your brother."

Ramzy looked toward the window.

"His martyr's death has been recorded on the front page of every paper in the Arab world. There were violent demonstrations here in Marjeh Square after it happened. It's indicative of the love the people have for you, Ramzy Awwad."

Ramzy turned back. "They could have stopped him. They didn't have to kill him."

"They probably knew he was your brother. It would be like them to punish you this way for what you do."

Ramzy was silent.

"Fawaz was only a warning. Eventually they will see to it that you die. You are too dangerous to them."

"I have killed them before," Ramzy said as his other mind wondered whether the Abu Nidal information officer was right.

A smile played on Abdul Rahman's mouth. "Yes, you have."

Just then there was a sharp rapping on the door.

"Yes," Abdul Rahman said with impatience.

The guard who had been monitoring the security screen burst in excitedly. "Excuse me, it's the news. It's all over the radio. A bomb, at Phalangist headquarters. They say nearly eight hundred kilograms. The mur-

derer Bashir Gemayel is dead, along with dozens of his
followers. They don't know exactly how many yet.''

"Are they certain it's confirmed?"

The man nodded quickly. "The French and Americans are reporting it, too. There's no doubt."

The Syrians had succeeded. Abdul Rahman grinned.
"Brief me immediately with any further reports."

The security guard turned quickly and closed the door
behind him.

"So much for the Israelis counting on their relationship with the Phalangists. All that is left is Amin. He's
too weak. Their fighters do not respect him, will not be
bullied into becoming such a close ally of Israel under
him. He's the older brother. The family would not have
passed him over in favor of Bashir, shaming him, if he had
any qualities of a leader. Not that Bashir wouldn't have
turned on the Israelis in the end when he had what he
wanted from them." Abdul Rahman moved behind his
desk, sat and leaned back. "An unusual day. The end of
Bashir Gemayel and the appearance of Ramzy Awwad."

"You know why I'm here."

Abdul Rahman laughed. "It is not, I take it, to ask my
opinion of your latest book."

"Your way is the only way left for me now."

"And your men in Europe?"

"I will speak to them. Some, I'm sure will come with
me."

"Quite a prize. Ramzy Awwad and a number of his
men." Abdul Rahman came forward, his hands gripping the desk. "First, there will be a rite of initiation."
His face eased abruptly, and he sat more naturally in the

chair. "Farouq al-Hout commands the force in the Sha-tilla refugee camp Arafat left behind when he ran away. The Israelis say there are two thousand fighters still in the camps. Kill al-Hout. Seal the bargain in his blood."

Ramzy had not expected this. He sat silent, then rose. "I'll leave for Beirut in the morning."

Abdul Rahman came out from behind his desk and hugged him with both arms. "I'm sorry it took your brother's murder to bring you to us," he said gently. "I would have preferred another way."

Ramzy broke the embrace, lifted his bag from the floor, then stopped. "I'll need a handgun, preferably small caliber."

Abdul Rahman smiled. "I suppose you won't have any trouble getting near him, will you?" He moved to the door. "Come, we should have something to accommo-date you."

Outside, Ramzy walked back to the as-Saghir Gate. As he hailed a cab, he gazed up at the hilly suburbs north of the city. Above them rose the brown Mount Kassioun with white mosques and schools jutting from her slopes. He saw the UNRWA school and again felt Dalal, so near. Tonight he would be with her.

"Just drive," Ramzy said to the young man behind the wheel as he settled into the rear seat.

"Where to?"

"Anywhere, it doesn't matter. Into the desert."

The taxi headed south along the road to Jerusalem, past the austere stone chapel of the shrine to St. Paul. Ramzy stared out the window. He had to figure out some way to make it appear that he had killed Farouq al-Hout.

## 14 September 15 • Albufeira, Portugal

SHAI PICKED RESTLESSLY at the bougainvillea on the balcony of his room in the Montechoro Hotel, waiting for the package that was his first lead in the search for Abu Nidal. The four-day International opened in the hotel on September 24. There was not much time.

Below him on the grass area in front of the ten-story blinding-white building people descended the minibus that shuttled guests to the nearby Albufeira beach. He heard a knock, hurried into the room and turned the knob on the front door. A young Israeli agent stood there with a manila envelope.

"Come in," Shai said, and shut the door behind him. "What do you have?"

"We've been photographing arrivals on all European flights from Damascus, as you suggested. You were right. It appears he's brought in a fresh team from there."

Shai took the large envelope from him and opened it.

"There was a flight to Madrid the day before yesterday," the agent went on. "After we processed the film and went through the files, we identified two of the arrivals as members of the Abu Nidal faction."

Shai studied the photographs. "Names?"

"The younger one is Marwan Nasir. The older mustachioed man is Ismail al-Qasim, though we can't assume he still has the mustache."

"Get copies to all our people and have them spread the coast with them. Every bar, café, restaurant. Offer a large reward for any information."

"I'll have the pictures distributed by tonight. Anything else?"

"Not for now."

After the agent left, Shai went to the desk and grabbed his keys. He would work the seaside bars in the provincial capital of Faro himself and make his way to those who ran the underside of the fishing coast.

OPPOSITE THE SEMICIRCULAR Kuwaiti embassy in south Beirut, Ramzy entered the Shatilla refugee camp through the main dirt road. He stood motionless and stared at the destruction. The acrid smell of the fires still hung in the air despite the sea breezes. Every building over one story was pockmarked or crumbling. Windows had been blown out, boarded over, then reboarded. Life existed only at ground level. The camp had endured seven years of devastating civil war with the Christians, with no incentive to rebuild. A hundred thousand had died on both sides—and then the Israelis had bombed them.

The anger and frustration built quietly inside Ramzy. He continued into the noisy, dirty camp. The main road was filled with women, children and old men. Occasional stray goats picked at the garbage. Bomb craters dotted the dirt. Women with large tin containers on their heads walked to the communal water taps as apparently the running water was out again. As he moved farther into Shatilla, to his puzzlement, Ramzy passed only a few armed fedayeen, usually walking with teenaged boys carrying AK-47s.

Ramzy quickened his pace. He would have to find Farouq al-Hout and somehow convince him, while all was quiet here, to play dead for several days or more—until he could eliminate Abu Nidal.

Suddenly Israeli F-15s and Skyhawks thundered overhead. He heard the thud of shelling coming from the gunboats offshore, the whistle, then the explosion. To the north and east, smoke rose. They were striking just this side of the green line. These shells seemed to be aimed below the port where the leftist Mourabitoun militia had taken up positions previously held by the withdrawn Palestinians. Abruptly there was shelling behind him, near the airport. Ramzy felt the ground shake, saw the smoke billowing nearby from the Bourj el Barajneh camp between Sabra and Shatilla and the runways. The people in the alleys ran, the women screaming. Shells shrieked, hitting the southern end of Shatilla. Explosions rocked the camp.

Ramzy ran through the warren of dirt alleys, flanked by heavily damaged cinder-block structures. He had to reach Farouq al-Hout's headquarters. This was not a massive punishing attack as the camps had suffered before, but a layer of exploding protection for their tank columns. There was no other possible reason for this bombing now. Israelis would be sweeping northward from their positions in the hills. Ramzy was furious. They were taking West Beirut.

He reached the two-story building that had been Farouq al-Hout's headquarters. It had been bombed apart, sandbags sprayed in all directions. The damage did not appear recent. A shell suddenly exploded behind him, deafening. He turned. The roof of a small building slid into the dirt alley. Another explosion shook the earth, horrifyingly close, almost pitching him to the ground. A shard of concrete sliced his cheek, stinging. He felt a trickle of blood.

"Here, quickly." A young boy was motioning from the entrance of a partially standing cinder-block home. He heard the sounds of firing from the southern extremities of the camp.

Ramzy instinctively wiped his cheek with the back of his hand, saw the blood, then darted toward the boy, who closed the wooden door behind him.

The boy sat on the floor, his arms around an old woman, more comforting her than seeking protection. "I must find Farouq al-Hout, now," Ramzy said.

"He cannot go out," the woman said defiantly, hugging the boy to her chest.

But the shelling of Shatilla had stopped almost as soon as it had started. He could still hear the explosions in the north near the port.

The boy pulled away from the old woman. "Come," he said with the authority of twice his no more than ten years.

Outside, the alleys were deserted. There were no sounds anywhere nearby, only the dull thud of explosions in the northern distance. Suddenly another formation of Israeli Kfirs streaked high overhead, shattering the sound barrier, but dropped no bombs. As they passed over the northern coast, they arced high into the sky. In the distance Ramzy heard sporadic small-arms fire.

Ramzy followed the boy through a maze of alleys into an area where most of the buildings were now broken slabs of concrete and plaster. The boy moved among them, stepping on sheets of corrugated tin roofing twisted from the explosions. As more planes flew overhead, he stopped and waited at the edge of a bombed-out house. Across the dirt lane the floor of a second story jutted into the air, a sewing machine still on a table.

The boy ran ahead, then darted around a corner. Ramzy followed. The boy had stopped. Two keffiyehed men armed with AK-47s stood guard at the underground entrance to a bombed-out one-story concrete hut.

"There," the boy said, then ran back around a corner and disappeared.

Ramzy approached. The two men leveled their rifles at him and ordered him to halt.

"Tell Farouq al-Hout that Ramzy Awwad's here," he said, feeling the dust and dried blood on his face.

One man moved inside. He returned moments later and, pointing a rifle at Ramzy, motioned him down the underground steps flanked by walls of sandbags. Ramzy entered the stifling makeshift command center. The man followed him, still holding the rifle at his back. In the right corner, a man was hunched in front of a shortwave radio. Reports cackled over it. A naked light bulb hung from the ceiling, and sandbags were piled against the inside walls. Across the bunker, sweat beaded on his forehead, his uniform soaked under the arms, sat Farouq al-Hout.

"It is you," he said without emotion.

"Yes."

"Should I return outside?" the guard asked.

Al-Hout looked at him for a long moment without speaking, then as if suddenly remembering where he was, nodded. The guard turned abruptly and left.

Ramzy knew al-Hout could not stay out of sight and play dead in the midst of all this. The fear of Abu Nidal's success plunged through him.

"What's the status here?" Ramzy asked.

Al-Hout rose slowly and motioned his arms in all directions. "What's the status here? We're surrounded by the Israelis, completely. In a matter of minutes . . . there's no way out." The exhaustion was dark under his eyes. "They're broadcasting over the radio that they're taking up positions in West Beirut to prevent anarchy and bloodshed after Gemayel's assassination."

"The Israelis think there are two thousand fedayeen still in the camps," Ramzy said. "It's been all over the papers."

Al-Hout dropped back in the chair and laughed. "Does it look like we have two thousand fighters here?"

"Farouq," the man behind the radio called anxiously. "One of our radio operators in East Beirut is reporting in. The Phalangists are meeting. They're going to head for a staging area near the airport as soon as the Israelis

have secured their hold on the city.'' He yanked the ear-
phones from his head in horror. ''Then they're coming
into the camps.''

## 15 September 17 • Pedras d'el Rei, Portugal

TWO DAYS LATER, as the sunset touched the marshy beach at Pedras d'el Rei, Abu Nidal stood in the cabin with the female revolutionary, who had picked up Nasir and al-Qasim, holding on to his arm. Dozens of isolated cabanas dotted this beach area, twenty-five kilometers from the Spanish border.

"Hurry up," Abu Nidal snapped in the direction of the bedrooms. The two Palestinians entered the salon. They had crossed the open border at Alcoutim and had been waiting here since Tuesday. It was now Friday. "How long do we have to remain in this place?" Nasir asked.

"You are not to leave this cabana for the next week," Abu Nidal snapped. "This woman will bring you everything you need."

"Everything?" Marwan said, grinning at her.

Abu Nidal approached the young man, the fury quiet on his face. "You will think of nothing but the target. If you have doubts, I will bring in someone else, and it will be known that you could not complete the assignment."

The woman walked to the kitchen with the glazed blue-and-white *azulejos* tiles above the sink, turned on the water and bent to drink. Nasir sensed her movement, heard the water, but dared not look at her. "I understand, Abu Nidal."

Abu Nidal slapped him playfully, yet roughly, on the head. "Good." He turned to al-Qasim, who would pull the trigger. "Your bullets are the bullets that will bring us home."

"When will you return here?"

"I will not. You know what to do and when."

Al-Qasim nodded.

The dark young woman came back, the water still on her lips and face. Seductively she wiped her mouth on Abu Nidal's shoulder. Marwan watched her.

Abu Nidal followed Marwan's gaze. The boy looked very much like his older brother Mohammed, now in Nablus, who sold avocados and kiwi fruit to the Israelis. Maybe that was why he had chosen Marwan, he suddenly realized, to die. He thought about his nine brothers and sisters, all older than he. After the family had fled from Jaffa to Ashkelon, to Gaza, and then to Nablus, none of them had had time for him, had even noticed what he was doing. He had been the runt of the brood, neglected. If the Zionists had not come and forced them out of their home, it all would have been different.

"The guns," Abu Nidal said.

The woman picked up her large bag and pulled out a Smith & Wesson .38 and a WZ-63.

"Use them well," Abu Nidal said.

SHAI SAT IN THE DARK CAFÉ in the provincial capital of Faro. Through the window the last orange color of the sunset faded, ushering in the Rosh Hashanah holiday. Across from Shai, Antonio Sebastian poured more dark red wine into his glass and turned over a domino.

"These killers that have come to our peaceful coast," Sebastian said. "We may find them and then we may not. It depends very much on how clever they are." He turned over another domino, and a smile spread across his face as the pattern matched the end of his line. He slipped it in place. "If they are smart and do not move from where they are hiding, I'm afraid the task will be essentially impossible."

Shai turned over a domino but did not see the pattern. He was worried. It was now forty-eight hours since Ramzy was supposed to send a message, and there had been no word from him.

"The International opens in seven days," Shai said. "That is not so much time."

RAMZY PRESSED HIS BACK against a one-story cinder-block building, breathing hard. Despite the onset of the New Year's observance, for the second straight night Israeli 81 mm mortars outside the camps fired flare after flare, lighting the sky as the Phalangists combed the alleys.

It had started yesterday, just after dark. Farouq al-Hout's teenage scouts reported that some six hundred Christian fighters with the inscription *Keta'ib Lubnani-yeh* and a drawing of a cedar tree over their shirt pockets had moved past the Israeli tanks massed at the southern entrance to the camps.

The shooting, sometimes nonstop, sometimes sporadic, had haunted the long night. The sound of heavy feet, shouted orders, doors pulled open, people screaming, then the gunfire mixed with the constant thud as the flares arced, then hung, sizzling in the sky. With the morning's natural light, more Phalangists drove jeeps and bulldozers into the camps. One bulldozer had rumbled near where Ramzy was hiding, its scoop filled with bodies.

Ramzy squeezed his eyes. He heard the cackle of small-arms fire nearby, moving toward him. He had thought this area, already rampaged by the Phalangists, would be safe, but evidently others had the same idea and were filtering back here to hide. He looked around quickly, searching for a place to disappear that would not be discovered. Small fires burned all over the camp. The sounds of the heavy fighting where the last guerrillas here had resisted had disappeared by late last night. There were only the quieter bursts of the executioners now.

There was nowhere to hide. The Phalangists seemed in no hurry. They were searching everywhere in the iridescent, illuminated camp. Across from him at the base of a low cinder-block wall, a line of young men and boys lay on the ground. Each had been shot at point-blank range through the cheek. He could see the dried blood on their faces and hear the buzz of the cloud of flies that had settled over them.

The party of Phalangists was nearing, only seconds away. He heard the horrible shrieking of a woman, then a single shot and silence. He searched frantically around him. The line of bodies against the wall gave him an idea.

He walked quickly and silently past the corpse of a girl no more than three, her white dress muddy, the back of her head blown away. A sickly sweet smell hung in the air; the bodies killed yesterday scattered down the alleys, twisted together, had bloated in the heat.

Ramzy battled the nausea and moved down a narrow alley. On the street leading to the main road to his left, a bulldozer had smashed a clearing. Hands and feet protruded from the debris. He headed to the right, deeper into the warren of alleys where the bulldozers would not attempt to reach. The small-arms fire was still near, behind him and to the left. He passed another line of old men and boys beneath a redstone wall, maybe twenty of them, some fallen on top of others, shot in the back, some with their necks slashed. He hesitated, but the group was too large. The Phalangists might attempt to bury them.

Sweat coated his body. He hurried on, then saw it. A pile of recently killed—two women, an old man and a small child—sprawled in the rubble of a bombed-out house off the alley. He neared, then heard some Phalangists running in his direction. Quickly he bolted to the corpses, stuck his hand into the warm blood of a gaping wound in the top woman's stomach then smeared the blood across his neck. He heard them turning the corner. Ramzy lifted the heavy legs of the old pajamaed man and crawled beneath them. He rested on his side, his head between a woman's feet, showing his bloodied neck, his face in the dust.

He lay without moving, eyes closed, then heard the approach of a party of Phalangists, six, seven of them; he was not sure. They were walking now. "The will of God is being done," one said. "Maybe this will convince the rest of them to leave Christian Lebanon," another went on. They stopped only a few meters from him in the alley. Ramzy felt the dead bodies weighing on him, heard the strike of a match and the inhaling of a cigarette. "The boys will grow up to fight us and the girls will mother fighters," another voice said. And still another spoke, "It is God's will."

"Looks like someone just got those," one said. Ramzy concentrated all his will on not moving. Something small sailed past his face, landed near his cheek, hot, burning. A cigarette.

"They're everywhere in the rubble, especially the small boys. They're like rats."

The cigarette lay against his cheek, burning his skin. The pain seared through him. He only had to move a fraction, but he dared not.

"How long do we have?" one asked.

"Don't know. They haven't told us."

"We'll stay until it's finished. That is God's will."

The pain. His eyes teared. He smelled his flesh burning, tried to divert his mind, pictured Dalal as she slept peacefully, and he tried not to shift in the bed and wake her. If only they would walk a few meters. The pain was hot and cold, like burning ice on his cheek. He did not move.

"Damn flies," one said, swatting the air. "That's the worst part of it, and the stench."

Ramzy wanted to scream.

"Come on, let's get on with it before we get hauled in for standing around."

Ramzy listened to them walk off, counted the paces, one, two, three, four, five, six, seven, eight, each one more distant, then the voices muffled as they rounded a corner. He moved his face quickly, pushed the cigarette away with his hand and turned under the bodies onto his back. His breathing was heavy, his eyes watery.

His chest quieted gradually, and after a few moments his cheek hurt less. He felt the weight of the woman's legs on him and looked up. She still held a tiny baby to her body. The bullet that had passed through her breast had killed the baby, too. Above him flares burned, turning the sky a smoky iridescent white. He eased back on his side.

His fury at the butchering Phalangists was equaled only by his anger at the Israelis. Ramzy felt the corpses caressing him. Blood dripped down from the still-ripe wounds. The stench, the flies, the weight pressed on him. He clawed the ground with his nails. Flies swarmed in his hair, lighted on the wound on his cheek. He shook his head fiercely. The fires smoldered throughout the camp; the small-arms fire continued. He lay there without moving.

The hours crawled into one another, then agonizingly dropped away. His entire body was covered in sweat and itched. His back ached from the awkward position and the weight above him. His thirst was terrible.

He began writing a story in his head called "A Letter from Hebron," memorizing each sentence. It was about a young Palestinian who hated the occupied city, who had just been accepted to study civil engineering at the University of California. He would liberate himself there in green California, far from the stench of defeat that had filled his nostrils the past fifteen years.

The story took the form of the narrator writing a letter to a childhood friend who was already studying there. It explained how everything under this occupation reminded him of the decay of dying bodies. His flight was booked for two weeks hence; he had his ticket. He had gone into the office in the center of town to pick it up when a group of young armed Jews wearing skullcaps and T-shirts, with a squared fist inside a six-pointed star, sped down the main street in jeeps. They parked and started passing out leaflets that threatened the Arabs with death unless they left Judea and Samaria. Israeli soldiers came and removed the intruders, but the pamphlets still littered the street. No, the narrator wrote, he would not go to California, and he had no regrets. He would stay in Hebron in order to retain his dignity, not run from the debris of defeat. The story ended with the narrator imploring his friend to return, that they were all waiting for him.

Ramzy lay in the dirt, exhausted. He went over the story again in his mind, sentence by sentence. Several times groups of Phalangists passed his or adjacent alleys, but none stopped or noticed him. Occasionally he listened, and when he was certain there were no footfalls nearby, he shifted position to relieve a cramped muscle. Each time the carpet of flies rose in a buzzing cloud, then settled again.

He had not slept in nearly forty-eight hours. He stared at the dirt and forced his eyes to remain open. He could not allow himself to sleep, afraid he would snore. The sound of the flares fired into the sky suddenly stopped. The smoke dissipated, and for the first time in two days there was darkness. He closed his eyes.

With the brightening of dawn, the shooting gradually died away. For a long time, in the distance near the southern exit from Shatilla, he heard bulldozers and jeeps, and then all was deathly quiet. There were no sounds except the flies.

After the thirty-six hours of sporadic shooting, the silence was spectral. The early-morning sun creeping above the mountains bathed his face in warmth. He waited. The stench around him rose in the heat.

Then he heard heavy armored personnel carriers moving up the main road of the camp. A voice boomed over a loudspeaker into the silence: "This is the Israeli Defense Forces. We are only looking for terrorists. All men proceed immediately to the sports stadium with their identification papers. This is the Israeli Defense Forces..."

Ramzy felt the fury touch every part of him. He could not remain like this any longer. He pushed his way through the bodies, took the pistol from his front pocket, threw it on the ground and moved along the alleys. Passing Farouq al-Hout's headquarters, he saw al-Hout's body, disemboweled over a sandbag. It made no difference now. He reached the main dirt street.

Israeli commandos crouched low as they ran from building to building. Ramzy walked into the street,

watched them and started to laugh loudly, dementedly.
A commando rushed at him, his rifle pointed.

As the soldier led him away, he kept laughing. They
were still looking for terrorists. They headed to the sports
stadium. *If you want to see murderers and terrorists, look in
a mirror,* he thought.

**16** September 18 • Jerusalem, Israel

LATER SATURDAY MORNING, Yehuda Shamir moved quickly through the vacant corridors toward Meir Carmon's office. He had been summoned by one of Carmon's aides from the small synagogue in Nachlaot on this special Rosh Hashanah Shabbat. As they pulled away from the curb into the deserted streets, his aide briefed him on the disaster in the refugee camps; he had stared out the window and not spoken for the rest of the drive.

He walked past Tami's empty desk and knocked quietly on the inner-office door.

"Come in," Carmon said loudly.

Shamir moved into the office.

Carmon rose nervously. "Yehuda, you heard?"

Shamir nodded. "How many?"

"We don't know yet. Maybe eight hundred. They buried a lot of them."

Yehuda swore silently.

Carmon quickly lit a cigarette. "We never thought they'd do this with us standing there. Didn't they know what a position this would put us in?"

"Apparently they didn't care."

"They were supposed to kill the terrorists. Okay, maybe a few civilians would go in the process, that's inevitable. But there weren't any terrorists in the camps."

"They all left on the ships?"

"I don't know. We had firm intelligence reports. Arafat was planning to leave two thousand behind. He even left six months' salaries for them. The money's there. We know where it is."

"We'll have to find out what went wrong."

"I've been on the phone to the prime minister's office. The Foreign Office is going to issue a statement saying once we realized what was happening we fired on the Phalangists to try to stop them."

"Is it true?"

"I don't know. There are some reports—"

Suddenly Yehuda felt a sharp stab of pain in his chest. He gripped the arm of the chair.

"Yehuda, are you all right?" Carmon asked, seeing the small man's face whiten.

The pain slowly subsided. Yehuda nodded. "Yes," he said.

"Are you sure? Can I get you some water?"

"No, I'm fine. It's just a little indigestion. The big meal last night. I can't take the spicy food anymore, that and the tension."

"You're sure you're okay?"

Yehuda nodded.

Carmon picked up his half-moon reading glasses and looked at one of the piles of red-tipped memos on his desk. "This is your baby," he said, pushing the memo across the desk. "They've got Ramzy Awwad in Beirut.

He was in Shatilla during the massacre, saw the whole damn thing and survived somehow. They want to know what to do with him.''

"What was he doing in Shatilla?"

"How the hell do I know?'' Carmon pulled his glasses off. "God knows what he thinks of us now. Have them lock him up indefinitely. We'll deal with him later."

"Maybe there's a chance he's still willing to cooperate with us?"

"After he spent thirty-six hours watching God knows how many of his people slaughtered while we not only let the killers in but lit up the goddamned sky for them? He'd probably blow Shai's head off if we let him near him. We'll consider ourselves lucky that he's under lock and key. Have Awwad brought to Megiddo, maximum security."

"Meir, I think someone should talk to him first."

"We're in the middle of what by midafternoon is going to be a full-blown international crisis. I don't have time to argue this with you. We'll protect Peres on our own."

"It was because of Awwad that we found out about Portugal."

"And it was because of him that Abu Nidal escaped in Vienna. No more arguments, Yehuda. Get him to Megiddo and locked up. Now. Then have someone get Tami here. I need her."

Yehuda rose, resigned. "All right."

SHAI PARKED THE CAR across from the two brick airplane hangar-sized buildings along the harbor of Olhao, eight kilometers beyond Faro. The call to come imme-

diately had come from Antonio Sebastian, the provincial
boss he had drunk with in the Algarve's capital. On the
narrow roads, it had frustratingly taken, with one of his
agents in the passenger seat, almost an hour to reach the
fishing town.

Men in front-peaked corduroy or plaid hats and knee-
high rubber boots carried buckets of silvery fish from the
small, colorful boats bobbing in the water. The air was
heavy with the smell. As they walked by the entrance to
the first hangar, Shai saw row after row of square wood
tables with tile tops, piled high with every imaginable
variety of fish, many still squirming. Customers made
their way between the rows, while near the door a dog sat
on the wet floor, munching a fish that had fallen.

They hurriedly crossed the street to the Casarao Restaurant. The high-ceilinged, open-fronted restaurant had
arches on all four walls, burgundy tablecloths and white
paper placemats. On one pillar a calendar, with a woman
whose red-and-white-striped skirt was pulled high ex-
posing her thigh, advertised Sagres beer. Shai pointed his
head at a man sitting alone at a back table, a small
espresso cup on his soiled placemat.

Shai and the agent sat at the table. Antonio Sebastian
lifted his cup and sipped. "You are not as quick as you
should be."

"I came as soon as I received the message," Shai said.

"You may be too late." He held his cup in both of his
roughened hands. "I do not know."

"Then you know where they are?"

"I know where they were. Then they may still be there,
but for certain, only our Lord knows."

"You're sure it's Nasir and al-Qasim?" Shai asked.

"Nasir and al-Qasim?" His breath smelled of fish and wine. "The names. No, there is no one by those names. But the faces." The old Portuguese shrugged. "The faces in the photographs you showed me. Yes, these two men have those faces."

Shai reached into his front pocket and placed an American hundred-dollar bill on the table. "For your time."

Suddenly the old man struck the table hard with his fist, rattling the cup. "You insult me. You think I do this, hand you these foreign killers who come to murder on our coast for . . . for your money?"

Shai was worried about the time. "My apologies. I thought only that Antonio Sebastian knows many people, some of whom may be in need of assistance. If the money could help them?"

"To help the poor," Sebastian sneered. "This small sum?"

Shai removed two additional hundred-dollar bills and set them on the table.

"The church in the hills above Monchique is in need of repair," Sebastian said.

Shai placed two more hundreds on the table and spread them out like a fan. Five of them. "Where are they?"

Sebastian reached for the money, and Shai let him gather it. "If they know how to enjoy a meal," he said smiling, "they are still with Madam Maria's girls. If they eat in a hurry. . ." He lifted his arms in a sign of it not being his fault, then abruptly clapped his hands together twice. A small boy came running out from the kitchen. "It is not far if you know the way. He will take you. The madam is expecting you and will help, but be careful not to wound any of her girls. If you do, there will be an extra charge for their care."

"Thank you," Shai said.

"It is the widows and orphans of the Algarve who thank you."

"Yes, of course."

Outside, they hurried into the car, the boy giving Shai instructions. Shai drove quickly along the harbor toward the huge trawlers, then at the boy's pointing, turned in immediately. The quiet sun-drenched streets reminded him of North Africa. Instead of the red terracotta roofs seen everywhere else in the Algarve, the white houses had narrow outside stairways climbing to flat roofs. Patterned enamel tiles filled the fronts of many of the two- and three-story homes.

The boy pointed to a house covered with square green tiles, and Shai parked. The boy jumped out and hurried away. Down the potholed street, two plaid-capped fishermen were untangling a long length of nylon net.

Shai approached the house and knocked on the door. A middle-aged Portuguese woman in a long white dress answered.

"Do you speak English?" Shai asked.

*"Français,"* the woman said.

Shai nodded and switched to simple French. "Are you Madam Maria?"

"Yes."

"We come from Antonio Sebastian."

She stepped back to let them in, then closed the door. The interior walls were cleanly whitewashed. A wooden staircase led to the second floor.

"Rooms five and seven at the top of the stairs, to your right," she said. "The girls were instructed to keep them there. There are no locks."

So they could get in if someone was beating one of the women, Shai realized. He turned to the agent. "I want at least one of them alive. I'll take number seven."

The young man nodded.

They climbed the stairs, guns drawn. At the top blue and white tiles covered the floor. Moving quietly, they made their way to the rooms. If the girls had followed their instructions, the terrorists would still be naked in bed, easy targets. Shai felt the nervousness in his stomach. He wished they had had time to call for help.

Shai moved ahead toward number seven, sensed the agent approaching number five. He glanced at him; with a nod they would burst in simultaneously.

Suddenly the door to number five opened. Startled, the agent recognized the younger Marwan Nasir, and in the same instant saw the gun in his hand. The young agent fired too quickly and hit him high. Nasir fell back and at the same time squeezed off his own shot, at close range.

The agent felt an explosion in his stomach and searing pain; he was vaguely aware as he fell to the ground of Shai's firing a fusillade at Nasir, striking him repeatedly. The agent grabbed his stomach and felt the warm blood through his fingers. The woman beyond the open doorway bolted past him.

Shai stared at the boy and hesitated. He could not tell if he was dead or alive. Quickly he ran to the stairs, yelled at the madam to call an ambulance, then headed for number seven.

Shai approached the edge of the door and pressed himself against the wall. He reached out the short distance, turned the knob and pushed the door open. He remained against the wall and listened. The woman inside was crying.

Suddenly the teenage girl ran out, completely naked, hands in the air, shouting, tears on her face. The madam was running up the stairs now. Other doors opened and people peeked out.

The girl collapsed into Madam Maria's arms, crying and sputtering in Portuguese.

"He's gone," the madam said to Shai. "Out the window."

Shai burst into the room. The window was open, wind blowing the curtain. A chair was toppled on the floor with men's clothes tangled in the legs. Shai looked out. They were on the second floor; if al-Qasim had hung from the ledge, it would not have been such a hard drop. He searched the bright street but saw no sign of him. The singsong whine of the ambulance echoed in the distance, speeding nearer.

Shai hurried back into the hall and saw the bullet-ridden body of Nasir slumped in the doorway. Nasir must have either heard something or had finished and had his gun out for protection. The madam was bent over the young agent, pressing a handkerchief futilely to the wound. He heard the ambulance slam to a halt outside, then the sound of men running in.

The madam's hands were covered with blood. "He's dead," she said.

Shai looked at the boy for a long time, then went back into the room and gripped the top frame of the window with both hands until his knuckles whitened. He hoped with everything inside him that the young man was not married. He stared down the quiet street again. There were six days before the International, and his only lead had disappeared. Al-Qasim would remain hidden now.

RAMZY RETURNED from the bathroom in the municipal sports stadium at the edge of the Sabra camp, accompanied by an Israeli soldier carrying an Uzi. A main dirt road separated Sabra from Shatilla. He had been questioned in the morning and, still in shock, had given them his real name, which he would not have done normally. He had only just now come out of the numbness enough to use the facilities and wash the blood and dirt from his body. The guard, who on his own accord had left him alone and unwatched, had returned a long time later with some red antiseptic for his wounds. He then escorted him back past a chain-link fence, behind which dozens of women were pushing and shouting. He watched the wives and sisters of many of those inside, begging the reporters waiting at the gate, kissing them up and down on the arm, if only they would go in and find out what was happening to their loved ones.

They neared the area, under several tiers of the stadium, where some four or five hundred men of a broad range of ages sat. He had watched the Israelis' faces tighten into confusion, nervousness and finally shame as they had gone through the identification papers of the Syrian laborers, poor southern Shiites and Kurds who had settled around the edges of Sabra and Shatilla to avail themselves of the water and electricity UNRWA provided the camps. The Israelis had immediately brought chocolate cookies and small plastic sacks of milk to those confined here.

As the guard silently led Ramzy back to his seat, a sergeant approached.

"Is that Ramzy Awwad?" he asked the guard.

"I don't know," the soldier said. "I was just ordered to keep him separate from the others."

"Are you Awwad?" the sergeant asked in Arabic.

"I am *samid*," Ramzy said, speaking the term for steadfast, persevering, that Arabs under occupation in the West Bank used.

The sergeant looked at him, his face suddenly shaken. "I understand," he said quietly. "Today I, too, am *samid*. If you are Awwad, then you must come with me. The delay it takes for identification will not change anything."

Ramzy looked at him, then rose, silent, feeling the hate break through the numbness.

The sergeant turned to the guard. "You can return to the others now." The guard nodded and hurried quickly down the concrete steps of the aisle to where the bulk of the detainees were being held.

Ramzy followed the sergeant as they entered the tunnel that led away from the field. The sergeant accompanied him down the outside stairs, past the guards at the base, to a jeep parked across the street below the Akka Hospital. A half-dozen Israeli tanks rested on the street like elephants that had strayed from the jungle. Their treads had torn the pavement. The driver started the engine as soon as they approached. The sergeant pointed to the front seat and climbed in the back himself. Ramzy stepped in and sat.

They drove to the four-lane highway that circled the Bourj el Barajneh camp and headed south toward the airport and Israeli lines. Every hundred meters, Ramzy saw the Phalangist symbol—a triangle inside a circle— sprayed on the walls of buildings.

He turned to the man in the back seat. "Is that how you directed the Phalangists, painted the way for them?"

"We didn't think they would do this."

"What did you think they would do, two days after the murder of Bashir Gemayel?"

"There were supposed to be two thousand fighters in the camps," the sergeant said quietly. "We just wanted to protect our boys."

Ramzy turned away from him.

The two crossed landing strips of the silent airport were visible off to the right. Ahead of them stretched the ocean and the coastal road. At the junction, to Ramzy's surprise, instead of countinuing south the driver made a sharp left up the steep road that wound into the mountains. He did not wonder where they were taking him. It did not matter at all.

The jeep climbed through the forest, passing magnificent vistas of Beirut below. They drove through stone towns with red roofs and passed opulent villas and resort hotels set back among the pines. Then the road steepened and the landscape grew more lush.

As they approached the narrow streets of Bahamdoun, Ramzy saw Israeli military vehicles everywhere. They continued through the beautiful town nestled in the pines, quiet but still functioning with its shops open. The mountain air was crisp. On the narrow road beyond Bahamdoun, they approached the barreled barrier, with soldiers guarding it, that marked the eastern extremity of Israeli lines. The driver stopped, and the sergeant jumped out and approached the soldiers, removing a piece of paper from his pocket. Moments later he returned.

"You're free to go," the sergeant said.

Ramzy looked at him and laughed.

"I mean it. You can go."

"To do what?"

The sergeant looked down. "I don't know. Whatever it is you do."

Ramzy laughed again.

"It's no trick."

"Isn't it?" Ramzy climbed out of the jeep.

"Let's go," the sergeant ordered the driver as he pulled himself into the front seat.

Ramzy watched the vehicle turn and speed away, the laughter dead. They were trying it again, so he would agree to continue working with them. He walked past the

open roadblock toward Syrian lines. This time it would
not work. Let Peres die. What difference did it make?
The Israelis would never grant them their own state anyway.

LATE IN THE AFTERNOON on Sunday, Shai walked through Francisco Gomes Square in Faro, biting small pieces of fish off a wooden skewer that comprised the lunch he had been too busy to eat. Though he should not have taken the time, he had accompanied the coffin of the dead agent to the Faro airport for the flight to Lisbon.

Shai dropped into his car seat, tossed the skewer on the floor and pulled out of the square. Without a better lead, they would concentrate the search near Olhao, where al-Qasim had escaped. Still, the assassin could have traveled any distance there to cover his tracks.

Shai drove toward the village of Moncarapacho, a few kilometers in the hills behind Olhao. He felt the tiredness like a physical sadness, like the moment after making love with the wrong woman. He suddenly thought about Tami, wanted to talk to her, hear her voice. He would call her later.

On the main road, Shai passed orchards surrounded by low rock walls with grass and wildflowers growing through the red earth between the trees. A headache pressed from behind his eyes. He had still not heard from

Ramzy. It was beginning to look as if Abu Nidal's people had killed him. In any event, there would be no infiltration from the inside. It was all up to him. He gripped the steering wheel. There were only five days now until the Socialist International.

AS THE SUN SET over the desert, casting an orange sheen on the stone buildings and minarets of Damascus, Ramzy approached the UNRWA school in the hills. Dalal, in her long skirt and dark blue scarf, was sitting on the low wall of the courtyard with another teacher, eating an apricot. As the two women saw him approach, the other teacher excused herself and walked quickly toward the former convent building.

Dalal remained on the wall. The happiness of seeing him again so soon mixed with the depression over news of the massacre in Beirut. As he neared, she saw the cut and the pus of the cheek burn. Fear for his safety darted through her, even though he was here.

He did not embrace or touch her; he remained silent.

"What happened?" she asked after a long time, her voice soft.

He looked below at the orchards and the winding arteries of the Barada, watched over by drooping myrtle saplings. He turned to her and spoke without emotion. "I was in Shatilla. I saw it."

Horror pinched her face. "Ramzy, no."

He gazed back at the orchards.

She wanted to hold him, comfort him, but waited.

After a moment, he looked at his petite wife, took in her creamy brown skin, delicate nose and mouth, followed the black ends of the hair near her forehead that disappeared below her scarf.

"I want us to go away for a while together," he said. "Someplace far from all this."

"You talking about a vacation?"

"I guess so, yes."

"For how long?"

"I don't know."

"You're sure this is what you want?"

"Yes."

Her large coal-black eyes found his. "I'd love a vacation, but not now."

He had not expected that; he stared down at the groves glutted with figs, mulberries, mandarins.

Her voice was gentle. "Why do you want to go now?"

"I'm tired," he said. "I've had enough of being away from you."

"We've been together more, recently, than we have in years. You're here now."

"I want to stay."

"Why suddenly today?"

He said nothing.

"You want to stay, or you don't want to go back?"

"All right. I don't want to go back. Dalal, it doesn't matter what I do out there. It doesn't make any difference. The Palestinians have less than when I started."

"Then if you want, we'll go away. But tell me, how long will it be before the frustration eats at you? A week? A month? Two months? And how long before you turn that frustration on me?"

He shut his eyes. "I love you."

She slid nearer on the wall. He felt her small hands in his hair. "I love you, too." Her voice faltered. "I've lived without you. I will not live with you for the wrong reasons."

He saw her lips quiver and held her tight against him. The warm wind carried the scent of the orchards.

She touched gently around the burn on his cheek with a finger, frightened. "Whatever it is, don't stop in the middle."

He was amazed that she knew, yet it felt wonderful that she did. He circled his hand around hers and clasped it. "Dalal, I was working with the Israelis to stop Abu Nidal, but after Sabra and Shatilla . . ."

"If there was a good enough reason for you to work with them before," she said softly, "then nothing has changed."

He looked at the determination in her eyes, and a smile came involuntarily to his lips. He nodded, and to his surprise much of the burden dropped from him. He kissed her, joining the deep softness of her mouth. "I can stay tonight," he said.

She slid off the wall into his arms. "Let's walk through the desert, like we did when we first met."

IN THE MORNING Ramzy approached Abu Nidal's office outside the southern walls of Old Damascus. When he thought about having anything further to do with the Israelis, the rage rose in him, and he saw them at the entrance to Sabra and Shatilla as the Phalangists proceeded through their lines. Still, if Abu Nidal killed Peres, it would be the Palestinians that would suffer.

Ramzy moved under the surveillance cameras, walked past the guards lounging outside and continued up the stairs. Two new guards were stationed at the second-floor landing, but the same man sat behind the television monitor.

"Please go in," he said, swiveling toward Ramzy. "I've informed Abdul Rahman that you're here."

As the two guards stepped aside, Ramzy entered the stark office. "Ramzy," Abdul Rahman said without rising. "I've been worried about you. We're all in shock here."

Ramzy approached the desk. "Farouq al-Hout's dead. I killed him."

"Sit, please," Abdul Rahman said, motioning to the chair. "It's obvious what you've been through. First, we'll have some tea."

"No tea. No delays." Ramzy unleashed a hatred that was no act. "They sealed off the camp. Fed the Phalangists when they grew tired from the butchering, so they could go back in."

Abdul Rahman pointed at the chair. "Please, Ramzy. Sit."

Ramzy stared at him, then walked over and fell into the chair.

"They will pay for this," Abdul Rahman said evenly. "Both the Phalangists and the Zionists." He laced his fingers together and hesitated for a long moment. "Now, please, you will excuse my questioning. But how are we to know it was you who killed al-Hout and not the Christians?"

Ramzy stood. "What do you think I was doing in Shatilla if I didn't go there to kill him? Where do you think I got this from?" Ramzy turned his cheek to Abdul Rahman. "I hid in a pile of bodies."

"Understand," Abdul Rahman said, "the questioning is not to be considered a personal insult."

"I do not need to explain the reasons for my change any further." Ramzy turned and headed for the door.

He twisted the knob and walked out.

"Wait, please," Abdul Rahman called after him. He came out from behind his desk. "I have spoken with Abu Nidal." Ramzy took a single step back into the room. "Abu Nidal would like to talk to you and would like you to stay in comfort, as his guest. Check into the Ritz Hotel in Lisbon. Someone will contact you there."

# 18 September 22 • Lisbon, Portugal

SHAI SAT IN THE MODEST Bonjardim Restaurant in the narrow, short street beside Lisbon's main post office. He had not ordered. Around him noisy Portuguese were eating their one o'clock meal of the restaurant's specialties of barbecued suckling pig and spit-roasted chicken. Two days remained before the International, and still he had no leads.

Shai saw Ramzy coming through the door. The message had come unexpectedly late last night, and fortunately there had been a seat on the ten a.m. flight from Faro, otherwise he would have had to drive the three hundred kilometers to the capital.

"I'm glad to see you," Shai said as Ramzy sat without speaking. He took in his injured cheek. "I was worried about you."

"Worried about me? Or the operation?"

"I was worried about the operation and about you. What happened to you?"

"Nothing. How's my brother?"

"Fine. He's staying in my apartment in Haifa. He's a little disoriented and uncertain about what he's agreed to, but he's going along with it."

Ramzy nodded.

Shai leaned forward on his elbows. He spoke in a soft tone. "Ramzy, did Abu Nidal's men torture you?"

"No. Actually, I received the wounds in Shatilla. You've heard of the Sabra and Shatilla refugee camps, haven't you? Oh, sure you have. Your troops moved into West Beirut to prevent anarchy and bloodshed. Isn't that what your prime minister announced?"

Shai went pale. He must have witnessed the Phalangist rampage and somehow survived it. "My people are outraged at what happened."

"My people are dead."

Shai remained silent. To say he was sorry was meaningless. In Ramzy's place, he would want no platitudes. The noise of the restaurant suddenly became audible.

"Since you called," Shai said, "I assume you're still willing to help us."

"I want Abu Nidal dead. What progress have you made here?"

Shai told him about Nasir's death, and al-Qasim's escape.

When he was finished, Ramzy said, "I was successful in Damascus."

"Great."

"Abu Nidal will leave the country as soon as they shoot Peres or attempt to. If they've sent me here, he'll contact me before then."

When they did, Awwad would be walking in there, alone. "You obviously won't be able to take a gun in with you the first time," Shai said. "We have a directional transmitter we can fit into the sole of your shoe."

"No. We both know what will happen if they find it."

"And we both know what will happen if you're in trouble and you're alone. There's always the chance that somehow they'll learn about your brother. Too many people know."

"And you're saying you can't guarantee Fawaz's being alive won't leak out." Ramzy's eyes hardened. "You mean purposely, don't you? A lot of your people would rather have Abu Nidal around killing those like me. No one will ever pressure you to negotiate with him."

Shai worried about what Carmon was capable of doing. "I want you to take the transmitter. Please. As you say, they have no reason to suspect you at the moment, and it's virtually undetectable."

Ramzy thought about the mistakes in Vienna. "All right," he said reluctantly.

"Now, we have to set up a system of communicating so we won't be seen together."

Ramzy nodded. And then we wait, he told himself. He did not think it would be too long.


INSIDE THE ISRAELI EMBASSY in Lisbon, Shai did not sit as the young head of their intelligence in Portugal offered him a chair.

"I need two vans with monitoring equipment immediately. I want one driven down to Faro and one here."

Shai had to be ready in the event Ramzy flew to the provincial capital.

"What else?"

"I need a team from the Algarve brought here on the next flight. Set them up in a hotel."

"You want anybody in particular?"

Shai thought for a moment. "Get me Cilla. Her British accent throws off suspicion."

The agent lifted the phone and dialed an internal connection.

Less than two full days before the International, Shai thought, feeling his first optimism since he had lost al-Qasim.


KHALID MONSOUR SAT at a corner table in the Metro Bar in Amsterdam, finishing his cheap genever. He set the glass down sharply and shoved it away. He lit another Rothman's, hating the harsh taste. He had failed a course in statistical thermodynamics in the spring and was having to take it over now.

He removed the cigarette from his mouth and brushed against the several days' old stubble on his chin. The bell over the door jingled, and Dani and Yusuf, two Arab friends from the university, entered unsteadily. They saw Khalid, came over to the table and sat.

"We just came from the windows," Dani said, laughing. "Yusuf tried to get his money back because his pecker wouldn't stand at full mast. I don't know what he did, but she called the police, and we had to run for it."

"I slapped her, that was all." Yusuf motioned to the bartender. "Beers for my friends," he said.

Drunkenly Dani leaned back in his chair. "Speaking of women, whatever happened to that poetess you were with? What was her name?"

"Leila," Yusuf chimed in. "Leila Fahdi. She was hot, wasn't she, Khalid? You could tell by looking at her. I bet she really screamed when you did it?"

"Shut up."

"What did happen to her?" Dani asked.

"I got rid of her."

Yusuf grinned. "That's not what I heard."

The bartender arrived, placed three mugs of foamy Amstel on the table, then left.

"What did you hear?" Dani asked, grabbing a beer. Some of it spilled on the table as he swept it near.

"I heard that she walked out on old Khalid without a word. Didn't even say bye-bye."

Dani drank some of the cold beer. "Well, maybe our friend Khalid couldn't keep her happy. Let's take him to the windows. That big black Surinamese can teach him a few things. Then maybe he won't lose the next one." Dani broke up laughing, and Yusuf slapped him on the back, laughing, too.

"Just shut up, you two. Shut up or I'll—"

"Or you'll what?" Yusuf said. "Take our girlfriends away from us?" He looked at Dani, and the two collapsed into laughter again.

Khalid took his beer, every part of him aching in humiliation and fury, and drank half of it. "I'll show you," he said, holding the mug so tightly with both hands that he thought it would break.

"What are you going to do?" Dani asked, smiling.

Khalid drank the rest of the beer in one long swallow. "I'm going to find her, bring her back here." He wiped his mouth with the back of his hand. "Then we'll see who's laughing."

"Come on, Khalid. Forget it. It's not that important. She's only a woman."

"She left with Abu Nidal."

Dani laughed, motioned to the bartender for another round of beers, then turned back to Khalid. "Who told you that story?"

"Her roommate."

Dani tapped Yusuf on the shoulder. "And he believes her? To the windows immediately. This man has a problem with women that must be solved."

"It's true," Khalid said angrily. "Ramzy Awwad came to the houseboat asking if I knew where she was."

"Abu Nidal and Ramzy Awwad," Dani said in mock seriousness. "Forget the windows. We better go back to his houseboat immediately in case Arafat calls personally for his help."

"I'll show you," Khalid said, livid. "I'll show everyone. I'll go to Abu Nidal's headquarters and inform him about Ramzy Awwad, then they'll tell me where she is."

The bartender set the fresh beers in the center of the table. Dani pushed one at Khalid, unsuccessfully suppressing his laugh. "Sure, Khalid, we all know that's what you're going to do, but in the meantime, why don't you have another beer?"

---

TWO DAYS LATER, Shai's optimism had withered into worry. He stood on the grass in front of the Montechoro Hotel as the delegates of the sixteenth Socialist International milled in recess after the opening session. Ninety-odd hours—the attack could come any time between now and the close of the final session, scheduled for two o'clock on Monday, the twenty-seventh. As of several hours ago, Ramzy, still in Lisbon, had not been approached.

To make matters worse, since the International delegates comprised only a small portion of the eight hundred guests in the fully booked hotel, the management had denied them permission to set up metal detectors and check the identification of those who entered the lobby. The delay and questioning might spark a panic that would empty the hotel.

Shai moved through the glass doors into the white high-ceilinged lobby. He strode across the adobe-colored tile floor to the pay phones, dropped in his escudoes and dialed the centrally located Hotel Principe Real in Lisbon. By now he knew the number by heart.

Apparently nobody in the hotel suspected that the British honeymoon couple, who understandably rarely left the room and ordered bottles of champagne with each meal, were Israeli agents, as were the others who surreptitiously entered the room from down the hall, when they did leave. All were waiting for the call from Ramzy, signaling that Abu Nidal had made contact. He asked for room 412.

"It's Johnny," Shai said in English when Cilla answered. "You want to meet for a late dinner?"

"No, luv," Cilla said, "afraid not."

He laughed into the receiver. "Enjoying yourself, I take it?"

"I'm having a frightfully good time, thank you. If honeybuns can find his trousers, maybe we'll join you tomorrow. Why don't you ring then?"

"Fine," he said. "All best."

He hung up. Still nothing. Shai returned to the main lobby and saw Shimon Peres's familiar head, with its receding white hair, moving toward the elevators that would carry him back up to the tenth-floor convention facilities. As he waited with the other delegates for the doors to part, Shai recognized the phalanx of Israeli plainclothes security men surrounding him.

AS THE PAIR of Israeli agents escorted Khalid Monsour into the security room at the Israeli embassy in The Hague, the Palestinian felt clever. He would not have to travel all the way to Abu Nidal's headquarters to locate Leila Fahdi. He would have the Israelis find her for him.

"You may sit there," the darker Israeli said in Arabic, and pointed to a table surrounded by chairs.

As Monsour lowered himself into a chair at one end, the two agents sat opposite him. The dark agent wore a shirt without jacket or tie. "You said over the phone that you had something important for us?"

"I know how you can find Abu Nidal."

"You're unhappy with the way he's killing your own people?" the Israeli asked.

Monsour glared at them. "I didn't come here to answer questions. I came here to tell you how to find Abu Nidal."

The Israeli nodded. "Please, go on."

"I want something from you in return."

"That depends. If it's something we can provide..."

"I want to know that someone with him won't be harmed."

"If you tell us who it is, we'll try our best."

Monsour rose restlessly from the chair and paced several steps toward the wall and back. "This is how you can find him. He's with a woman. A...friend of mine. If you find her, she's with him. But before I tell you who she is, you have to promise not to hurt her."

"The women with him are of no interest to us."

Monsour neared the table again then spoke loudly. "I want your word that you will not harm her."

"Please, sit down. I promise you, protecting the woman will not be a problem."

Monsour stood there. "If you're lying. If anything happens to her, I'll—"

"We are not lying. Please, sit."

Monsour stared at the two men, then dropped into the chair.

"What is the woman's name?" the dark Israeli asked.

Monsour was silent.

"If you do not tell us her name, obviously we cannot help you."

"Leila Fahdi," Monsour said loudly.

"Do you know where they are?"

"No. The last I heard from her she was in Vienna, but that was a month ago."

The dark Israeli touched his partner on the arm, motioned his head toward the door, then turned to Monsour. "Please excuse us for a moment. We won't be long."

In the hall outside the soundproof room with the heavy steel doors, the dark Israeli leaned against the wall. "What do you think?"

"I don't know. Either it's a clever trap of some sort or he's in love with the woman."

"Send a telex to Jerusalem and see if they know anything about this. In the meantime, let's cut him off, follow him and see what he does."

The Israeli nodded.

They reentered the room. Monsour was seated, one hand tapping the table.

"I'm sorry," the dark Israeli said, "but unfortunately this information is of no use to us."

The tapping stopped, and Monsour's fingers closed into a fist. He glared at them. He should not have come here in the first place. He shoved the chair back. He should have gone directly to Abu Nidal.

RAMZY SAT AT HIS DESK in the elegant Ritz Hotel, rested a moment from his writing and gazed out the window. Below the high, grand building lay Eduardo VII Park and to the right of the grass, the long tree-lined Avenida da Liberdade. Already this early in the morning, people crowded the open-air cafés and strolled among the statues and trees.

Though Ramzy would have preferred to scour the Algarve, he did not mind remaining in the hotel and waiting for Abu Nidal to come to him. From the day he had first stood in line at age twelve for the monthly UNRWA food parcel, he had grown accustomed to waiting. Ramzy returned to writing the ''Letter from Hebron'' that he had composed in Shatilla. He wrote in longhand with small, evenly curled letters. He loved the look of handwritten Arabic and never used a typewriter.

The phone rang, jarring him from his thoughts. After the second ring, he lifted the receiver.

''Hello, Ramzy. It's Wasif,'' the voice said in Arabic.

He knew no Wasif. ''How are you, my friend?'' Ramzy asked.

"Excellent. Why don't you meet me at Tofa's on the Avenida da Liberdade? You know it?"

"I'll find it."

"Good. See you in fifteen minutes?"

The phone went dead. Ramzy pushed the button, received a line, then dialed the number at the Hotel Principe Real. He asked for room 412. When the woman answered, he said in English, "I'm sorry, Cilla, but I won't be able to come by and have breakfast with you."

"Oh, what a shame. We were so looking forward to it."

"Something's come up. An old friend. You will forgive me?"

"All right," she laughed. "Make sure you enjoy yourself, and she better be stunning if we'll have to do without you."

"Sorry for the last-minute cancellation."

"Oh, not to worry. I'm sure we'll find something to do."

Ramzy hung up, slipped on his shoes with the transmitter in the sole and headed for the door.

SHAI CAUGHT the eleven o'clock flight to Lisbon, and since the airport was only a few minutes from the center of the city, he arrived at the Hotel Principe Real before noon. Certain that the van receiving signals from the transmitter in Ramzy's shoe was following him at a discreet distance, he had the woman code-named Cilla order sandwiches and coffee, and they settled in for the wait. There were almost exactly forty-eight hours left of the Socialist International.

A little after three the phone rang, and Cilla snatched up the receiver and listened. A few seconds later she hung up. She looked at Shai on the bed. An agent from the embassy in Lisbon sat in a chair.

"They're heading out of the city," she said excitedly. "South."

Shai grabbed his small traveling bag from the floor. "Let's go."

Outside, they jumped into the resident agent's car. Shai sat in the passenger seat, with Cilla in the back, as they lurched from the curb. Shai spoke into the walkie-talkie. "Are they still headed toward the destination?"

A voice cackled over the speaker from the van. "Affirmative."

"Anything from the destination itself?"

"Just spoke to them a few minutes ago. It's quiet."

"All right." Shai placed the walkie-talkie back on the floor and tried to relax in the seat. It would take them over three hours to reach the nearest point on the coast.

"It appears it's all going smashingly," the long-blond-haired Cilla said from the rear seat.

"Yes," Shai said, turning to her.

"But it might take some time, don't you think, for him to get alone with Abu Nidal to kill him?"

"We'll just have to wait," Shai said.

"Don't like that, really."

"Either do I, but if we move without being certain he's with Abu Nidal, we risk everything. It took a lot to get Ramzy inside. We have to let him find a place and time to handle it."

KHALID MONSOUR, tired after the flight from Amsterdam, pressed through the crowd of bearded Druze sheikhs, black-veiled women, peasant women in colored full-length *festan*, slight mustachioed men and dark-eyed miniskirted Damascene girls. High overhead, thin streams of sunlight slanted through the bullet holes in the arched corrugated iron roof of the long Street Called Straight. The roof somehow shielded the dark souk from the oppressive heat outside.

Khalid pushed through the people, hating all this backwardness. The air stank of unrefrigerated foods. Shopkeepers called out from the entrances to their small electrically lit stores, hawking prayer carpets, camel bone and rosewood mosaicked boxes and tables, Ottoman daggers, lustrous damask silk brocades. There was no change here, no progress. Three-wheeled motorized carts wove through the crowd of pedestrians and donkeys to make deliveries to the shops.

So angry at the Israelis that he wanted to smash something, Khalid turned down an alley that headed toward the shoe sellers' souk. The high-pitched singing of Feiruz with the background whine of the oud blared from a transistor radio. The song was one of those stupid folk stories of flirtation, love, courtship and marriage. He would like to take some of these people to the red-light district in Amsterdam and show them what the modern world was like. Only hours here, he already longed to return to the cool cleanliness of Holland with its open relations between men and women.

He turned into the shoe sellers' souk. It was dark and quiet here, the air redolent with leather. Footwear dropped from stands on both sides of him: slippers, sandals glittering with cut glass, tartan boots.

An elderly man in a keffiyeh was seated on a stool in front of an old leather-cutting machine. As he worked, he sucked on the long tube of a narghile; the water that cooled the smoke bubbled in the glass jar on the ground.

"Uncle Shawkat," Khalid said.

The elderly man turned from his machine, a look of surprise in his eyes. "Khalid." A smile came to his face. "It is you."

Khalid came near, bent and hugged his uncle, who ran a hand affectionately through his nephew's thick dark hair. His uncle placed both hands on his face, then called to some unseen boy in the lane to bring them coffee.

"Come, sit," Shawkat said, pointing to a wooden stool with a woven hemp seat. "You must tell me everything about your life in Holland. How are you doing at the university?"

"Yes, tonight," Khalid said, not moving toward the chair. "First, I need something from you. Now."

"For the son of my brother, if it is in my power, of course."

"Do you know where Abu Nidal's headquarters in Damascus is?"

The old man lifted the snake of the water pipe. "Why do you ask?"

"I must go there. Immediately."

"I see." He drew slowly on the narghile. "You have left your studies?"

"Uncle, I cannot explain it to you. There is something I must do. I ask that you help me, or I will have to go to someone else to ask for that help."

Shawkat looked up at him from his stool. "This thing you must do burns in you. And you will abandon your studies for it?"

"No. I shall return to them."

Just then a small boy arrived carrying a heavy copper tray with small porcelain cups. He set it on the wooden stand in the corner, then disappeared.

"First, we will have our coffee," Shawkat said.

"Then you will take me?"

Shawkat rose unsteadily and moved to the tray. "If that is what you wish."

Some twenty minutes later, with Khalid's promise that he would be his guest at a special restaurant meal that evening of his boyhood favorites of stuffed vine leaves and chopped mutton soaked in goat's milk, Shawkat left his nephew in the street below the southern walls. Khalid, who hated those foods now, had agreed so as not to insult his uncle.

He saw the fists holding the crossed rifles and the camera over the entrance and walked boldly into the structure. At the second floor, he strode up to the man sitting at the monitor as the two guards fixed their machine pistols on him.

"I want to speak to whoever's in charge here," Khalid demanded.

"Search him," the man said.

One guard kept his gun pointed at Khalid's head while the other patted him down. When it was clear he was unarmed, the man at the monitor nodded and both guards resumed their positions by the stairs.

"What is your business?" the man asked.

"I will only speak to whoever's in charge."

"At the moment, I'm in charge. What do you want?"

There was a clear path to the door. Khalid moved toward it. He was tired of taking insults from those so obviously below him. With lightning, graceful power, the man behind the monitor got out of his chair. As Khalid's hand touched the knob, he grabbed him at the back of his shoulders, turned him around and threw him against the door. "Show him out," he said to one of the guards.

"No," Khalid said loudly. His head rang. "I know something, something important."

The guard grabbed him by the shirt front, and pushed him toward the stairs.

"I'm warning you, it's important."

The man had returned to his monitoring screen, suddenly worried that he had been lured away from the cameras as part of some plot. "Throw him out the front door, then return immediately," he said.

"No. I'm telling you. I know who's trying to kill Abu Nidal."

The guard shoved him down several stairs.

"Wait," the man said, still keeping his eyes on the monitor. "Bring him here, then go check the street."

The guard deposited Khalid next to him, then hurried down the stairs. "What do you know?" the man asked, still looking at the monitor. The street was clear.

"I'll only speak to whoever's in charge."

211 BULLETS OF PALESTINE

Even now. This boy probably knew nothing. Still, something told him that Abdul Rahman would want to listen, but he would not let him near him alone, whether he had a weapon or not. "Wait," he said. After a few minutes, the guard trotted back up the stairs in a military cadence.

"No one's seen anything unusual outside," he said.

The man looked up from the screen, then crossed to the door and went in. He returned several minutes later. "Go in," he said to Khalid, then turned to the guard. "Don't let him near the desk."

Abdul Rahman did not get up as the guard brought Khalid into the office and ordered him to stop in front of the doorway. "I am the chief information officer for the Palestine National Liberation Movement," Abdul Rahman Rahim said. "What is it you know?"

"I want something first," Khalid said, coming forward. The guard grabbed his shoulder and riveted him in place, hurting him.

Abdul Rahman nodded for the guard to release him. "What is it that you want?"

"There's a woman named Leila Fahdi with Abu Nidal." Khalid rubbed his shoulder. She had to still be with him, since she had not returned to Amsterdam. "I want you to tell me where I can find her."

"I see," Abdul Rahman said. "Then this is a personal matter?"

"Yes."

"Well, then if you have information for us, we will, of course, help."

"How do I know I can trust you?"

"I swear on my honor. Is that not sufficient?"

Khalid nodded.

"Now, who is it you think wants to kill Abu Nidal?"

"Ramzy Awwad," Khalid said.

Abdul Rahman stopped breathing. "How do you know this?" he asked quickly.

"Awwad questioned me in Amsterdam looking for Leila after she disappeared with Abu Nidal."

"How long ago?"

"A month. Maybe a little more."

Long before Ramzy had shown up here. Abdul Rahman felt the fear inside him. If Monsour was telling the truth, Awwad had used him to get to Abu Nidal, and now, Abu Nidal was in danger. Still, maybe this man worked for Arafat and was attempting to destroy Awwad's usefulness. First, he would check Monsour's story about this Leila Fahdi.

"This may prove of use," Abdul Rahman said. "As soon as I learn the woman's address, where can I locate you?"

Khalid gave him his uncle's location in the shoe sellers' souk off the Street Called Straight.

"Please escort him out," Abdul Rahman said to the guard. "And inform those outside that he is to be treated as my most honored guest."

"Thank you," Khalid said. "How soon will I hear from you?"

"In a day or two, three at the most." If the woman was or had been with Abu Nidal, he would tell this boy nothing.

After they left, Abdul Rahman picked up the phone. He had to investigate this. It was old information, and this Monsour hardly seemed reliable, but still there was the possibility he was telling the truth.

"IT MEANS VERY MUCH to us that you're joining us," the shabbily dressed Wasif said to Ramzy as they walked through the darkness in the cool hills overlooking the coastal plain. Below them, eucalyptus, pine and mimosa blanketed the descent to the lights and tile-roofed port town of Portimao.

Ramzy walked next to him to the secluded house, the two men about the same height and build. The brisk smell of the mountain herbs and flowers was so different from the warm beaches they had driven along before turning up here.

"When will I see Abu Nidal?" Ramzy asked.

"He hasn't told me. I have to phone and let him know that we've arrived."

Wasif opened the front door of the whitewashed house, set off from the narrow mountain highway by a dirt road. As they stepped inside, three men rose from chairs in the living room, where they had been drinking wine and smoking heavily. The odor of the cigarettes created a sharp contrast to the crispness outside.

"These are some of our other members," Wasif said. Ramzy nodded.

"Abu Nidal believes that the Israelis are here, after us."

"So he's brought in extra people?"

Wasif smiled. "He has a surprise for the Socialist International. An assassin that is absolutely undetectable."

"Good," Ramzy said, suddenly scared that even if he stopped Abu Nidal, this assassin might already be in place.

"Would you like something to eat or drink?"

"Juice would be fine, or water if you don't have any."

"Follow me." Wasif headed to the kitchen, pulled open the refrigerator and took out a bottle of apple juice. He poured Ramzy a glass. "I prefer wine," he said. "I hope it doesn't insult you."

"No."

Wasif removed an open bottle of red wine from the refrigerator and yanked the cork from its lip. He had been incommunicado for the almost four hours it had taken them to drive here. "Now, if you'll excuse me, I want to make that call to Abu Nidal."

"Tell him I look forward to greeting him."

"I'm sure he'll send you the same message in return."

Ramzy watched Wasif head toward the back bedrooms, the fear climbing in him with each of the man's steps. Too much could go wrong here.

THAT SAME NIGHT, after the Sabbath had disappeared with the darkness, Yehuda Shamir stood on the fringe of the sea of people in the Square of the Kings of Israel in Tel Aviv. Emotion tight in his throat, for the moment he ignored the transmission from his agents in Damascus that had been troubling him about this Khalid Monsour.

People flowed across the pavement of the immense square, into the streets, totally blocking traffic. Others stood in the balconies of the five-story apartment buildings that surrounded the rectangular area; still others sat in the trees. From every direction they were moving to the square, a crowd impossible to estimate, maybe four hundred thousand and still swelling—over ten percent of Israel's Jewish population—joined together in a single act of anguish.

Huge lights illuminated the square; the people of Israel had come to mourn the Palestinian victims of Sabra and Shatilla and demand a full judicial inquiry into the massacre. In the week since the killings, Prime Minister Begin had defiantly told the Cabinet that "the very appointment of such a commission amounts to an admission of guilt." Then he had fought off a Knesset motion for an independent inquiry by forty-eight votes to forty-two.

The prime minister had spoken, and now the people were wrenching the issue from his hands. They needed the inquiry for themselves, in agony that the prophet Samuel's call for the people of Israel to be "a light onto the nations" could turn into their soldiers firing flares that illuminated the way for the murderers.

Yehuda knew now what had happened to the two thousand fighters that were supposed to be in the camps. On August 23, the second day of the twelve-day PLO evacuation, Bashir Gemayel had been elected president of Lebanon. The PLO were terrified that the blood-hungry Bashir would move into West Beirut. At the final moment, with the promise that the multinational force would protect the camps, more than half of the two thousand had boarded the ships. Those that remained were not military units, but people who worked in offices, in bakeries, held normal jobs. Organized into underground cells, Arafat had intended to resume contact with them later. The multinational force of French, Italians and Americans, despite the understanding, had considered their work accomplished with the evacuation and they had set sail shortly after the Palestinians.

Yehuda read the banners: Will the Sword Eat Forever? from the Book of Lamentations; Rosh Hashanah of Shame; Children's Blood Is Not Water. No other country in the Middle East would demand a moral account from its leaders, he thought with pride. In the Arab world nobody had even paid much attention when, earlier in the year, President Assad of Syria had ordered his troops to raze the Muslim Brotherhood stronghold in the city of Hama and killed twenty thousand rebels and civilians. Yehuda loved that his people asked so much of themselves.

An amplified voice emanated from the podium, far away, above the reed-filled fountains at the head of the square. Yehuda pushed his mind back to the problem that had been nagging at him. This Khalid Monsour, who had turned up at the embassy in The Hague, had been received and later escorted out of Abu Nidal's information headquarters in Damascus with importance.

So Monsour was one of Abu Nidal's men. Still, something did not mesh. Why approach them with the Leila Fahdi story? Where was the trap? They already knew about Fahdi, and Abu Nidal would know they knew, after he had abandoned her at the scene of the shooting in Vienna. It made no sense. He wished Shai would send more detailed reports while the operation was in progress as they had demanded so many times. It was often in this kind of paper checking that crucial links were found. He had gone through the reports already, and there was no mention of a Khalid Monsour.

Yehuda had begun to walk back to his car when a thought occurred to him. Sometimes he could see the veins on an elephant's skin but not the elephant. What if this Monsour was, incredibly, exactly what he seemed—an irrational, scorned lover? He would have no way of knowing that Leila Fahdi had been left behind if she had not contacted him. But if this was the case, why was he treated with such honor?

The speeches echoed through the loudspeakers several blocks behind him. If Monsour was treated with such respect, that meant he had something significant to offer them in exchange for Leila's whereabouts. And then he saw it; the pieces of the puzzle locked together. Yehuda started to walk faster. He seemed to remember in the reports that Awwad had used his real identity to break Leila Fahdi. If Awwad used his stature as part of his tradecraft and had used it in Amsterdam with Monsour, then Monsour could very well know Awwad was after Abu Nidal. Yehuda ran to his car. He had to notify Shai immediately. If they verified Monsour's story quickly enough, Awwad would be walking into a trap.

WASIF RETURNED from speaking to Abu Nidal on the phone and entered the living room. He turned to Ramzy.

"I need to talk to these men for a moment. Will you wait for me in the first bedroom?"

Ramzy set his glass of juice down, concerned. "Of course." He moved down the adobe-tiled hallway and entered the bedroom. There was a large brass bed against one wall. He could feel his breathing.

Moments later Wasif entered. The three Arabs followed, each carrying a folding chair. Wasif had a wine bottle in his hand and drank from it.

"Traitor," Wasif said with menace in his voice.

To his surprise Ramzy felt little fear. Somehow he had been expecting it. "What are you talking about?" he countered, feigning confusion.

"Shut up," Wasif shouted, raising the bottle over his head as a club, "or I'll—" He abruptly turned to the three other Arabs. "Welcome him to the Palestine National Liberation Movement."

A fat Arab approached and pummeled Ramzy twice in the stomach. Ramzy staggered back in pain. The fat Arab then struck him again with a tremendous blow to the face, bloodying his nose.

"Wait, stop," Wasif commanded. He approached Ramzy, studied him. "Let's not get blood on his shirt." He unbuttoned it and pulled it off Ramzy. He took the wallet from Ramzy's rear pocket, saw the large amount of bills and beamed. Next he unhooked Ramzy's belt, then caressed his genitals. "Take your pants off." Wasif looked down. "And those shoes, too."

Ramzy hoped that he would not remove the shoes from the house. Even if he was dead, they would lead the Israeli here. Ramzy bent and complied.

"Now the watch."

Ramzy handed it to him. Wasif pushed the wallet and watch into his front pockets, took the belt from Ramzy's pants, slipped it through his own loops, then sat on the bed and yanked off his worn shoes. He tried on Ramzy's. A smile lit his face as he realized they fit. Wasif slung the shirt and trousers over his shoulder.

"These men are only going to enjoy themselves," Wasif said, his smile growing. "Abu Nidal wants to finish the job personally."

As he walked out of the bedroom, he heard the thuds of the beating starting up again. The three of them liked to work one at a time, while the other two sat in chairs, drank wine and watched. Wasif changed into Ramzy's clothes, felt the weight of Ramzy's wallet in his pocket and headed for the front door, thinking how much he would enjoy spending the traitor's money on dinner and some young tourists in one of Albufeira's many discotheques. He smiled at the way the light-skinned foreigners, particularly the German and Scandinavian women, loved to sleep with dark Arabs.

YEHUDA SHAMIR DROVE up Kaplan Street through Government Center, praying he was not too late and that Shai was somewhere where he could be reached immediately. A chain-link fence topped with barbed wire surrounded the Defense Ministry. Every twenty meters yellow signs in Hebrew, Arabic, English and French warned against photographing the area. Yehuda turned left into the driveway blocked by a black-and-white iron gate and stopped as the white-helmeted, armed military police officer approached his window. The large square block area in the middle of the city, only minutes from the Square of the Kings of Israel, was filled with small huts and structures. Ahead of him towered the main Ministry building crowned with a mélange of antennae and satellite dishes.

The guard took Shamir's laminated photograph identification back into the military hut and picked up the phone. Ramzy was in Portugal already, Yehuda thought to himself. He had checked with the operation there after he had released Awwad against Carmon's explicit orders—a move that would end his career as soon as it was discovered.

The guard slid the heavy gate open, then approached the car window and handed back the identification card. "Go ahead, sir," he said.

Yehuda took the card quickly from him and drove the short distance into the compound. He parked in front of the main building, moved toward the empty entrance and then he felt the pain burst in his chest. Panic flashed through him. Not now, he whispered. There was no one in front of him, and he could never climb the steps. The guard. He turned and tried to keep walking. The pressure in his chest felt like a balloon was being blown up in there, larger and larger. He was dizzy. The guard stood only ten meters away, facing the street. He had to tell him, have him send word to Shai. He could not go any farther. The pressure, the dizziness. He sat on a low wall in front of some shrubbery.

"Help me," he called hoarsely.

The guard turned, saw him and hurried to the small man.

Yehuda felt cold and clammy, dizzy. It was as if a truck had slammed into his chest, and the pressure was moving up into his jaw. He was icy cold now and sweaty.

The guard was almost there.

The pain was excruciating. The guard arrived. He tried to form the words, but his mouth would not move. Suddenly he was so cold. He fell forward.

The guard caught the small man before he hit the pavement. His skin was ashen. He reached for a pulse on his damp neck, then searched to make certain he had not missed it. There was none. The man was dead.

IT WAS AFTER THREE A.M. when, alone in the car, parked on one of the steep streets in Albufeira, Shai picked up the walkie-talkie and listened to the voice from the van.

"He hasn't moved for forty-five minutes now. We pinpoint him at the Hotel Sol E Mar."

"All right. Stay on him the whole night if necessary, and call me if he leaves."

"You'll be in your room?"

"Yes."

Cold, stiff and exhausted, Shai started the motor and pulled on the headlights, which stabbed through the still darkness. Albufeira was the largest resort area on the Algarve. They had followed Ramzy along the coast, into the hills, back to several stops in Albufeira, then to this hotel, where apparently he would spend the night. Shai eased from the curb, turned the car around and headed back up toward the high-rise Montechoro, thankfully only a few minutes away. There was another day and a half left of the Socialist International. He felt confident that Abu Nidal would see Ramzy soon. And as long as Ramzy was moving around freely like this, that meant he was safe.

THE EARLY MORNING SUN, slanting through the window, threw a patch of light on the white plaster wall opposite the bed where Ramzy was tied spread-eagle, his arms and legs lashed painfully to the brass frame. Soon the rays of brightness widened and began to move warmly across his body. Instinctively he tried to sit up, and his body was torn with such pain that he had to force himself not to cry out. He dropped back against his restraints. His body was stiff and bruised, his groin ached and his bare feet were numb. He felt the bruises and dried blood on his upper lip and down the left side of his mouth.

He had heard movement in the house for what seemed like over an hour now, the sounds of the toilet flushing, plates banging in the kitchen. He had no appetite, but his mouth was dry and sticky, and he was thirsty. Finally, he guessed somewhere around ten, he heard a car pull up in front.

When Abu Nidal entered the room alone, Ramzy felt more anger than fear. He did not let his hate show.

"I came to join you," Ramzy said hoarsely.

Abu Nidal stood over him and said nothing.

"Why are you doing this?" Ramzy asked.

Abu Nidal turned, walked to the window and looked out. He watched the wisps of white clouds move in the sky. "When I first heard you wanted to join us, I could not remember when I had such feelings," he said finally. He spun around, his broad face hard. "Then I learned you've come to kill me."

"Kill you?" Ramzy edged surprise into his voice. He tried to pull against his binds, but sank back in pain. "It's not true. You're being tricked by someone who wants me dead."

"No. I was almost tricked by *you*."

"My brother was murdered," Ramzy said loudly.

"You are as clever with your tongue as you are with your pen. You used your brother's death as a ruse to enter my camp. When we were alone, you would have killed me."

"Is that how you think I would honor the memory of my brother, by killing you instead of those who murdered him?"

"In your deceit, you cared nothing for the memory of your brother."

Every part of him ached. Ramzy tried to think clearly through the pain. So he did not know Fawaz was alive.

"What makes you think I'm deceiving you?"

Abu Nidal pulled the gun from the belt underneath his nylon windbreaker and approached the bed. He thrust the muzzle at Ramzy's temple. "I am going to rid our people of you," he said furiously. Here was another traitor, like his brothers.

The fear caught in Ramzy's throat. "Abu Nidal, what makes you think I'm deceiving you?"

"Khalid Monsour."

The surprise ran icily through him. It had never occurred to him as a possibility. "He's lying," Ramzy said.

"Lying." Abu Nidal pulled the hammer back on the revolver. "He seems to have quite a believable story. He says you came to him looking for Leila Fahdi, so she could lead you to me. More than a month ago."

"You believe him?" Ramzy said, searching desperately for a way out, the ropes tearing his skin. "He's unstable."

Abu Nidal's mouth tightened. "So you admit to knowing him?"

"Of course," Ramzy said. He had to come up with something. "Monsour was sent to me early in the year from Beirut. He was stationed in Amsterdam undercover as an engineering student. I made him part of a cell operating out of Paris. But he couldn't keep his mouth shut. He kept bragging to people that he was a PLO agent. When I found out about it, I threw him out." Ramzy felt the hard tip of the revolver against his forehead. "He went crazy, started yelling, How dare I do this to him, that I must be a traitor working for the Israelis. He said he didn't care how long it took, but he would get me. Apparently, he's trying to."

"Then how did he know you were going to join forces with me?"

"That wouldn't have been hard. I told my people on the Continent, gave them the option of coming with me. What I was doing was no secret. On the contrary, I was proud of it. All my people were talking about it. He could have easily come across the information from any of them he knew.''

Abu Nidal held the gun where it was and said nothing.

''I know Khalid had a girlfriend named Leila Fahdi,'' Ramzy said, ''but I never met her. What does she have to do with you?''

''I met her in Amsterdam, took her with me.''

''If I'm right about Monsour, he'd go crazy at that.''

Abu Nidal thought about the way Leila had described Monsour as irrationally jealous whenever she was late.

''Don't you see?'' Ramzy said, the revolver still hard against his forehead, the sweat heavy at his back and underarms. ''He's found a way to get even with both of us. He'll get you to kill me and have the last laugh after you destroyed what otherwise would have been such a prize for you. He'll probably even brag to the Fahdi woman about it to get her back.''

Angry, Abu Nidal pressed the gun deeper into Ramzy's forehead, against the bone. He did not like this. It was too fantastic a coincidence that Monsour had been involved with Leila Fahdi and had worked for Awwad. He would just kill him now.

Abruptly, though, he pushed the gun into his belt. ''Monsour's still in Damascus. I'll have him questioned. He won't stand up under torture. Soon we'll know the truth.'' He left the Palestinian poet tied up and walked out the door. Ramzy sank back against the bonds.

IN JERUSALEM the weather seemed to have shifted overnight. Cold winds whipped down from Mount Scopus, howling through the narrow stone corridors of the Old City and spreading dampness through the insufficiently warmed New City, where imported heating oil posed a major expense. It had been snowing more and more the past few years, the Colonel thought as he pushed his way against the late afternoon wind up Mount Herzl, carrying a bag. Wrapped in his heavy European coat, gloves and muffler, he was glad he lived in the kibbutz along the warming sea, instead of in these mountains where in his last winters here the dampness had rarely left him.

At the pink geranium-lined stone plaza that housed the tombs of the former prime ministers, the Colonel rested for a moment. Then he continued down the dirt path to the graves of the military cemetery that covered the far slopes of the mountain. They seemed endless: coffin-sized, stone-bordered plots, with a uniform green plant trimmed meticulously on each grave to the top of the stones. Between the headstones ran fresh dirt with plants. Other plants and flowers in pots rested on the graves themselves.

The Colonel found Yehuda Shamir's freshly hewn grave easily, in the place of honor closest to the tombs of the leaders of the country. The Colonel bent beside the grave. He had chosen to avoid all the officiousness and eulogizing of the funeral earlier that afternoon.

He opened the plastic bag at his side and removed the small rose plant that he had grown himself. He pulled off his gloves with his teeth. The cold wind blew at his back; heavy gray clouds moved through the sky. He worked the dirt in the border above the grave with his fingers, then planted the small rose bush. He covered the roots with dirt, confident that it would rain soon and that the care-takers would tend to the bush long after he was gone.

He picked up his gloves and rose with difficulty as he looked at the young bush wavering in the wind. "Good-bye, my friend," he said quietly. "It was my honor to know you."

He turned and headed back toward the stone plaza and the street that would take him down the hill. He wondered about Shai's relationship with Awwad. Regardless, Shai would have no more help from the inside.


IT WAS DARK Sunday night as Shai sat in the rear of the van parked on the road overlooking Albufeira and the ocean. Ramzy had been with Abu Nidal's people for al-most two full days now, moving freely around the Algarve. The Socialist International would close at two tomorrow.

"Is he still in the restaurant?" Shai asked the red-bearded Israeli who sat behind the computer terminal.

"Yes."

Shai nodded.

"Where'd you send Cilla?" the redhead asked.

"To the Montechoro for some photographs."

Two quick knocks sounded on the side door of the van, then a pause, and another two. Despite the correct code, Shai pulled the Hi-Standard .22 from his shoulder hol-ster, then slid the heavy door open. Cilla bounced in, holding a manila envelope.

"Have you looked at them?"

Cilla shook her head.

Shai pulled out the two enlargements of Ramzy Awwad. He handed the pictures to Cilla, who eyed them, moving closer to the light in the van's roof.

"Not bad-looking," she said.

"I want you to go in the restaurant and act like you're supposed to meet a date. When he's not in the front, check to see if he's waiting at a table. I want to know who Awwad's with and how it looks to you."

She smiled. "Be back in a jiff."

After she bounded outside, Shai slid the door closed. He kept the pistol in his hand, stood hunched over in the low van and waited. Ten minutes later the knocks sounded again, in the same pattern. Shai jerked the heavy door open.

Cilla looked pale. "He's not there."

Shai stared at the redhead.

"The signal's still there," the redhead said. "Absolutely no doubt. The transmitter's in that restaurant."

Shai turned to Cilla. "Stay here and get the door fast when I say so." He turned to the redhead. "Come with me."

The two of them clamored into the warm night. They turned the corner. Closed shops and several fish restaurants lined the narrow street at the upper extremities of Albufeira. They crossed the single lane toward the Catuna Restaurant, located in the trees down the hill from the street. Below it shone the lights of Albufeira.

"Just do what I say," Shai said as they descended the concrete steps. His gun and holster were covered by his light jacket now.

Inside the entrance, a cook was grilling various whole fish, including long silvery sardines, over a flaming wood fire. Shai continued into the spacious, glass-walled restaurant. He studied the tables, and then he saw a dark slim man dining with a light-skinned woman. He approached them, the redhead trailing. As Shai neared, he recognized the man's shoes.

"We're taking him with us," Shai said quietly. "Leave the girl, but get her purse. We'll deal with her later."

Shai moved near. The Arab was lifting a forkful of fish to his mouth. From behind, Shai grabbed the man around the neck. The fork flew out of his grasp. The restaurant abruptly fell silent. As the woman yelled, the redhead lifted her purse. Using his size and weight, Shai pulled the man out of his chair and dragged him toward the entrance. The restaurant was utterly silent; people watched but no one moved. The redhead was out in front, hand in his pocket. The Arab gagged on the food in his throat; Shai did not loosen his grip. The woman at the table began shouting in German. Still no one moved.

Outside, Shai dragged him up the stairs and along the street so quickly that the few people there were unsure what was happening. Shai called to Cilla, who yanked open the door of the van, and the redhead helped him lift the Arab inside. They both jumped in, and as the van jerked away, Shai slammed the door shut.

The Arab lay on his back on the floor, coughing hard, his face flushed. Shai searched him quickly; he was unarmed.

"Where is Ramzy Awwad?" Shai asked in Arabic.

"I don't know what you're talking about," Wasif said.

Shai smashed him hard across the face with the butt of his pistol. He screamed, and blood spurted from his nose. The van bounced lightly over the cobbled streets.

"I have no time for this," Shai said. "We'll go to the countryside, and I will shoot the fingers off your hands, one by one. If you don't tell me what I want to know, I will then work on your toes. Then your ears, nose, eyes."

The man lay huddled on the floor. "No, please. I don't know anything."

Shai turned to the redhead. "Tell the driver to take us someplace where we won't be disturbed."

"No." The Arab squirmed on the floor. "I beg you."

"Where is Ramzy Awwad?"

"I don't know. I swear it."

Shai removed the Swiss army knife from his pocket and spoke to the redhead. "Spread his hand out on the floor. We'll start here."

The redhead took the Arab's hand, flattened it out, then stepped on his wrist to immobilize the fingers. Wasif screamed.

Shai pulled the blade from the body of the knife and snapped it into place. He bent to his knees.

"He's at a house in the hills above Portimao," the Arab shrieked. "But they were going to kill him. That's all I know, I swear."

"We trailed the subject to a house there last night," the redhead said.

Shai rose. "Tell the driver to hurry."

After the instructions were given and the van turned left with a screech, the redhead looked at Shai's pale face in the dim light of the van. ''What do you want me to do with him?'' he asked.

''You have any rope back here and something to gag him with?''

''Yes.''

Shai dropped into the seat, the sweat dripping through his thinning hair. ''The interrogators will want him.''

As the redhead and Cilla bound the Arab, Shai thought ahead. There were Uzis in the rear compartment. He knew there was little chance Awwad was alive.

He felt the bumps in the road as the van raced over them. He leaned back against the wall, the vibrations bouncing off it. They turned onto the smooth two-lane highway that traversed the Algarve. Fifteen, twenty minutes passed. A half hour. He closed his eyes. Then he felt the van turning right and climbing. It would not be long now.

The van rocked back and forth, accelerated in lower gear and bore its heavy way through the hills. Soon the driver's voice cracked over the intercom. ''How close do you want to get?''

Shai looked at the man sitting at the screen. ''Tell him to stay far enough away so that they won't hear the van approaching.''

Seconds after the message was relayed, they pulled onto a dirt road and stopped. ''What should we do about him?'' the redhead asked, looking at Wasif.

''Just leave him here and get the Uzis.''

Shai pulled open the door and stepped into the brisk air. Stars winked in the clear sky. Fortunately there was only a sliver of a moon illuminating the trees. The driver and the redhead moved past him and around to the back of the vehicle. Cilla joined them, and the redhead distributed the four Uzis. Shai stood in the light of the door and held up Ramzy's photograph.

"This man's important to us. As you know, he's an Arab by the name of Ramzy Awwad. If he's still alive, he's being held prisoner. Abu Nidal may be inside, he may not, and Ramzy may already be dead. We're going to have to go in and find out."

"Any idea how many people are inside?" the driver, Moshe, asked.

"No."

"It doesn't matter," the redhead said. "I'll see if there's a guard. *Yalla*, let's go."

Shai nodded.

The redhead moved ahead up the narrow dirt road bounded on both sides by tall pines. Tire tracks showed in the soft ground even in the dim light. Shai felt his hands damp on the cold metal of the Uzi as they moved forward until they could see the lights of the house with the red-tiled roof off to their left. The redhead had disappeared ahead of them. A dog barked somewhere in the distance.

They stopped and waited. Crickets sounded loudly in the silence. The redhead returned and whispered, "There are no guards outside. There's a front window with drapes pulled back and good visibility. I'll go in the front door followed by Moshe." He turned to Cilla. "You take the window." Cilla nodded. The redhead turned to Shai. "Sir, you watch the back door, and make sure none of them get out that way."

Shai shook his head. It was his responsibility. "I'll be first in the door," he said.

"Sorry, there's no time to argue. Come on, *hevra*, let's go."

The three of them moved off, and Shai remained there for a moment, remembering how the generation of 1948 had worried that their sons would not be able to defend the country as they had. He followed the three young people moving soundlessly through the night, then circled to the right.

The three stooped and waited; the redhead watched Shai disappear around the rear of the house. The redhead nodded, and they ran forward in a crouch through the wild grass, Cilla slightly ahead. They hit the stairs at full stride. The redhead shot off the doorknob and lock, sending wood chips flying, then slammed against the wood and was inside, Moshe at his heels. Two men at the table, cards dropped, were reaching for their machine pistols. Cilla sprayed a burst through the window catching one, missing the other. The redhead cut him down in a noisy fusillade, shattering plates, puncturing the wooden walls. Blood leaked from the two corpses.

From the hallway a single shot rang out, striking the redhead in the shoulder, and he dropped.

Shai charged through the back door, ran ahead and caught a glimpse of an Arab as he ducked into a room. He ran with every ounce of strength he had and reached the doorway just as the figure pointed a pistol. Someone was tied to the bed.

Shai fired a burst high at the Arab's back and head, afraid the bullets would pass through him and strike the bed. The man's shot struck the wall, and he fell to the floor. Shai saw Ramzy sag against his binds, alive. The Israeli ran back into the hall, then into the living room. All was quiet. Moshe and Cilla were searching the rest of the house. Shai saw the redhead sitting on the floor, his face pinched in pain, clutching his shoulder.

The driver, Moshe, came back to the room. "That's it," he said. "The three of them."

Shai looked at him, then said, "Gather up whatever documents you can, from the bodies, too." He turned to the redhead. "We'll have you on the way to the hospital in two minutes." He headed back to the bedroom. Ramzy wore only underwear. Shai removed his knife, approached the bed and sliced the ropes binding Ramzy to the corners of the bed.

Ramzy tried to sit up and fell back, his face a web of pain. He lay there and rubbed his wrists. "Thank you," he said in a hoarse whisper.

Shai went to the closet and found a tattered pair of pants and a shirt that looked as though they would fit Ramzy. There were no shoes. Shai crossed the room, the clothes over his arm.

"Let me help you up." Shai held Ramzy around the waist and lifted him into a sitting position.

Ramzy tried to stand; the pain shot through his ankles, and Shai grabbed him to keep him from falling. Shai's whole body was damp through his shirt. After a few more steps, Ramzy was able to hobble on his own. Shai handed him the clothes and left him to dress.

When Ramzy entered the main room, he saw the young redhead sitting on the floor, clutching his shoulder. Shai gave Ramzy a pair of sandals he had removed from one of the corpses.

"Abu Nidal should be returning," Ramzy said. "We can't—"

Just then they heard the high-pitched sound of a sports car, spinning its wheels down the dirt road and accelerating onto the highway. Shai knew what had happened.

Cilla had removed a blanket from the bedroom and was wrapping it around the redhead.

"I'll bring the van up," Moshe said.

Shai nodded. He left Ramzy leaning against the wall, and with Cilla's help, he lifted the redhead to his feet.

"I didn't check the body in the bedroom," Cilla said.

Moshe pulled up, then ran inside. "The Arab from the back of the van is gone."

"I know."

As Moshe and Cilla helped the redhead outside, Shai entered the bedroom where Ramzy had been. He turned over the dead Arab to search him and recognized the face of Ismail al-Qasim, the man who had escaped from the Olhao brothel. Shai wondered what it meant to Abu Nidal's plan that these three, in addition to Marwan Nasir, were dead.

Shai came back into the main room and looked at Ramzy. "Is there anything I need to know, now?"

Ramzy forced a nod. "One of them told me they have an assassin nobody will be able to detect."

"Shit," Shai said.

ABU NIDAL STARED out the window at the red stone walls
and turrets of the Crusader Castle on the hill overlooking the tile roofs and citrus groves of Silves. The rage that
had initially torn through him at Ramzy Awwad's escape
had quieted into satisfaction. He would like to see
Awwad's face in a few hours, after the strike.

He could not comprehend those like Awwad who
would talk to the Zionists. At the thought, the anger
pushed hot against his face. Though he had been only six
when the fighting had started, he remembered how his
mother had locked all her jewelry in the closet in Jaffa,
certain they would return in a few days. They had fled to
their villa in Ashkelon.

In 1949 his family had abandoned Israeli-controlled
Ashkelon for Gaza, where they had remained for a year
before moving to Nablus. In Nablus they had been forced
to beg for a place to live from some of those who had
worked in his father's orchards.

He had loved playing in that twenty-room home in the
Ajami quarter of Jaffa that his father's family had built
in the nineteenth century. They had had the only phone

in Ajami. His family had been one of the wealthiest in Palestine. His father, Haj Khalil, had marketed ten percent of all Palestinian produce to Europe. Haj Khalil had had houses and orange groves in Ashkelon, stables in Yavneh and additional groves in Abu Khabit and Kfar Sava. Kibbutz Ramat Hacovesh still had a grove that bore his family's name. Abu Nidal bit his lower lip as he pictured the Zionists picking their fruit.

He remembered when Nablus had fallen to the Israelis in the June war of 1967 and the borders to the coast had suddenly been opened. They had been allowed to travel though not stay overnight anywhere inside the so-called "green line." His father had been dead by then, and his mother would not go. She had remained in their small kitchen and had told him over and over again about how she had lost everything. Mohammed had driven to the coast against her orders, then had fled back. The house in Jaffa had been turned into an Israeli police station.

Everything would have been so different if the Zionists had not invaded. In the struggle to survive in Nablus no one had had time for him, the youngest.

He turned from the window in the rented room and glanced at the revolver on the small table. Beside it was a photograph cut from a newspaper. He had intended to use Ismail al-Qasim to pull the trigger but had been forced after his and Marwan Nasir's idiocy, and the certainty of how close the pursuers were, to bring in a new man.

The assassin came into the salon from the bedroom, wearing a bathing suit, rubber zori and a T-shirt. He was a slim man, of medium height, with wavy blond hair and blue eyes. His British father had worked as an engineer in the Saudi oil fields. His mother was a Palestinian. His identification papers of a British tourist from Leeds were genuine. The Spanish woman's observation of the hotel indicated that the management was not allowing metal detectors or the search of people entering the lobby.

Abu Nidal took the newspaper photograph and handed it to the assassin.

"Study the target carefully," Abu Nidal said.

The assassin took the newsprint from him. The picture was good-sized, the features clear. He looked at the face of Dr. Issam Sartawi, the man who met publicly with those who occupied their land.

Abu Nidal watched the blonde. He again thought with pleasure about how Ramzy Awwad would feel when he failed to save Sartawi. He had been preparing the death of the traitor for months, the next to last step in his plan.

"Wasif reported that the men who held him spoke Hebrew," Abu Nidal said.

The assassin set the photograph back on the table. 'Maybe they think I am to kill Peres?"

"If so, it will only make the task easier."

Abu Nidal picked up the revolver, held it high over his head and said, "To you, Allah, the most magnificent, the most great, and to your servant the Prophet Mohammed. We ask for your assistance in successfully implementing the death sentence on a criminal and a traitor. The bullets in this weapon are the bullets of Palestine." He lowered the revolver to his mouth, kissed its muzzle and handed it to the man in the bathing attire.

The man took the gun, kissed the muzzle, then carried it to the towel he had left on the floor in the hallway. He placed it carefully inside the folds and lifted the towel and the plastic bottle of suntan lotion.

The man, forbidden to speak after the ceremony, did not turn back. He walked to the door, where the Spanish woman who had rented this room, the house above Portimao and the cabin in Pedras d'el Rei for Abu Nidal, waited to drive the killer to the Montechoro Hotel.

"You know what you are to do once you arrive there," Abu Nidal said to the woman.

"Yes," she said.

SHAI STOOD in the Montechoro Hotel corridor outside Shimon Peres's heavily guarded room. The hotel management had again refused them permission to set up metal detectors outside the entrances to the hotel for fear of panicking the guests. They had traced the German woman, from the purse lifted at the restaurant in Albufeira, to the Hotel Sol E Mar, where she turned out to be a bank teller from Cologne on a two-week holiday. In the event she was anything more, they snatched her from the hotel and were holding her until the Socialist International closed this afternoon.

Shai approached the door to Peres's suite. They had been allowed to hook up a surveillance camera at the end of the hall. As he waited in front of the door, it was opened by one of the three men inside. Shai walked into the room. Peres waved from the phone where he was talking. On his desk sat a breakfast tray. Shai had, with difficulty, finally persuaded the Labor Party leader to take breakfast in the room rather than the crowded restaurant downstairs, filled with hotel guests and walk-ins, as well as the delegates.

Peres hung up the phone and turned to Shai. "You're doing an excellent job," he said. "There are only a few hours left, then we go home for Yom Kippur."

"I'm going to stay with you now until the end."

"All right." Peres took off his glasses. "You think there's going to be an attempt today, despite all that's happened?"

"Yes."

"I assume now that they know we're onto them the assassin won't leave wherever he's holed up until he's ready to strike."

"That's our assumption."

"You'll just have to stop him, then."

Shai was worried. "That's what we're here to do," he said.

ISSAM SARTAWI ENTERED the small Albufeira Hospital room and saw Ramzy lying in bed awake. He winced silently at the swollen bruises and bandages on his friend's face.

"How did you . . . ?" Ramzy started to ask. It hurt his face to talk.

Sartawi sat in the wooden chair by the bed. "One of the Israelis came to me and explained what happened. He said his name was Shai."

Ramzy nodded, the pain evident as he moved.

The former heart surgeon, who had given up his practice in the United States after the 1967 war and returned to the Middle East, squeezed Ramzy's hand. "I spoke to the doctor. He showed me your chart. You'll be fine."

"The conference . . . ?" Ramzy asked.

Sartawi attempted to hide his disappointment. "They didn't allow me to speak. Only granted us observer status. I'm not sure how the Middle East Resolution's going to turn out. They're going to vote on it before lunch."

Ramzy was silent.

Sartawi, a chain smoker, had an urge for a cigarette. He stared past the bed. "If they kill Peres on top of everything else, I just don't know. Last week I met with Arieh Eliav in Paris. He's lost his Knesset seat—didn't get enough votes. I'd pinned so much hope on the Israeli doves. Before Eliav left, I turned to him and said—" Sartawi switched to English "—you and I, we are not peaceful, but peace fools."

"You're not."

Sartawi put a cigarette in his mouth without lighting it, then removed it. "Arafat's been invited to meet with the pope. Did you know?"

"No." Ramzy's voice was weak.

"Maybe something will come of that. We're scheduling a parliament-in-exile meeting in Algiers for after Rome. I've sent a request to Arafat to address the delegates about the need to recognize Israel. We have to move ahead, especially now that we've lost Lebanon." Sartawi rose. "But we'll talk later. You need your rest."

Ramzy forced a nod.

"I have to get back to the International, anyway."

"Thanks for coming."

Sartawi smiled. "I'll be back this afternoon. You take care of yourself, you hear. And rest. You'll be all right here. There's a police guard outside."

"Let me know immediately if anything happens at the International."

"I'll phone as soon as it's over."

SHAI STOOD in the spacious white high-ceilinged lobby of the Montechoro as Peres chatted with several of the delegates. The morning discussion sessions were scheduled for the smaller rooms off the lobby; at eleven the delegates would return to the upstairs conference hall for the plenary meeting.

Shai watched the heavy glass doors for signs of anyone unusual. The one great advantage they had was that Abu Nidal would use a recognizable Palestinian and not some indistinguishable Red Army Faction or Red Brigade sympathizer. He always wanted the world to know the Palestinians squeezed the trigger themselves. Shai watched the tourists—many of them on package deals from Manchester, Birmingham and other working-class British cities—enter and exit the hotel, some dressed for the beach, others for shopping or sight-seeing. He saw Dr. Sartawi come in and wondered if he had gone to see Ramzy. At the long marble reception desk, the French delegate, Jean-Bernard Curial, stretched out his hand as Sartawi approached.

Shai scanned the crowded lobby again, fingers wrapped around the pistol in his pocket. He wished the International had chosen a smaller hotel that they could have secured more easily. Out of the corner of his vision, he saw Peres still standing and talking in front of the elevators.

Across from the elevators, the small Spanish woman who had driven the blond assassin walked out of the souvenir shop. Pretending to be looking at the postcards she had purchased, her head came up to the men talking in front of the elevator doors. She crossed the lobby in front of the large reception desk, saw Sartawi and strolled outside.

The blond assassin was sitting on the grass, letting the sun strike his pale skin, which was heavily coated with suntan lotion.

The woman passed him without a word and stood at the stop for the minibus that shuttled hotel guests to the beach. At the signal, the assassin rose, slipped his feet into his zoris, took the towel folded neatly at his side and moved toward the hotel lobby. He passed the men standing around casually in lightweight suits—obviously armed Israelis.

Inside, Shai wished that Peres would hurry and head into the elevators. He would be safer seated in the convention hall. Only a few more hours, Shai thought. He kept his hand around his pistol.

Shai saw Peres shake hands with whomever he was talking to and smile that wide smile of his. Peres nodded, and his aide pushed the button between the two sets of elevators, lighting it.

Shai turned and surveyed the lobby again. Everything seemed fine. Then he saw something that struck him as a bit odd. A blond tourist was walking intently toward Issam Sartawi, his hand inside his towel. Suddenly Shai wondered if this was a diversion. He glanced at Peres moving to the elevator, not yet in. Israelis surrounded him.

Shai pushed through the people toward the blonde. He had a feeling. He saw the towel drop away, the assassin's gun. Shai aimed, fired. Two shots simultaneously exploded through the room. People screamed, ducked. A quarter of the blonde's forehead splattered across the lobby. Shai continued toward his body in a crouch, pistol extended. Seeing no other terrorists, he turned. Peres had disappeared into the elevator; he was safe.

Below the marble reception desk where he had slumped to the floor, blood spilled from Issam Sartawi's chest. Jean-Bernard Curial was bent over him, his face white, checking for a pulse. Flash photographers snapped pictures. "He's dead," the Frenchman whispered. "Sartawi's dead."

# BOOK IV: SHAI

## 23  September 28 • Damascus, Syria

ABDUL RAHMAN RAHIM stood behind his desk in Abu Nidal's Damascus headquarters, a smile on his lips as he looked at the *International Herald Tribune*'s front-page article. A quarter of the way down the page, across three columns, ran the headline: PEACE ADVOCATE SHOT IN PORTUGAL. A close-up photograph of Sartawi, lying dead on the hotel lobby floor, blood running from his mouth and down his cheek, filled the bottom corner of the page.

A knock echoed off the door. "Come in," Abdul Rahman said, setting the newspaper down.

Kamal Khalaf and Salah Madani entered, each carrying a suitcase.

"You are ready?" Abdul Rahman asked.

"Yes," Khalaf said.

"Do not rent the car at the airport in Zurich," Abdul Rahman reminded them.

Khalaf nodded.

"And do not ask for maps at the same place you rent the car. Buy them elsewhere."

"We know."

"You have plenty of time. There's no need to hurry. All eyes will be focused on Portugal now. No one should be watching for us to move again so soon."

"We have been over it many times. We are ready," Khalaf said.

"Abu Nidal will contact you once you have arrived in Rome. Wait for him, and do not do anything that could draw attention to yourselves."

Khalaf lifted his suitcase.

Abdul Rahman swept the hair away from his glasses and came out from behind his desk. He felt an almost sexual excitement. "Go now. What all of us have done before has merely been preparation for this moment."

RAMZY SAT BESIDE SHAI in the Concert-Café Pruckel in Vienna, waiting for Leila Fahdi. People at the small tables around them were eating pastry and drinking coffee, while others were reading newspapers supported down the middle with wooden sticks. Silent, the depression still tugged at Ramzy. After he had heard about Sartawi, he had checked himself out of the hospital, sat on the beach for hours, unmoving, and stared at the ocean. He felt he should have been there to protect Issam, should have suspected the danger.

Leila Fahdi approached, nervously clutching several sheets of her recent poetry. Shai watched her. Peres had been in the Montechoro lobby at the time of the shooting; the assassin had not come near him. They had to find out where they had gone wrong, see if there was a clue to Abu Nidal's trail in the killing.

Leila reached the table, saw Ramzy's battered face, and shaken, dropped into the chair. "What happened? It wasn't . . ." She stopped in midsentence.

"It was Abu Nidal." Ramzy nodded at Shai. "This is a friend of mine." He angrily remembered the Arab name Shai had used to fool Nadjla in Sidon. "Halim. Halim, Leila Fahdi."

Shai glanced at Ramzy, then turned to Leila. "I'm pleased to meet you."

Leila picked up the small spoon and clutched it in her lap, her eyes on Ramzy. "Is he alive? Does he know I helped you?"

"Abu Nidal's alive," Ramzy said. "But I don't believe you are in any danger."

"Are you sure?"

"He knows something about Khalid Monsour, and that I saw him in August when I was looking for you. Abu Nidal does not know that we spoke. He mentioned your name only in the context of Monsour. I don't think he'll come after you."

She looked down. "What did he say about me?"

"Nothing. He only alluded that you told him how irrationally jealous Monsour could become."

She nodded quickly.

"He said nothing else. Leila, whatever happened between you is in the past. No one need know."

She tried to force a smile, but it failed.

"Leila, the information you gave me was not fully accurate."

She held the spoon tighter. "I didn't know about Sartawi." Her voice broke. "I didn't."

"We have to go over it again."

She remained silent, both hands in her lap.

"What did the newspaper article you read say?"

She looked at her hands. "It was in English. It said that Shimon Peres was to attend the Socialist International in Portugal. It had the date and the place in Portugal underlined."

"Was Sartawi's name mentioned in the article?" Shai asked.

Leila turned to Ramzy, who nodded that she should answer. "I don't know," she said, her voice shaking. "He was in the shower. I was afraid of what he'd do if he caught me searching through his pockets. I just glanced at it."

Shai handed her a photocopy of a newspaper clipping from the London *Jewish Chronicle*. Abu Nidal had been in England prior to Amsterdam. Shai had phoned ahead to the embassy and had them search the *Jewish Chronicle*, London papers and the *International Herald Tribune*.

She stared at the article. "This looks like it, but I don't know. I'm not sure...maybe. It seems so long ago. I only glanced at it for a few seconds." Tears rose in her eyes. "I'm sorry about Sartawi." She looked at Ramzy. "I'm sorry about what happened to you."

"Did Abu Nidal ever mention Peres as the target, by name?" Shai asked.

"He said it was a big attack. It was supposed to be Peres. I wasn't lying." Tears rolled down her face. Her eyes darted to Ramzy, then back to the questioner. "He never actually said Peres, but he wouldn't have told me anything like that."

"What else did he say about the attack?" Shai went on.

"I don't know." She wiped at the tears, smearing mascara across her cheeks. "He said it was not going to be just another killing. That's why I knew it was Peres."

"You told me he said something about waiting for the target to come to Europe," Ramzy said.

She nodded. "He was very excited. Said he had to wait. That he had a timetable. That until the target arrived, he had something else planned. That's why he . . . we attacked Hamshari here."

"But Sartawi lived in Paris," Shai said. "He didn't have to wait for him to arrive in Europe. He was already here. How do you explain that, Leila?"

"I don't know. Maybe he couldn't get close enough to Peres, so he decided to kill Sartawi."

"Peres was in the lobby of the hotel at the time of the shooting. The assassin ignored him completely."

"I don't know," she said, the tears coming harder. She bent the head of the spoon back. "He said this was the biggest thing that he had ever done, the biggest thing that any Palestinian could do for his people. The end of a long struggle. He was waiting until he arrived in Europe to do it in front of a world audience. He had the clipping about the Socialist International. It was supposed to be Peres. I don't know what happened."

Shai looked at Ramzy who was reaching across the small table for her loose sheets of paper. "I'm glad you brought your poetry," he said.

She wiped her cheeks again with the back of her hand. "I wouldn't have, but you kept saying on the phone—"

"I meant what I told you before about wanting to help you." He began to read the first poem.

She put her hand over the page. "No, not in front of me."

He nodded. "I understand. I'll read them later. Would you rather I called you or made comments on the paper?"

"Comments on the paper," she said abruptly.

"Fine."

She put the bent spoon on the table. "If there's nothing else, I want to go now. If it's all right?"

"Of course, and thank you for coming, Leila. You've been a great help."

Her voice rose with a note of hope. "Have I?"

"Very much so. And I'll get these back to you very soon."

Leila nodded several times and stood. "Thank you," she said. Then she hurried away.

Shai watched her, feeling sympathy for how the Palestinian dilemma and her own difficulty in knowing which way to turn had caused her such pain. He retrieved the *Jewish Chronicle* clipping. The second-to-last paragraph reported that Dr. Issam Sartawi would be attending the Socialist International. Abu Nidal had probably first learned about Sartawi's participation in the meetings by reading about it in the Jewish newspaper.

"Sartawi was the target in Portugal, all along," Shai said.

Ramzy nodded. "In Portugal, yes."

"She misinterpreted everything he was saying because she saw that article."

"She reached the only possible conclusion with what she knew." Ramzy watched the condensation on his water glass. " 'The biggest thing that any Palestinian could

do for his people. The end of his long struggle.' Abu Nidal did have a timetable, only it wasn't the Socialist International." He turned to Shai. "It was the siege of
Beirut. He's after Yasser Arafat and has been the whole
time."

"It all makes sense now. Sartawi's stature in Europe
was a threat to him. Sartawi was an important strike while
the clock was ticking down on the real target. As soon as
we besieged Beirut, Abu Nidal knew Arafat would eventually be forced out. He's been waiting for Arafat to come
to Europe as he does after each setback, trying to turn it
into a victory. Abu Nidal wants to kill him where the assassination will have his world audience."

"Arafat's due in Rome October fourth," Ramzy said
quietly. "That's in six days."

Shai remained silent. Peres was safe. Shai thought
about the Israelis Awwad had murdered and Carmon's
orders to kill him.

"With the defeat in Lebanon and Arafat dead, I'm
afraid large numbers of my people will welcome Abu Nidal's leadership," Ramzy said.

"Then we're going to have to eliminate Abu Nidal this
time."

Ramzy studied the Israeli. "You'd help me save Arafat?"

"To stop Abu Nidal from replacing him, I'll do everything I can. We'll leave for Rome on the morning flight."

Ramzy continued to look at Shai. There was no danger to any of them now. It occurred to him that this might
have turned out perfectly for the Israelis. This Israeli
could be luring him to where they would pump him with
bullets, then let Abu Nidal kill Arafat. With he and Ara-

fat dead, in addition to Sartawi, the PLO would be terminally crippled. They had attacked that house in the Algarve because they had believed Abu Nidal's operatives inside were a threat to Shimon Peres. He would make his own calls and have his men meet him in Rome.

"Thank you," Ramzy said. "I appreciate the help."

Shai nodded. "Maybe you've been standing out in the rain alone long enough."

OUTSIDE LUGANO, Switzerland, the two Israeli agents, David and Avi, who had followed Khalid Monsour from Amsterdam to Damascus, sped south along the mountain lake in a two-seater Triumph Spitfire. Both accomplished painters, the youthful, long-haired agents traveled alternately as struggling bohemians or successful artists, depending on the exigencies of the assignment. Non-Jewish-owned galleries in London, at the quiet behest of Jewish friends, carried works of the two in their British cover names.

Sudden and excited activity at Abu Nidal's information headquarters in Damascus had piqued their curiosity, and they had stayed with the two men who had been seen repeatedly at the information offices. The previous day they had boarded a flight from Damascus to Zurich. While David had kept them under surveillance, Avi had broken into the Palestinians' Zurich hotel rooms and learned they were traveling under the names Kamal Khalaf and Salah Madani. No destination could be determined from the papers they had left in the rooms. While Khalaf and Madani were dining at a moderately priced restaurant, David had slipped a directional trans-

mitter inside the rear bumper of their rented burgundy
Peugeot.

With the directional equipment on hand at every Israeli embassy, when the Palestinians drove south out of
Zurich a team followed in a van. Avi and David had originally rented a sleek Citroën in the event the Palestinians' Peugeot raced beyond the heavier van's directional
range. So far, the two times that had occurred, they had
been able to keep within visual distance. In Bellinzona,
the capital of the southern Ticino canton, some thirty
kilometers behind them, they had exchanged cars in the
event the Citroën had been seen.

Avi drove relaxed at the wheel as David held the walkie-
talkie on his lap. The Palestinians had stopped for lunch
in Bellinzona and given the van time to catch up.

"It doesn't seem like they're out to see the sights,"
David said as he unwrapped the hunk of cheese he had
bought while Avi had rented the Triumph. He cut off a
slice. "You want some?"

Avi nodded and David handed him the hard cheese
with an end of fresh bread. The cool mountain air whis-
tled through the window. Beautiful villas and a path
where geese waddled surrounded the lake. "There
doesn't seem to be much doubt where they're going," Avi
said, taking the food but not removing his eyes from the
road.

"No, we should be at the Italian border in another ten
minutes. From Como they'll probably head to Milan and
pick up the autostrada."

"All right. As soon as we cross and can stop, we'll call
it in."

RAMZY SAT HIGH on one of the hundreds of marble steps of the Vittorio Emanuele Monument in Rome. Below him he saw Shai move past the bearded Jesus-like figure who was drawing a huge Madonna on the sidewalk in pastels; beside the artist sat his collection box. As Shai climbed the white steps, Ramzy surveyed the Piazza Venezia. He felt safer here, where he could see for a distance in all directions. Cars parked everywhere in the square were squeezed without space against one another. Yellowish-orange buses crammed with people, fleets of yellow Fiat taxis, cars and young Romans on motorbikes circled the central grass area. As the Israeli sat, Ramzy saw no one suspicious.

"They've left Zurich," Shai said, breathing hard.

"Are they headed here?"

"We'll know soon." He wiped the dampness from his forehead with his handkerchief. It was cool out. "I'm going to call in a few minutes and check. I wanted to see you first."

Ramzy nodded. "Assuming they are moving here, I suggest this time that we wait until they lead us to Abu Nidal. We don't want to alert him in time for him to bring in another assassin again."

"Agreed."

"Arafat will be here in five days," Ramzy said. "He's planning to stay two. He's scheduled to meet with Foreign Minister Colombo and President Pertini on Monday before his audience with the pope. The mayor of Rome has invited him to a reception in his honor, Tuesday."

Shai did not let his anger at the red carpet being rolled out for the terrorist leader show. "I'll need a schedule, as close as you have it."

"All right, this afternoon."

"You have any new leads from your side?" Shai asked.

"There are some vague reports about a movement of WZ-63s out of Sofia. We're attempting to follow it up."

Shai stood. "These two from Zurich seem to be heading here. Let me make that call and find out where they are."

Ramzy rose. "I'll wait lower down."

Shai patted his stomach. "It's all right. I can use the exercise."

Ramzy started down the stairs with him. "If you want the exercise, some of my men would be happy to chase you around Europe."

"I'm sure. The question is what you'd want them to do if they caught me."

Without waiting for a response, Shai left him and quickened his pace down the stairs. Ramzy sat and watched the Israeli cross the black cobbled square. He was suspicious that the Israelis would help him protect Yasser Arafat. It was one thing that he had agreed to try to prevent Abu Nidal from killing Peres—if Abu Nidal had killed the important Israeli, the PLO would have been blamed, despite their denials. Besides, he had personal reasons for wanting Abu Nidal, enough to cooperate with them.

He wondered if the Israelis would really do this solely to prevent the radicals from taking over the PLO. With Abu Nidal's successes, he worried about Arafat's safety and welcomed the assistance. Ramzy waited.

At the north end of the square, he saw Shai come out of the Bar Brasile. The Israeli moved quickly past the tourist carriages and scraggy brown horses in front of the famous Palazzo where Mussolini had harangued the masses from the balcony beneath where Shai now walked. Something about the intensity of his gait told Ramzy there was news.

Shai climbed the stairs and sat beside him, silent for a long moment before he said, "Khalaf and Madani have crossed into Italy. There's no doubt that they're headed here."

Ramzy felt confident. They would not make the mistakes they had in Vienna and Portugal. "Good."

Shai stared toward the square. He had reported his progress upon arrival in Rome, and the orders had just come into the embassy. "There's something else. I've been called back to Jerusalem for consultations. I have to leave immediately."

A sarcastic smile outlined Ramzy's lips. "I see."

Shai turned to him. "It won't take long. I should be able to be back in Rome by the day after tomorrow."

"Certainly, fine."

"I'll be here."

Ramzy rose. "As I said, fine."

"Ramzy, I know what you're thinking. It's not true. I believe Abu Nidal must be eliminated."

"Of course you do. The question is whether you believe he should be stopped right now."

Worried about what was waiting for him in Jerusalem, Shai remained silent.

Ramzy did not look at him. "What about the two coming from Switzerland?"

"There's a team on them. They'll keep them under surveillance until I return. There's time. It's only Wednesday. We have until Monday."

Ramzy started down the stairs. "Have a good flight."

"Thank you," Shai said quietly.

---

CARMON LIT A CIGARETTE. The sun was setting through the window in his office, behind where Shai sat.

"So where is this Ramzy Awwad now?" Carmon betrayed none of the anger that had billowed through him when he had learned Yehuda had ordered the Arab's release.

"In Rome."

"You were there with him?"

"You know that."

Carmon smiled. "Yes, I suppose I do. What did you tell him?"

"I told him I'd been called to Jerusalem for consultations and that I'd return immediately."

Carmon drew on his cigarette and studied his agent. "How would you feel if I ordered you to return there and kill him?"

Shai stared out the window, feeling the tiredness from all the traveling. He turned back and said, "When Awwad thought Abu Nidal was after Peres, he helped us."

"In the attempt to save Peres or get Abu Nidal?"

"At the time, it was the same."

"Then he really wasn't attempting to help us, was he?"

"What else do you want?" Shai said. "He did everything he said he would and more. Abu Nidal's men beat him like a punching bag."

"And you rescued him. Because of Peres, of course." Carmon leaned back in his chair, the cigarette burning between his fingers. "You don't have to concern yourself, Shai. I don't want you to kill Awwad. In fact, I don't want you to do anything of the sort."

"What are you saying?"

"You've been at it nonstop the past few months. Too long for someone your age. I think you should take some time off. It's still warm in Eilat. Go down there for a week or so. Take Tami with you. I can spare her for a little while."

Shai watched Carmon smoke and knew what he was doing. "I don't want any time off."

"It wasn't a request."

"If Abu Nidal gets Arafat, with Syria's backing he'll be a step away from taking over the PLO."

"That's none of our affair," Carmon said. "It's an inter-Palestinian dispute."

Shai's expression was icy. "You'd love it if the hardliners succeeded. The end of Arafat might even break the West Bank Arabs identification with the PLO, make it easier for you to sell them local autonomy. Do what your whole war in Lebanon failed to do."

"I will not risk you or any of my agents to protect Yasser Arafat."

"How many more people are we going to lose to terrorist shootings if Abu Nidal takes over the PLO?"

"I don't know. How many buses do you think are going to be blown up here while Arafat has to placate the radicals to stay in power?"

Shai had to convince him. "The hard-liners have rejected Arafat completely now. He doesn't have to cater to them anymore. That's given him more maneuvering room. Despite whatever else Arafat is, he's a moderating force out there. The fact that he wants to negotiate now, even if it's on his own terms, is a start. There's at least a possibility with him."

"Since he hasn't sworn off putting bombs in our supermarkets and buses, the distinction between one terrorist and the other is, I'm afraid, lost on me."

"It's Abu Nidal who's the real danger," Shai said. "Don't you see? He'll kill any moderate who arises."

Carmon knocked the end of the cigarette into his ashtray. "Which only shows you the danger in dealing with any individual Arab peace spokesman."

Shai was shaking inside. "But how long can we go on like this? We lost over six hundred boys, more than three thousand wounded trying to destroy Arafat. And what did we achieve in the end? Maybe we can salvage something from this war yet. Arafat's been destroyed militarily. No Arab government will risk itself to give him a base for his armed struggle. He knows that. That's why he's willing to talk now. In time, he has to move toward recognizing us in return for our willingness to exchange land for peace. He has no other choice. I'm not saying that we should invite him to Jerusalem, as his position stands, but you make peace ultimately with your enemies." Shai's face reddened. "If he's killed and Abu Nidal's butchers take over, we'll have no chance. We have to eliminate Abu

Nidal, the far greater threat, and he's in our reach in Rome.''

''We'll get Abu Nidal later.'' Carmon reached forward and ground his cigarette out. ''You really don't understand, Shai. The settlement has proceeded too far. It's irreversible now. Judea and Samaria are an inseparable part of the Land of Israel. There will be no rescuing Arafat, no giving him a state there or in Jordan. You're on vacation. In Israel.''

Shai said nothing, did not move.

''Report here in a week, Shai.''

Shai sat there depressed and worried about where Israel was heading. He forced his way to his feet. ''This stinks.''

''If the world was fair,'' Carmon said, ''we would have found some oil under our sand, too.''

ABU NIDAL STOOD at the tall iron fence that ringed the great domed synagogue by the Tiber. He calculated how many people after Saturday services would be crowded into the small gardened plaza below the steps that led to the columns at the synagogue entrance. Hundreds, if he was lucky. To his right, traffic crawled up the tree-lined, river-fronted Lungotevere d'Cenci Highway. The lights above the water shone in the darkness

Abu Nidal moved around the far side of the synagogue, where a garden of palm trees was enclosed by the high fence. A yellowed peeling building looked down on the narrow Via Catalana, which ran along this side of the synagogue. It was Thursday night. The two that had just arrived from Switzerland would park on the Via Cata-

lana and spray bullets through the fence into the crowd
as soon as services were over. Trapped, the targets would
have no place to run. The world would see how the Palestinians treated the Jews at the same moment the pope
and Italy's leaders had invited Arafat to Rome. In people's minds the PLO would be identified with the attack. More important, it would divert attention from Abu
Nidal's real target, Arafat himself. According to newspapers, the traitor would arrive on Monday the fourth.
Abu Nidal's final victory was within his grasp now. Two
other teams were at the moment making their way to
Rome.

Abu Nidal continued through the cold evening around
to the Tiber side of the synagogue. The two from Switzerland were eating across the river in Trastevere. Let
them dine well after the long drive, he thought. He would
see them late tonight and diagram Saturday morning's
massacre for them.


IN TRASTEVERE the Israeli agent, David, came back
from the phone, then joined Avi at the window table of
the Ristorante La Cisterna. The two Arabs were eating
across the small black cobbled piazza inside the Ristorante Paris. The tables outside both restaurants were
empty in the chilly fall night.

David did not touch the plate of pasta that had arrived
in his absence. "I don't believe it," he said.

"Don't believe what?" Avi speared more of the soft
gnocci dumplings with his fork.

"The orders."

"Yeah, what don't you believe about them?"

"We're supposed to stop following those two."

Avi put his fork down. "What?"

"As I said, we're supposed to stop following them."

"And do what?"

"That's it. Nothing."

"I don't understand."

"Neither do I, but you're not going to believe this next part."

"Try me," Avi said.

"We're supposed to take a vacation. The embassy suggests Bologna. They say the university's about to open and the city's swarming with young attractive women."


"IS IT BECAUSE you promised Awwad that you would return to Rome?" Tami asked, massaging the hard muscles in Shai's bare back as he sat on the corner of the bed in her apartment.

"No." Seated on the mattress, her smooth legs stretched on both sides of him. "I know in the long term that the hard-liners are much more dangerous," Shai said.

"Did you try to convince Carmon?"

Shai laughed. "This situation is tailor-made for him. He gets rid of Arafat, and since the Palestinians do it themselves, there's no martyrdom. That's more important to him than who among us Abu Nidal might kill next."

"Maybe Ramzy will be able to stop it on his own?"

"Maybe, but there are only four days left." He felt her thumb moving in circles over a hard spot. He ran his hand along her bare thigh. "You're good at this."

"Thanks."

He leaned back, and she bent forward and kissed him, her hair sweeping his shoulder. Then she jabbed his side. "Sit up straight. I'm not done here."

"Yes, Sergeant."

She grabbed him around the neck with both hands. "I'll have you know that I was a lieutenant."

He reached behind him and pulled her closer. "I think I still outrank you."

She rested her chin on his shoulder. "What are you planning to do?"

Already part of the tiredness of the long weeks in Portugal and all the flying from there to Vienna to Israel was beginning to lift. "The idea of a week like this in Eilat isn't exactly torturous. How do you think Carmon knew about us anyway?"

She encircled his stomach with her hands. "I don't know. I certainly didn't tell him. I mentioned it to a few friends. I suppose that was enough."

He kissed the inside of her arm. "Where was I?"

"You were telling me, the idea of a week together in Eilat didn't exactly sound terrible. And I was waiting for the but."

Shai was silent.

"There is a but. That much about you I know. You couldn't just go down there and lay on the sand and forget about Rome."

"No, I couldn't."

"So?"

"If I disobey, my career's over. It doesn't matter how valuable I am. Carmon won't put up with ignoring a direct order of this magnitude, and in that he's right."

"You've been out there a long time," she said. "If you really believe in this, maybe you should help Awwad. You can always go back to the kibbutz afterward. You told me once how much you enjoyed working in the desert."

"And we could be together."

"I must admit that the thought did occur to me." She let go of him. "But that's not why I suggested it."

He turned around in her lap and touched her hair. "The idea of being together all the time . . ."

She said nothing.

"But I really can't go back to the kibbutz and be happy. That belonged to another life, with another woman. If we went there, I'd never be free of that, and you'd never have all of me. And, Tami, I'm not cut out for a job in the city, not yet anyway."

"What does that mean?"

"It means that I love you, I want to be with you every moment I can, but I'm going to Rome."

"What about your career?"

"I'll have to worry about that later."

She looked at him, and then a smile crossed her face. "You say you love me, huh?"

He gave a small nod.

"So, when are you leaving for Rome?"

"In the morning."

The smile gone, she wrapped her arms around his shoulders and pulled him down onto the bed with her. "Then there's the rest of tonight," she said.

# 26 October 1 • Rome, Italy

THE ISRAELI EMBASSY in Rome was beginning to close Friday afternoon in preparation for the Sabbath when Shai strode into the cultural attaché's office. Zev, the slim, curly-haired man in his late thirties, oversaw all Israeli intelligence activities in Italy.

"Shai," he said, taking off his glasses and looking up from the papers he was reading. "I didn't expect to see you back here."

Shai came across the room and shook Zev's hand. The assistant cultural attaché remained seated as he took it.

"There's been a change in plans," Shai said.

Zev looked puzzled. "Yes?"

"What happened to those two from Switzerland David and Avi were following?"

"We let them go—Jerusalem's orders."

"Where are they now?"

"I don't know. Remember, I said we let them go."

"What about David and Avi?"

"They're out of town." He smiled at his suggestion of Bologna. "With any luck, enjoying themselves."

"You have a phone number for them?"

"Of course."

"I want to speak to them."

"Why? I understand everybody's been called off this one."

"I've been put back on," Shai lied. "Carmon's orders."

Zev began twirling his glasses in his fingers. "I haven't heard a word about it."

"I just landed at the airport. You can telex Jerusalem if you like."

"You know I won't get a response on something like this until after Shabbat."

"I just want to speak to them," Shai said, hoping the transmitter would still be operative on the Palestinians' Peugeot. "And I want a directionally equipped van."

Zev laughed. "Anything else?"

"Yes. I want weapons in the van."

Zev placed his glasses on the desk. "Shai, I had specific orders when you were called back to shut down this operation, completely."

"Well, now there are new orders."

Zev leaned forward. "Shit, Shai. There aren't any new orders. What the hell are you doing?"

"The number and the van," Shai said. "Then you won't hear from me again."

"Does Carmon even know you're here?"

"He will as soon as you telex. Cover yourself. Send it priority. By the time you get a response, I'll be long gone."

"Do you know what you're doing to yourself?" Zev asked.

"Yes."

"Shai, it's not worth it, not for Arafat. Come on, we'll go out and get drunk, forget all this."

Shai remained silent for a long moment, staring at the younger man. "You were no more than a kid when I parachuted into the Sinai in '56. I fought the Egyptians again in '67 and once more in '73. The hate for Sadat in '73 was awesome, attacking on Yom Kippur. Everywhere we talked about his collaboration with the Nazis during the Second World War. You remember? Then he came to Jerusalem. If you would have told me anytime before then that in my lifetime Israeli families would be flying to Cairo and touring the pyramids, I would have thought you were nuts. If we help Arafat now, he may be induced to take even a greater step. Either way, we'll be much worse off with him dead and the extremists running rampant."

Zev looked at the older man who had fought in two more wars than he had. He thought about his own son, now eight, and wondered what future both sides were preparing for him.

"All right," Zev said. "The phone number, the van and weapons. But as soon as you're out the door, I'm sending that telex."

"Thanks," Shai said.

Outside, Shai drove along the greenery of the Villa Borghese just beyond the embassy. He had reached Avi. They had no idea where the two Palestinians were staying and had only tailed them to a restaurant in Trastevere before being pulled off, but as Shai hoped, they had left the directional transmitter operative on the Palestinians' burgundy Peugeot 504.

Shai stopped in the parking area above the Spanish Steps, turned off the motor and waited for Ramzy. From the hill here he had a panoramic view of Rome. In the humid summer, men in T-shirts and women in light blouses sat on the roofs of the rose-colored buildings, some eating, others watching television. Now the railing-enclosed roofs were empty. Two magnificent domes rose straight ahead of him, one behind the other: the dark Church of St. Carlo, and across the river, the magnificent St. Peter's.

Shai heard a quiet knocking on the passenger window. He reached over and pulled the handle up, and Ramzy climbed into the van.

Ramzy felt the weapon in his pocket, knowing the Israeli could be here to kill him and ensure Abu Nidal's success. "I didn't think you would return."

Shai glanced at him. "Are you saying you missed me?"

Ramzy allowed himself a small smile. "It has been a while since I've seen my wife."

"Well, how about if we stop Abu Nidal, then you can have a long visit. You have any leads?"

"Nothing verifiable. There's been some more movement in Sofia, but we're not sure yet if it has anything to do with here. What about the two that drove down from Switzerland?"

"The transmitter's still on their car. That's why I have the van. We're going to have to find them."

Ramzy had already suspected that the Israelis had let them go. He wondered what had happened to make them change their mind, if they had. He would be on guard every second for the trap. "Do you have any idea where they are?"

Shai shook his head. "We're going to have to search the city, then the outlying areas." Shai opened his door. "You drive."

As the Israeli moved around the van and yanked the side handle, Ramzy slid into the driver's seat. If the target car was moving, they could miss each other's paths indefinitely without coming in range. Still, it was late, and if the car was parked somewhere in Rome itself or in a nearby outlying district, they had a chance of finding it if they searched systematically. Ramzy started the motor. He would try a general drive through the city first, to see if they turned lucky. If not, he would begin a north-to-south grid search.

CARMON HEARD Tami's familiar walk in the empty outer office and her soft knock on his door. Fuming after receiving Zev's cable, he had phoned her apartment and found her home, obviously not on vacation with Shai.

"Come in," he said loudly.

Tami entered, pushed the door shut behind her and stood there.

"Where is he?"

"Who do you mean?" she asked.

"You know damn well I mean Shai."

He had instructed her, if questioned, to tell everything she knew. "He's in Rome."

"I know he's in Rome," Carmon shouted. "Where in Rome? Where's he staying?"

"He didn't say."

"I want to know, Tami. Now."

"He didn't tell me. He didn't want me to know."

"You mean he figured I might find out he was there and you'd have to answer to me."

"No. He said it was best I didn't know, that it's always safer if people don't know where he is."

Carmon laughed sarcastically. "Which side is he trying to protect himself from?"

"I don't think he'd ever tell me where he was staying."

Carmon reached for his cigarettes, and then his demeanor softened. "No, come to think of it, I guess you're right. It's probably best if you don't know where he is."

His change of attitude worried her. "What's going to happen to him?"

Carmon removed a cigarette. "He's finished, your friend. Out. He has his sand and desert now, the way the Colonel has his roses."

"He's doing what he believes in."

"You can go now, Tami. Finish your vacation."

"Maybe you ought to fire me, too," she said, then turned abruptly and left.

Carmon drew on his cigarette. She would calm down by next week. Then, with renewed pleasure, he picked up the cable that had arrived the previous day from their highly placed agent in Damascus—Operative 66. Operative 66 had worked his way into the upper echelons of the Mukhabarat, one of Syria's two security services. With the rush of activity around Abu Nidal, he had ordered Operative 66, if possible, without endangering his cover, to see what he could discover about the terrorist's plans.

Carmon read the cable again. Operative 66 confirmed that Abu Nidal had sent three teams to Rome to eliminate Arafat. Carmon wheeled back in his chair and bent to open the safe hidden below one of the stone squares of the floor. The information would remain here.

A LITTLE AFTER TWO A.M., Ramzy drove the van through the Via Guglielmo Marconi toward one of the southern bends of the Tiber. Eight-story peeling buildings lined the wide road, each roof crowded with television antennae. Ramzy had been driving for almost ten hours now, and they had eaten in the van while moving. His back and arms ached. He ignored the tiredness. He would drive the entire night and next day, too, if necessary.

Seated behind the computer screen, Shai rubbed both eyelids hard, trying to keep awake. He leaned back in the small chair and thought about Tami, felt the smooth warmth of her skin as she had slept against him, could sense her scent. Amazed, he had never expected to have this again. He pictured her in bed in her apartment now, her dark hair spilled over the pillow. He glanced over in his tired reverie, and then he saw it. A small green light on the screen, not moving.

He flipped the switch on the microphone, then punched up a map. "Ramzy," he said excitedly. "We've got them, and they're not moving."

"Where?" came the even reply.

Shai waited as the new map formed line by line. The green light was near the center of it now. "You know where EUR is."

"Yes, south."

Shai felt the van picking up speed. EUR was the recently developed southern suburb of Rome, originally set aside by Mussolini for the World's Fair, canceled because of the Second World War. Shai watched the screen, periodically giving Ramzy directions. He felt the adrenaline released through him. They would find out where Khalaf and Madani were, then take turns napping, and this time follow them to Abu Nidal.

Soon, as they neared the modern residential quarter, Shai tapped the keyboard with a new set of instructions. The grid around the green light came up in greater detail. "It should be just at the end of the artificial lake," Shai said, speaking into the microphone.

"We're along the lake now."

The van pulled off to the right and eased to a stop. Shai checked the pistol in his shoulder holster. "Do you see the Peugeot?" he asked.

"You better come up here."

"Do you see the Peugeot?"

"Yes."

Puzzled at Ramzy's reaction, Shai slid open the side door and stepped into the cool night. A tall green glass building with the ENI logo of the Italian Petroleum Agency rose beside him. He moved to the front of the van, saw Ramzy motionless behind the wheel, followed his line of sight and then he saw it across the street. The burgundy Peugeot 504 was sitting with a number of other cars inside a parking lot surrounded by a chain-link fence. Shai felt the excitement escape him, like air leaving a balloon. There was a small building at the front of the lot with a large unlit sign. The familiar white letters

on the red background spelled AVIS. Khalaf and Madani had returned the rented car.

Shai opened the van door. Ramzy was still staring at the
Peugeot.

''We'll come back in the morning,'' Shai said. ''We'll
figure out a way to find out if they've rented something
else.''

SATURDAY MORNING, two days before Arafat's arrival in Rome, Khalaf and Madani sat in their hotel room waiting for breakfast to arrive. Abu Nidal had ordered them to stay in the room until they left for the assault on the synagogue. The Jews would arrive to pray at various times, Abu Nidal had explained; he wanted the strike at 12:30 when they disgorged from the building together. They would remain here until a quarter of noon.

The knock sounded on the door, and Madani rose to answer it.

"Wait," Khalaf said.

The muzzle of a WZ-63 protruded from one of the packs on the floor near the window. Khalaf crossed the room, zipped the pack closed, then nodded to Madani standing near the door. Madani opened it, and the waiter wheeled in a cart. Khalaf gazed out the window and checked that their black Fiat Mirafiori was parked where he had left it on the side street behind the hotel. It was.

AT 10:40 SATURDAY MORNING as the Avis office opened forty minutes late, Shai stepped through the door. They had decided that one of them alone would be less intimidating and more likely to achieve success with a bribe. It was agreed that Shai, with his lighter skin, would fare better. They had also briefly discussed the possibility of breaking into the office last night but had opted against it. The information was computerized, and since they did not know for certain how to call it up, they would effect a break-in, and in the morning be faced with a police investigation at the office rather than what they hoped would be an underpaid clerk.

Shai chose between the two clerks and approached the light-skinned, blond, northern Italian woman at the far end of the counter.

"I'd like some help," he said in English.

"Yes. What kind of car did you want?"

He took the two hundred-dollar bills from his pocket and pushed them along the side of her computer terminal so the man to her right would not see. "I have two friends," he said softly. "I dropped them off here a few days ago and unfortunately lost their address. They returned the burgundy Peugeot 504 outside. I wanted to see if you have an address for them."

The woman glanced quickly to her right, then opened her drawer and swept the bills inside. "You have the license of the car?" she asked quietly.

"Z, six, five, zero, zero, three, three."

She tapped the keys. "Kamal Khalaf?"

"Yes."

"He's at the Hotel Napoleon in the Piazza Vittorio Emanuele."

Shai removed another hundred-dollar bill and placed it beside the computer. "Did he rent another car?"

The woman opened her drawer again and quickly drew the bill inside. "Yes. A black Fiat Mirafiori."

"You have the license plate number?"

She looked at him and waited, apparently expecting another hundred.

"You have the license plate number?" Shai repeated.

She shrugged and looked at the screen. "Roma, six, six, six, three, one, five."

"Thank you," Shai said, and left.

More than forty-five minutes later, Ramzy sped through the last of the heavy traffic and pulled onto the Piazza Vittorio Emanuele. Ramzy glanced at his watch—11:40. As Shai climbed out, headed through the outdoor flower market in the middle of the square and entered the hotel, Ramzy dropped his head back on the seat. He dared not hope. As he waited, the cold fear inside him made him suddenly remember how afraid he had been as a boy with his father, his mustache white as the anti-Lebanon snowcaps, sitting on the floor of the concrete hut in the Ein Hilweh Camp, muttering to himself.

Almost immediately Shai returned, walking quickly. He stuck his head through the open passenger window.

"Nothing," he said. "The address was a phony."

Ramzy stared straight ahead. "There must be tens of thousands of black Fiat Mirafioris in Rome."

ABU NIDAL SAT parked in the Alfa Romeo on the Via Catalana that ran along the far side of the magnificent synagogue by the Tiber. The sun stood high in the sky. The worshippers would be coming out momentarily. He peered to his right at the two rows of original columned arcades of the Theater of Marcellus. The Orsini family palace sat atop the ancient white stone ruins, using them as a foundation. He would live in a house like that, he thought, in Jerusalem, built atop the Jews' remains.

He saw the well-dressed people coming down the front steps of the synagogue. They began to gather in the garden area encircled, like the rest of the synagogue, by the high iron fence. He could not have envisioned a more perfect setting. The crowd gradually swelled. The men, women and children remained inside the garden talking. Then some began kissing one another on the cheeks, shaking hands and moving toward the two gates in the fence. The anger rose inside Abu Nidal. Where were they? If they arrived too late, he would . . . Then he saw the black Fiat Mirafiori emerge from the far side of the apartment building opposite the synagogue. The Fiat turned left onto the Via Catalana and parked across the street from the sidewalk surrounding the synagogue.

Several children were playing on the grass near the fence. Khalaf and Madani opened both doors of the car and came out with their WZ-63s lowered at their sides, the doors left open. Abu Nidal watched the people inside. No one noticed the two Arabs approach the fence, raise the small machine pistols and point them through the tall vertical bars.

Both men fired into the crowd, the sounds like small pops. Those hit, fell to the pavement. People screamed and scattered. Bullets ricocheted off the stone pavement and steps of the synagogue, the shards and metal slicing into the shrieking people. Some tried to run up the high steps. Khalaf sprayed from left to right and cut them down. Bodies slumped to the ground, leaking blood. People crowded at the two gates, shouting and moaning.

A fusillade of bullets exploded at them, dropping many. Two small boys sat on the grass right in front of the fence, wide-eyed, not moving. Khalaf stepped back, pointed the WZ-63 at the small blond boy on the left and fired at his face. The child toppled over, a bloodied mess. His brother bolted up, ran, and a burst from Madani caught him in the back and head. The boy pitched forward from the grass and skidded, face first, on the pavement, bloodying the stones. Khalaf kept firing at the face of the first boy, only an arm's length from him, splattering his features across the green grass. The small corpse twitched with each hit, and then finally with the dull click of metal against metal Khalaf's clip emptied.

As the two Palestinians ran to the black Fiat amid the crying and screaming, Abu Nidal slipped the Alfa Romeo into gear and roared toward the Tiber. He turned right on the tree-lined highway and raced past Tiberina Island. This was only the beginning. As he swung the car off the too-visible highway into the Via Giulia, his mind turned to the two teams about to arrive in Rome—one from Sofia and the other waiting in Florence—who would rid their people of Yasser Arafat. The two from Sofia would do the job, but in the event they were apprehended or silenced at the scene, the two driving here from Florence would be hidden in such a way that no one would be able to stop them.

THE ISRAELI AGENT, Avi, sat on the stone steps of the Colosseum in the darkness, ripping the evening newspaper with the front-page photograph of the synagogue slaughter into increasingly small shreds. His anger grew with each tear. After hearing the news in Bologna, David and he had raced back to Rome.

He listened to the steps of the man he was waiting for and flung the shreds of newsprint into the wind. From the arches of the Roman theater, wild cats hissed and shrieked, the way they did in the alleys of Jerusalem. Avi's longtime friend sat beside him. They had met during basic training in the elite Golani paratrooper unit, had proudly worn the green oak-tree patch and brown beret on their leaves together in Tel Aviv. Avi had later joined the external service. His friend was now a correspondent for *Maariv*, specializing in the Palestinians. As Avi expected, he had been sent to Rome to cover Arafat's visit.

"Are you all right?" the newspaperman asked his friend.

Avi was bent forward on his elbows, his head in his hands. "No." He straightened and looked at the reporter. "The slaughter in the synagogue, it could have been prevented. We were following the killers." The eyewitness descriptions matched Khalaf and Madani, exactly. "For some reason we were called off. I want you to print what happened, every goddamn word of it. Someone in Jerusalem's responsible for these deaths."

THE FRONT GATES padlocked by the police, Shai stood outside the Great Synagogue waiting for Ramzy. He wrapped both hands around the black iron bars and stared at the blood soaked into the pavement.

The facade of the building and the steps mounting to the entrance were pockmarked from the 9 mm slugs. The pages of an open prayer book, with a bullet hole through it, flapped in the breeze in front of him. Beside the prayer book, the grass was stained, and Shai saw what looked like bits of brain matter. He squeezed the bars.

The morning papers had revealed that the black Fiat Mirafiori, which witnesses reported at the scene of the attack the previous day, had been abandoned near the main train station. Fourteen had died so far, including two small brothers; half a dozen others still hovered on the critical list.

The iron cut into Shai's flesh, and suddenly aware of how hard he was gripping the bars, he let go. If Carmon had not pulled their agents off . . .

Shai saw Ramzy walking toward him on the sidewalk and rubbed his wrinkled fingers to restore the circulation. He fully understood, for the first time, what killing

Abu Nidal meant to Ramzy. Ramzy had implied on the phone that he had news. Shai was more determined than ever. Arafat arrived tomorrow.

Ramzy looked at the bloodied pavement, then at Shai. "This was avoidable."

"Yes," Shai whispered.

"As your people mourn for Sabra and Shatilla, I feel your pain about this."

"Thank you." Shai stared at the stained pavement. "Tell me, what did you feel before you shot that unarmed man and woman at our embassy in Paraguay?"

"Alone," Ramzy said. "A Palestinian alone in a world that cared nothing about him."

Shai nodded. "That's something Jews understand."

"The movement from Sofia's been confirmed," Ramzy said. "Two of Abu Nidal's people arrived in Dubrovnik last night and left this morning by boat for Naples. They'll dock late this afternoon."

"All right," Shai said. "Let's go."


MEIR CARMON KNOCKED on the deputy prime minister's office door, not knowing why he had been asked to appear.

"Come in," the voice said from inside.

Carmon entered. The deputy prime minister was seated at his desk. But to his surprise, standing at the window looking out, Carmon saw his head of intelligence for Italy, Zev. The deputy prime minister did not offer the customary handshake.

"Sit down, Meir," he said.

Carmon glanced at Zev, who was still staring out the window, then lowered himself into the soft chair opposite the desk and crossed one leg over the other.

"I asked Zev to fly in to confirm a report I had been given early this morning," the deputy prime minister said. "I understand we had the terrorists who attacked the Rome synagogue under surveillance."

Carmon uncrossed his legs. "Yes, but—"

"And you ordered our boys off?" he interrupted.

"Yes, but as I started to say, there's an explanation."

The deputy prime minister's face reddened. "I know there's an explanation. I just heard it. Your explanation cost fourteen innocent people their lives."

"That was unforeseen. I'm as upset about their deaths as anyone, but it will bring all Israel to safety sooner as the world sees the PLO for what it is."

Zev turned sharply from the window. "You know what Abu Nidal's done, how many of us he's killed, that he's going to continue to kill. But you're going to allow him to go on, to have him do your dirty work for you."

"That he would attack the synagogue in Rome was unexpected," Carmon said to the deputy prime minister. "Nobody suggested the possibility. It was not in any of the scenarios."

"Then maybe we need someone in your place who can direct a better set of scenarios?"

"No one could have foreseen it," Carmon said loudly. "What's important now is that we have the chance to get rid of Arafat free and clear, with no stain on us."

"No stain on us," the deputy prime minister repeated, nodding. "Don't you wonder how I suddenly happened onto all of this?" His face tightened in fury.

"The editor of *Maariv* dropped over early this morning. He wanted to do me the favor of warning me before they ran the story tomorrow of how we had the synagogue killers under surveillance then ordered our boys off them. That's the half they have. Now, how long, Meir, using your professional judgment, would you say it will be before they put together the rest of it?"

Carmon wiped a hand nervously on his pant leg. "How'd they find out?"

"Confidential sources. He wouldn't say, and I don't care. It's Sabra and Shatilla all over again. What matters is that it's going to look like we're responsible for Arafat's death. All of Judea and Sumaria will explode. And, Meir, have you thought by any chance of what's going to happen, with all this out in the open, if President Pertini, Foreign Minister Colombo or—I can't even begin to imagine the repercussions—the pope is killed along with Arafat in the attack?"

"This shouldn't have become public," Carmon said.

The deputy prime minister pounded his desk with his fist. "The prime minister blames you personally for this fiasco. I kept him out of here, otherwise he would have had your head. When I left him, he had the newspaper photograph of those two young brothers lying dead at the synagogue in front of him on his desk."

Carmon said nothing, reached in his pocket for a cigarette and matches and, his fingers damp, struck the match three times before it flared.

"The orders from this government are to kill Abu Nidal immediately. Is that clear? Before he can launch another attack. Now, where's this Shai Shaham Zev told me about? Zev says if there are any leads, Shaham will have them.''

''He's out on his own,'' Carmon said evenly. ''He went to Rome against direct orders. We have no way of contacting him.''

''He's your agent. You damn well better find a way. And I don't mean three days from now. The prime minister wants to be briefed every four hours until midnight, then again starting at six a.m. That means I want to hear from you personally, Meir, starting four hours from now. I want to know before he wakes up in the morning that we're in touch with Shaham. I'm not going to want to have to tell the prime minister, in addition to everything else, that you have an agent who's on top of this, but you can't locate him. Am I making myself clear enough?''

''Yes,'' Carmon said, his face pale.

He understood Abu Nidal's plan. Khalaf and Madani had accomplished their mission. Abu Nidal had two teams left now. Shai and the Palestinian would be searching for one fresh team; even if they found it, they would have no way of knowing about the other. Carmon had to send word to Shai about there being two hit teams, but there was no way of reaching him.

SHAI SAT BEHIND the wheel of the van with Ramzy at his side as they sped on the autostrada toward Naples. Shai looked into the rearview mirror. Two of Ramzy's agents followed in a two-seater Fiat X 1/9. He thought about Carmon's orders to identify Ramzy's operatives. It seemed so unimportant now.

"Is there any chance these two coming off the boat will recognize you?" Shai asked.

"They shouldn't," Ramzy said, "but we can't take a chance. My picture's often been printed with my stories."

"We'll have to figure out a way to get the directional transmitter on their car once we see which one it is."

"Assuming they don't take the train in."

"Between the four of us we should be able to stay with them if they do," Shai said quietly.

Ramzy watched the scenery flash by the window. He was worried that the Israeli had returned to ensure that he would fail. He kept the pistol near. "Those two who attacked the synagogue, I assume they're out of the country by now."

"That's virtually certain. Getting Arafat is Abu Nidal's moment of glory. He wouldn't risk using Khalaf and Madani. First of all, they've been seen by dozens of eyewitnesses, and secondly, he'd know my people are after them now."

"These two coming in have to be the assassins."

Shai navigated an easy bend in the highway. "There's no other reason for them to be arriving in Italy."

"We don't seem to be very excited that we're onto them, do we?"

"We're excited. We just don't know it."

Ramzy nodded. "It must be that we're so good at keeping secrets."

Shai smiled. As he drove in silence, he glanced again in the rearview mirror and saw the two Palestinians. There was no reason to contact the embassy. The killings in the synagogue would not change anything, he thought angrily. No Jews were in danger now. Carmon had no impetus to alter his decision. Even though they would soon have the assassins under surveillance, Shai felt uneasy.

"Can you get any more men here today?" Shai asked.

"I have more men in the city," Ramzy said. "You'll meet them tonight."

So Ramzy had not wanted him to be able to identify his other operatives. Well, he had no goddamn choice now. Still, Shai wished he had use of his own agents. Despite Ramzy's acumen, he knew from years of Israel's successes that the PLO personnel had nowhere near the training and skill of his people. He did not underestimate Abu Nidal.

"What time's Arafat's plane due tomorrow?" Shai asked.

"Eleven a.m. You know that."

"Yes, I suppose I do." Shai kicked down on the accelerator, suddenly worried since he could identify so many of Ramzy's operatives that they would be tempted, once this was over, to kill him.

ABU NIDAL SAT on the concrete edge of the Trevi Fountain, waiting for Jabr and Zayyad, the two who had arrived from Florence. The fountain, filling most of the tiny piazza, was alive with rushing waters and marble sea creatures commanded by an imperious Neptune. Tourists of all nationalities crowded the steps and benches surrounding it on three sides. As a precaution, the two assassination teams would never meet. The team from Sofia would approach Arafat openly on the street. In the unlikely event they were apprehended or silenced at the scene, Jabr and Zayyad would be hidden in such a way that no one would be able to stop their bullets.

Jabr and Zayyad walked through the narrow streets along the Palazzo Poli, whose columned, statued facade rose behind the fountain. Abu Nidal watched them approach and saw no one following them. They joined him on the concrete edge of the fountain.

"I have the robes and coins here," Abu Nidal said quietly. The noise of the water covered their conversation.

Zayyad saw the suitcase at his feet and nodded.

"He is scheduled to meet the pope at four tomorrow. If the others fail, you will see to it that he never reaches the meeting."

"No one will see us," Zayyad said.

"You know how to enter the Vatican offices from the rear?"

"Yes."

"There are no guards there, and if asked any questions, you have the coins. They will understand enough from your Spanish. When you turn the corner of the corridor, it is the eighth door."

"We have surveyed the building from the outside."

"Don't arrive too early, in case anyone comes to the office."

"We shall be there exactly as you instructed. We have timed the drive."

"You have been chosen for this most important moment. Allah is with you. Fear not, your lives are in his hands. He will protect you."

"Our lives are unimportant," Zayyad said, bending for the suitcase. "We will succeed."

SHAI SAT in the back of the van and watched the green light halt as the vehicle climbed through the Castelli Romani. They were about thirty minutes south of Rome, in the Alban Hills. The isolated weekend and summer villas sprinkled around the volcanic lakes would provide the perfect hiding place for the assassins.

Shai spoke into the microphone to Ramzy, who was driving. "They've stopped," he said. "Pull over."

Shai felt the van ease to the side of the road. A car had been waiting at the dock for the assassins. One of Ramzy's men had attached the directional transmitter under the chassis while the two had stopped in Naples to eat.

Shai pulled the van door open and Ramzy climbed out. "Where are they?" Ramzy asked.

"A few hundred meters off the road to the left. If we look, I'm sure we'll find a comfortable villa."

"I'll call some men to watch it."

Shai nodded. "Maybe we'll get lucky and Abu Nidal will show up here to give them their final instructions."

"Luck isn't something we've seen a lot of lately."

Though Shai worked most of his life on his own, to his surprise, he felt isolated and lonely now, cut off from contact with the embassy and Jerusalem.

"At least we know where the killers are," Shai said.

"That should be enough. They'll lead us to the scene of the attack and to Abu Nidal."

"Even if something happens and we can't spot Abu Nidal, at least there's no doubt we'll be able to stop the assassination."

FROM HIS COTTAGE, the Colonel heard the helicopter landing beside the greenhouse. He unscrewed the cedar-lined aluminum tube with satisfaction and slipped the Dunhill Montecruz into his hand. The call had come less than an hour ago. He placed the cigar in his mouth, savoring the taste before he struck the match. It was the small pleasures he had never really paid much attention to before returning to the kibbutz that meant so much to him now.

There was a knock on the door. He rose from the couch, cluttered with books and newspapers in a half-dozen languages, and made his way slowly to the door, the unlit cigar still in his mouth. He twisted and pulled the handle.

Meir Carmon stood there in his starched white shirt and sports jacket, every hair on his tall head immaculate. The Colonel removed the cigar from his lips.

"Come in," he said.

"Thank you for seeing me so quickly," Carmon said as he moved past him.

The Colonel shut the door. "You said it was important, didn't you?"

"Yes, I did."

The Colonel padded to the armchair across from the couch, picked the newspapers and magazines off it and placed them on the coffee table, which was similarly crowded. "Please, sit," he said. "If you'd like a drink, I'm sure I can find some Scotch for you. Always have some, for guests, that is."

"No." Carmon sat. "That won't be necessary."

The Colonel lowered himself onto the couch, searched the coffee table for some matches and finally found some under a book. He struck one, held the flame to the end of the cigar and drew on it several times until it lit.

"Marvelous thing, a good cigar," he said. "These are handmade in the Canary Islands. You ought to try one. I'll give you some if you like."

"Thank you, but I'll stick to cigarettes."

"All right. Your choice, of course. But they're much worse for you, you know. The inhaling."

Carmon laced his fingers tightly together. "I know you must despise me for what I did, but I believe it was best for the country."

"Yes, yes, of course. But then the other side does, too, don't they? Believe they're doing what is best for their country, I mean."

Carmon hated this, wanted to walk out of there, but remained seated. "I need your help," he said.

The Colonel puffed on his cigar and said nothing.

"I wouldn't have come to you if there was any other way."

The Colonel removed his cigar. "No, I don't suppose you would."

"I need to find Shai, now," Carmon said.

The Colonel nodded. "The best we've got, Shai. I recruited him personally. Always quite proud of that." He slowly set his cigar in the ashtray. "How is it that you don't know where he is?"

"It's a long story," Carmon said, exhaling audibly. "Abu Nidal's after Arafat. Shai's working with Ramzy Awwad in Rome trying to stop it. I don't know where he is at the moment."

"Why not? Strange. He'd report in. Unless..." The Colonel reached for his cigar.

"I ordered him off the case," Carmon said firmly, the anger deep in his voice. "He disobeyed a direct order, but that has nothing to do with this at the moment."

"I see."

"Shai's the only one who may have any lead as to where Abu Nidal is."

"But you ordered him off the case, didn't you?" The Colonel puffed on his cigar. "Ugly attack on the synagogue there. You order Shai off before it?"

"I want Abu Nidal. Now. If we have to save Arafat to get him, then I'll goddamn save Arafat."

"Yes, yes, I understand, but then why did you call Shai off in the first place?"

"All right, damn it. I'd rather they kill the bastard. But *Maariv*'s got the story that I called our boys off. They're coming out with it tomorrow. If the terrorists get Arafat or the pope or the president of Italy, it's going to look like we're responsible. Is that what you want to hear?"

The Colonel knocked the ash into the wastebasket by the coffee table. "Just want to have all the pieces. Need them. Can't see the puzzle clearly with too many missing."

"Shai's been working with Ramzy Awwad for a month trying to get Abu Nidal."

"Really?" the Colonel said, feigning surprise.

"That's why I'm here. They don't know it, but there are two Abu Nidal assassin teams in Rome after Arafat. They'll only be watching for one. I have to get word to Shai." Sweat beaded on Carmon's brow. "The only people who know where Shai and Awwad are, are the Palestinians."

"You mean you have to go to the other side to locate your own agent. Rather unusual situation. Well, I've been out for years now, you remember. You must have far better contacts with the Arabs."

Carmon's voice was tight. "I don't."

"I see, yes. I suppose you don't go in much for that kind of association, do you?"

"We want Abu Nidal stopped."

"Yes, you said."

Carmon removed the cigarettes from his inside coat pocket, extracted one and looked down at it. "I know you have a good relationship with Renate Pohle in East Berlin. Yehuda mentioned it several times. She'll know where Awwad is or be able to find him."

"Yes, she probably does or certainly can find out."

Carmon slowly replaced the pack of cigarettes in his pocket. "I would like you to call her immediately."

"If I do, we'll have to trade her something for the information, of course."

"Fine, whatever I have she wants."

"She may prefer to take the favor on account."

"All right. I don't care. However."

The Colonel reached over to the wastebasket and gently stubbed out the cigar on the metal side. "No point letting it burn and wasting it, is there? I'll use the phone in the bedroom, if you don't mind. We'll have to wait for her to call back. Actually, why don't you give me your number in Jerusalem? We'll have her call us there."

"Why?"

"Oh, while we wait for her to receive the message, you have a few things of mine you're going to return. You remember, don't you? My letters, the photographs with

Josra in Paris. I'll want the copies, too, from your office."

Carmon quickly lit his cigarette, pulled on it, then exhaled. "All right."

The Colonel put his hand on the arm of the sofa and pushed his way to his feet, then looked at Carmon. "The number?"

"Eight, one, four, seven, four, two."

"Ramat Eshkol. Nice neighborhood. By the way, you don't mind the East Germans having your home number, do you?"

"Make the call," Carmon whispered.

The Colonel crossed halfway to the bedroom, then stopped and turned. "Oh, there's one more thing before I do. I want complete amnesty for Shai and a promotion for him, with a pay raise. There's a pen and paper somewhere on the desk. You can put that in writing, now."

Carmon looked at him, his face hot, then drew hard on his cigarette. As the Colonel waited, he bent forward and found a pad of paper.

"It's too bad about this *Maariv* business," the Colonel said. "After all, we really don't want a witch hunt in the Service, do we?"

SHAI AND RAMZY sat in the back of the van, parked on the side road in the Castelli Romani near Lake Albano. Shai looked at his watch, which read 2:10. "Arafat should be finished lunching with President Pertini."

Ramzy nodded. "He's due at Foreign Minister Colombo's office at two-thirty."

"The Vatican at four and city hall tomorrow at ten to be received by the mayor," Shai said, more to himself than to Ramzy. "The attack should come today, before all the publicity of Arafat's success hits the papers."

"My guess is Abu Nidal won't show. They probably had their orders before they arrived in Italy, and the weapons, like the car in Naples, waiting for them."

"It doesn't matter. Wherever the strike's intended, Abu Nidal will be there, and we have the assassins."

Ramzy felt torn. He had left Sartawi. He should be with Arafat now, but he did not want to abandon the killers' presence, especially with the Israeli here.

"I know how you must be feeling about Arafat," Shai said. "I went through the same thing with Peres, with only hours left before the Socialist International closed. It's the hardest part, isn't it, the waiting?"

"Not always." Ramzy looked directly at the Israeli. "What are your orders after we kill Abu Nidal, assuming we succeed?"

Shai was not surprised that Ramzy had expected it. "I've already disobeyed my orders," he said.

"I'm supposed to believe that you won't try to kill me, now or later?"

"Our slate is wiped clean. If you're not personally involved in attacking my people again, it will stay that way. What will you do now that I can identify so many of your people?"

A voice abruptly cackled over the walkie-talkie from Ramzy's single agent in the Fiat X 1/9. "I just called in," the voice said. "There's an urgent message from East Berlin for your friend to call the Wolf."

Ramzy looked at Shai.

Zev, Shai thought. Zev in Hebrew meant wolf. "I have to get to a phone," Shai said excitedly. He did not know how the call had come from East Berlin and at the moment did not care.

Ramzy spoke into the walkie-talkie. "Drive up."

Seconds later, the low, sleek X 1/9 pulled alongside them. "I'll be back in a few minutes," Shai said, yanking open the door.

As the wheels spun in the dirt and the car broke away, Shai saw the Arab climb into the back of the van. There was a vineyard a few kilometers away that would have a phone he could use.

Ramzy took out his pistol, placed it on his knee and stared at it. This was too suspicious. The Israelis at this very moment could be plotting his death and Abu Nidal's victory. The Israelis, so far, had done nothing to help him in Rome, had abandoned the only lead they had uncovered, and equally likely, had sent Shai to monitor his success and thwart him. He wondered if he should kill the Israeli when he returned. If he did not and Arafat died because of it, he knew that failure would break him, along with the PLO.

A quarter of an hour later, Ramzy heard a car skid to a halt near the van and then a knock on the metal exterior. He replaced the gun in his coat pocket, for the moment, and opened the door. Shai bounded in.

"There's a second assassination team," Shai said hurriedly. "There's been a change of position in Jerusalem. They're going to help. My people are going to meet me in town. I'll take the walkie-talkie in the car."

Ramzy was silent.

"It's no trick," Shai said.

"Then why the sudden change?"

"I don't know. There's no time. It doesn't matter now. This man I spoke to, Zev, I trust him."

Ramzy felt the gun in his pocket. All logic told him to use it.

"Ramzy, did you hear what I said? There's a second assassination team out there somewhere."

Ramzy could not believe all the Israeli was saying, not at the last minute, when he had the assassins. It had to be a ruse to divert him. Scared for Arafat's life and worried he was committing a fatal error, he left the gun where it was. If by chance there was another team, he would need the Israelis. "I'll raise you if there's any movement here."

Shai nodded and moved quickly to the Fiat.

After he left, Ramzy picked up his walkie-talkie and ordered the bodyguards around Arafat to be alert for hidden assassins. Then he stared at the blank wall of the van. That the pair here would lead him to the scene of the attack offered little consolation.

ABU NIDAL DROVE his Alfa Romeo off the Tiber-fronted highway and parked in front of the massive round mausoleum of Castel Sant'Angelo. From Hadrian's tomb, crowned with a winged statue, it was a short, straight drive down the Via della Concilizione into Saint Peter's Square. Seconds later the small Spanish woman, who had been so valuable in Portugal, turned her blue Volkswagen Golf off the highway and parked behind him. Climbing out of her car, she approached Abu Nidal's with quick, small steps and climbed in.

She leaned over, placed her small hands on his shoulders and kissed him. He immediately broke the embrace.

"What time does your watch say?"

She drew the white cotton sweater away from her wrist. "Two fifty-one."

"Arafat's due to meet the pope at four. I want you to drive past the Palace of the Holy Office at three-thirty, then report to me at the northern end of the Janiculum where I showed you. I want to know everything you see."

She nodded.

He reached under the seat, pulled out a plastic Benetton shopping bag with a WZ-63 inside and handed it to her. "Once it's time, you stay behind me. If anyone's pursuing me, kill them."

She draped her arms around his neck and eased her body close to his. He kissed her hard, without feeling.

"Go now," he said.

DRESSED IN Franciscan friars' robes with hoods, Jabr and Zayyad left the sidewalk café in the oval Piazza del Popolo and moved to their car parked below the obelisk in the center of the vast asphalt. Young Romans on motorbikes sped through the crowded traffic with bravado.

Zayyad opened the trunk and, assured that the two suitcases of foreign commemorative coins with the Browning automatic pistols and WZ-63s at the bottom were still there, slammed it shut. He moved around to the driver's side and joined Jabr who was already seated beside him.

A short distance across the river, the dome of St. Peter's reigned above the skyline. Zayyad started the motor, drove around the circumference of the piazza and sped out the long, straight boulevard that led to the Vatican.

IN THE PARKING LOT of the Basilica of St. Paul's Outside the Walls, Zev stepped into Shai's small Fiat X 1/9.

"What do you need?" Zev asked.

Shai had been thinking on the drive in from the southern hills. The knowledge of a rogue team somewhere out there and simultaneously his full resources restored had altered everything.

"I want the fastest car you can get, and I want it in fifteen minutes," Shai said.

"All right. I'll call from my car in a moment. We have the two agents, David and Avi, and others if you need them—sharpshooters."

"David and Avi are artists, aren't they?"

"Yes."

"Okay, I'll use one of them that way. Get me some pastel chalk. I'll want high-powered rifles on all the surrounding buildings. Have everyone alerted for the second team. The Palestinians have the one coming down from the Castelli Romani under surveillance. It's the rogue team that poses the danger now."

"Where do you think the attempt will come?"

There was something that kept tapping on Shai's shoulder. "This has been well planned, so well, as far as we can tell, that Abu Nidal hasn't felt it necessary to see the assassins. Now what's the one meeting Abu Nidal could count on not being changed or the meeting place altered?"

"The pope." Zev nodded. "Shooting Arafat at the Vatican would give Abu Nidal banner headlines in every newspaper in the Western world."

"We have only a little more than an hour until the meeting. I want as many men as you can give me and that car at the north colonnade across from the fountain in Saint Peter's Square, as soon as possible."

Just then the walkie-talkie at Shai's feet cackled. He picked it up, and Ramzy's voice came over. "They're moving toward Rome."

"That confirms it," Shai said to Zev. He pushed the button on the walkie-talkie. "It looks like the Vatican. Follow them, and I'll meet you there."

"I'll let you know if there's a different destination."

"There won't be," Shai said.

JABR AND ZAYYAD approached the rear of the four-story square building with internal courtyard, opposite the Palace of the Holy Office. Each carried a heavy suitcase. Abu Nidal had ordered them to fire along with the two who had come from Sofia. There would be no missing. They entered the building that housed the Vatican newspaper, *l'Osservatore Romano*, the research offices of Radio Vaticano, the print shop, the Vatican stamp printing office and the small commemorative coin office, whose windows fronted the entrance of the Palace of the Holy Office.

They moved down the long hall in their robes without being questioned. The two killers turned left into the perpendicular wing, and Zayyad counted down eight doors, as Abu Nidal had instructed them, and saw the images of the papal coins on the door. They entered.

SHAI SHIFTED the V-12 Ferrari Boxer into gear, and the finned, red car roared away from the elliptical colonnade in St. Peter's Square. He drove out the main boulevard and circled quickly around the southern exterior of the colonnade until he saw the van parked to his right below the quadruple-deep columns. The four-story Palace of the Holy Office was just up ahead. Shai looked in his rearview mirror. The three Israelis were still in the car behind him.

Shai parked behind the van and honked twice quickly. Ramzy came out of the van's side door and strode toward him. The Israelis swept in front of the Ferrari and skidded to a halt by the van. Two of them jumped out and hurried inside it.

Ramzy approached the Ferrari. Though he still had difficulty believing it, there seemed to be little doubt that the Israelis were helping him. Otherwise, they would have tried to stop him in the van and kill him before he had arrived here, and they certainly never would have come to the Vatican where they could be implicated in the assassination. Had they wanted the murder to succeed, after eliminating him, they would have stayed far away.

Shai climbed out of the car and moved around to the passenger side. "You drive," he said, wanting to have the Uzi in his hands when all this was over. "I need to be free to direct the assault."

Ramzy nodded, and as he slid down behind the wheel, Shai pushed his way into the car, settling his legs between the two Uzis on the floor.

"Where are they?" Shai asked.

"About three blocks, that way." Ramzy pointed beyond the pope's offices. "What about the second team?"

"Nothing. I have my best men out there. If the rogue team's on the street, we'll stop them. Abu Nidal's assassins usually approach directly. But if by any chance they're hidden and cleverly...?" Shai did not look at him. "If you want, we can pick up the two we have now, call the whole thing off and divert Arafat. It's up to you."

"No," Ramzy said. He was certain Arafat would agree. "There'll just be another time when we're not prepared at all. We have to end this, finally." Ramzy's voice quivered with emotion. "I want Abu Nidal eliminated."

After the synagogue attack, Shai could taste how much he wanted him, too. "Good."

A voice cackled over the walkie-talkie beside Shai. "They're moving now, toward the palace."

As he eased from the curb, Ramzy checked his watch—3:40. "Abu Nidal will never outrun this," the Palestinian said.

"That's the idea."

"Where are your men?"

"We just got them positioned. They're on the roofs across from the entrance, in the street. There are no roadblocks. No Italian police. They're cooperating and have instructed that none of the pope's emissaries meet the car outside. The radio's announcing that the pope and Arafat will talk to the press inside Saint Peter's after Arafat's private audience. The press have all been diverted there. We're going to make it look easy for the killers. They have no way of knowing we're expecting anything. We'll try to spot Abu Nidal before we move on those two. If it gets too close, we'll have to take them."

"Abu Nidal will be there," Ramzy said. "He's come a long way for this. He'll want to watch."

INSIDE THE commemorative coin office, Zayyad eyed Jabr showing the two men behind the glass case, which held the papal coins, the Spanish sets they had brought with them. Zayyad moved to the water fountain near the door and bent to take a drink. He glanced up to make certain the two Italians behind the case were occupied, then reached out and turned the lock on the door.

He returned to his own suitcase, stooped then placed his sets of coins on the glass counter. One of the Italians moved close to examine them. Zayyad reached into his suitcase again and drew out the Browning automatic pistol with a silencer screwed onto its end. The Italian nearest him looked more puzzled than frightened.

Zayyad fired once into his chest, the sound like a muffled whoosh, then turned and fired twice at the second Italian, striking him in the head both times. As the man fell forward, about to crash into the commemorative coin case, Jabr reached out and caught him. Blood dripped onto the glass from the Italian's face. Jabr pushed him back, and he quietly slumped to the carpet. Zayyad came around the case and fired another bullet into each of the Italians' skulls to guarantee they were dead and could not call for help while he and Jabr stood at the windows.

AVI, HIS BEARD and long hair perfect for the role, knelt on the sidewalk in front of the Palace of the Holy Office, sketching a huge Madonna on the cement with pastel chalk. Beside him stretched a towel with the scattered coins of contributions, and near his legs his jacket bunched inconspicuously over his Uzi and walkie-talkie. He looked up from his work, as if to stretch, and saw his partner David sweeping the sidewalk along the length of the building. With no place to hide an Uzi, David carried a pistol at the small of his back.

Avi surveyed the area. Arafat was due any moment now, and there was no sign of any unusual movement. They had not had the time or the manpower to check out all the various buildings facing the palace, and they had not wanted to employ masses of Italian police for fear of scaring Abu Nidal away, to try again later, at a place of his choosing. They knew the exact location of the two assassins Shai had trailed down from the Castelli Romani. Avi wondered nervously where the other two were.

ABU NIDAL SAT in his Alfa Romeo parked on the hill beside the northern end of the vast green Janiculum, minutes from the Vatican. He checked his watch, then turned quickly and saw the blue Volkswagen Golf parked a half-block behind him. Fortunately the Palace of the Holy Office, nearby Audience Hall and the offices where Jabr and Zayyad had situated themselves by now lay outside the high Vatican City walls that turned inward before St. Peter's Square, allowing open access to the city. He would not have liked to have to enter the confined space inside the walls. He gazed at the sign on the corner pointing the direction to the nearby Holy Spirit Hospital. They would take Arafat there, he knew, but it would be too late. The traitor would not survive the shooting.

Abu Nidal lit a filterless French cigarette, inhaled with pleasure, then pulled slowly away from the curb. Seconds later the blue Volkswagen sped past him. He had explained his route to the woman, instructing her where to wait with her WZ-63. He descended the hill toward the Vatican without picking up much speed. He smoked leisurely. He would give her time to situate herself.

SHAI AND RAMZY sat parked in the Ferrari Boxer a block from the entrance to the Palace of the Holy Office. Ahead of them, they watched the two dark-skinned assassins walk along the street, wearing Mexican serapes with large silver crosses and cameras hanging from their necks. One carried a white plaster statue of Romulus and Remus sucking a she-wolf's nipples, the kind sold all over Rome, and the other held a map—both had tourist-type day packs on their backs.

The sharpshooters atop the building crouched out of sight. From the passenger seat, Shai watched Avi continue to sketch the large Madonna and David sweep the street. Words cracked over Shai's walkie-talkie, the voice coming from one of Ramzy's men several blocks in the direction of the river.

"Arafat's Volvo is approaching now," the Palestinian said. "It should be at the palace entrance in two minutes."

"Where the hell is the other team?" Shai swore.

Ramzy remained silent, his hands damp on the steering wheel. There was no one else in the street.

Shai watched Avi move closer to his jacket until he was touching it. Quickly Shai tried to raise him to tell him to leave the two in the street to the sharpshooters and concentrate on the nearby buildings, but there was no response. As he feared, Avi had turned off his walkie-talkie so the reports emitted from it would not alert the two killers walking nearby.

The Volvo raced even with them. Shai saw the scraggly bearded, keffiyehed Arafat sitting between two men in the back seat and felt a confusion of hatred and hope as the PLO leader sped by. Ramzy turned the ignition on the Ferrari and moved the Uzi across his lap. The assassins were bent on the sidewalk, a short distance from the entrance to the palace, studying the map spread on the cement, their packs off their backs.

Ramzy swept his head back and forth watching all the street entrances. He would not fail now.

Shai saw the Volvo rapidly approach the front of the nondescript Palace of the Holy Office. The brakes squealed as the car skidded to a halt.

Avi backed along his jacket, the light blue chalk still in his hand. The assassins were waiting right in front of him, in the open. They obviously were not expecting any trouble. He glanced at his jacket-covered Uzi near his right hand but continued to draw. Still, it was such a vulnerable assault. The other team had to be hidden somewhere, ready to fire. He watched the two on the sidewalk reach into their packs. He was the closest to them, the one who should take them out before they fired. He heard the car doors opening behind him. Troubled, he took his eyes from the assassins and again scanned the windows of the buildings that fronted the square.

Shai watched Arafat step out of the car behind a heavyset bodyguard. They could not wait for Abu Nidal or to find the other team. Shai pushed the button on the walkie-talkie. They had to take out these two and hustle Arafat inside.

"There," Ramzy said, quickly turning the ignition key, his fingers damp. A white Alfa Romeo with a man driving moved slowly toward them. "Abu Nidal."

"Fire," Shai shouted into the walkie-talkie as the Ferrari's engine roared.

Avi saw a glint in one of the windows to his left. Gun muzzles. Shots exploded from the four-story roof across the street. Avi grabbed the Uzi and dived on his stomach, firing at the window as he landed. Rushed bullets from the windows ripped into the Volvo. Arafat jumped to the ground, his bodyguard atop him. The glass above the window shattered as Avi continued firing, and the two assassins fell forward against the broken glass and frame. Out of the corner of his eye he saw the other two assassins spilling blood on the sidewalk where the sharp-shooters had punctured them.

The tires of the Alfa Romeo screeched as Abu Nidal turned and sped away. Ramzy jerked the Ferrari from the curb and spun it around, his heartbeat sounding in his ears. Shai had the Uzi leveled and was leaning out the window. Arafat was safe and Abu Nidal running, alone in the Alfa Romeo, no match for the V-12 Boxer. Ramzy punched the accelerator, emotion tight in his throat. He had him, finally.

Ramzy gripped the wheel, the only sounds the racing tires.

The small Spanish woman in the idling Volkswagen parked on the side of the street lifted the lightweight WZ-63 from the passenger seat. The red Ferrari had bolted from the curb and was chasing Abu Nidal. The Alfa Romeo flew past her. The Ferrari was gaining. She saw the man with the machine gun leaning out the window. She held the WZ-63 up, and as the Ferrari sped by, she squeezed hard and bullets burst from the muzzle.

Ramzy heard the shots, and stunned, felt them tear into the car, having no idea where they had come from. There was no power loss. He glanced at Shai, and horrified, saw the Israeli slump forward, his chest bloody. Ramzy pushed harder on the accelerator, gaining on the Alfa Romeo.

"Shai," he called out. "How bad is it?"

No response. He reached over and felt the Israeli's neck. There was a small pulse. He glanced up. The Alfa Romeo, only four short blocks ahead of him, quickly turned right. Ramzy shifted gear and tromped on the accelerator. It would take him almost no time to catch up, spray the Alfa Romeo with bullets and finish the man who was trying to destroy them, who had killed so many of his friends.

Ramzy flew to the corner, downshifted to take it, saw the Israeli out of the corner of his eye and knew he would die in a matter of minutes, exactly the way his friends had. Damn him, he thought, damn all of them for what they've done to my people.

He took the corner, shifted up again and saw Abu Nidal three blocks ahead. The Israeli moaned. Ramzy squeezed the wheel and closed the range, his fingers tight on the spongy leather. He blocked out the sound, felt how long he had waited for this. He reached the next intersection, gaining, his mouth dry, and glanced at the bleeding Israeli.

Ramzy brought his eyes back to the figure in the speeding car up ahead and riveted them on him. "I'll get you," he whispered. Then abruptly he turned in a screeching left and let the Alfa Romeo escape. Ramzy raced for the Holy Spirit Hospital, one of Rome's largest, and only seconds away.

# BOOK V: EPILOGUE

## 30 November 9 • Jerusalem, Israel

THERE WERE ONLY a small number of guests waiting for the ceremony to begin. They stood on the deep, bright balcony that looked out at the rocky hills north of Jerusalem, increasingly covered by young pine trees. Above the pines rose the olive trees of the Arab village of Shuafat, whose homes crowned the hill to the right.

The weather had turned unseasonably warm, and Tami's parents had insisted that they move the ceremony outside. With the lovely day and festive atmosphere, nobody seemed to mind the delay, although no one knew quite what it was about. The rabbi had arrived a half hour earlier, and Tami's best friend had come out, and when asked, had said that the bride was ready.

Shai's sister and her husband were there, their two daughters with their husbands, several old friends of Tami's, Tami's great aunt and her younger sister; her brother was in the army and couldn't make it. The Colonel stood talking to Shai's sister. An Arab woman, a guest of Shai's, sat alone near the balcony, her hands clasped together, looking away from the guests out at the hills.

When the doorbell sounded, Shai left Tami's younger, redheaded sister, Anat, and walked through the apartment to the front door. He opened it and saw Ramzy standing there, holding a poorly wrapped package.

Emotion filled Shai's voice. "Come in," he said, wrapping his arm around Ramzy's shoulder.

"I'm sorry I'm late," Ramzy said. "But despite your clearance, it took some time at the Allenby Bridge. I'm afraid they made a mess of the present."

"It doesn't matter. Come, we're about to start. There's a small ritual first. I have to lift the veil and check the bride to make certain I have the right woman. Jacob was tricked and ended up with Leah and not the younger sister, Rachel, whom he really wanted, though seven years later he did get the right one." Before they reached the balcony, Shai stopped. "Ramzy, I'm glad you came."

Ramzy turned to him. "When I first received the invitation, I didn't know if I would."

From the balcony the Colonel watched the two men. He would not tell Shai that this was what it had all been about from the beginning. He had hoped, though, that they would together, while developing a relationship, kill Abu Nidal. Two weeks earlier one of Abu Nidal's men had called Israeli Radio to take credit for the attack that morning in downtown Jerusalem. The three terrorists had used the open-border policy with Lebanon to cross into Israel and had successfully hidden their small WZ-63s and grenades somewhere in the car.

They had entered the Habira Sporting Goods Store, and speaking Arabic-accented English, had asked to try on some jeans. They had emerged from the dressing room brandishing grenades and WZ-63s, then had burst into bustling King George Street. Forty-eight had been wounded before Israeli storekeepers and pedestrians had pulled pistols and subdued them. One terrorist had been killed and two captured. Miraculously none of the forty-eight Israelis had died.

The Colonel suspected that the attack had come in retaliation for the obvious Israeli participation in foiling the Rome assassination. Ramzy was hunting Abu Nidal and so was a team of Israelis. Shai, still too weak to return to the field, was coordinating efforts between Ramzy and their squad.

Shai walked Ramzy across the large balcony, and then Ramzy suddenly saw her stand and face him. He was stunned.

"I think I interrupted your reunion in Sidon," Shai said.

Nadjla ran across the short distance, threw her arms around her brother and held him.

Shai watched them. He had driven Fawaz across the border into Israeli-occupied Sidon, affected a reunion and, with his help, had convinced Nadjla that it was safe to return to Israel with them, where she could see Ramzy. Fawaz had returned to the newspaper and had refused to answer incredulous questions about what had happened.

Shai approached the bearded rabbi and nodded. The rabbi took Shai's arm, then turned to the guests and spoke. "The Baal Shem Tov said that from every human being a light reaches straight to heaven. And when two souls that are destined to be together find each other, their streams of light flow together and a single brighter light goes forth from the united being. Come, let us go to the bride and stand in the presence of their light.''

## AUTHOR'S NOTE

Yakov Barsimantov, vice-consul at the Israeli embassy in Paris, Shlomo Argov, Israeli ambassador to Great Britain, Said Hammami, PLO representative to Great Britain, and Dr. Issam Sartawi, PLO roving envoy in Europe, are all historical personages gunned down by Abu Nidal's Palestine National Liberation Movement in the manner described. The Rome synagogue by the Tiber was attacked in the wake of Yasser Arafat's audience with the pope, as was King George Street in Jerusalem outside the Habira Sporting Goods Store. All particulars of Abu Nidal's operations are recounted as they happened.

''Spine tingling . . . Fascinating . . . Poignant.''
—*Time* Magazine

# JAMES O. JACKSON
# DZERZHINSKY SQUARE

Captured by the Nazis during World War II and then
falsely branded a collaborator, Grigory Nikolayevich
Malmudor must choose the one remaining road back
to his Soviet homeland . . . as a spy for the U.S. But he
is soon abandoned by his American masters in a world
of deadly shadows and constant terror, faced with the
promise of inevitable doom.

DS-1

''Plenty of suspense . . . Timely . . . Frighteningly authentic.''
—*People* Magazine